# THE SPONSOR

## DARREN GUEST

www.bloodhoundbooks.com


Print ISBN: 978-1-917449-9-46

"*A house is much more than a mere shelter – it should lift us emotionally and spiritually.*"

~ John Saladino

1

The doorbell rings and I can see a frosted silhouette through the glass, like a framed portrait of a ghost, and when I open the door it is a ghost of sorts, from my past.

'Hello, Mrs Young,' the man says with a pinched smile. 'My name's Detective Wallace...'

He holds up his ID, but I know who he is. I remember him from the trial, and from the day he drove me home from the police station. He seems to have forgotten me though.

'...and I wondered if I could steal a brief minute of your time?'

On the news this morning they said there's a good chance we'd be dipping into the nineties this month, not that it didn't feel that hot already. Despite this, Detective Wallace has his tie cinched tightly to his throat – an inoffensive mid-grey to go with his slightly darker suit. There was a time when I would automatically come up with the correct name for the colour – see it in the chart, along with the specific Pantone code that differentiated the shades between Pewter and Smoke, Graphite and Dove. For instance, the sweat stains spotting his underarms might be Pebble or Iron, I really couldn't tell anymore. Hard to believe I used to breathe these details like oxygen, before my passion for interior design was snuffed out like my daughter. All in the wink of an eye.

'Would that be a doorstep minute, Detective Wallace, or do you need to come inside?'

He squints up into a *Simpsons* sky as he puts his ID away. 'Inside, if that's convenient?'

I walk him into the kitchen. 'Would you like a tea or coffee?' I ask, but he doesn't seem to hear me. He's looking around the place, remembering he's been here before, noticing perhaps that it hasn't changed since the last time he was here. The bare plaster walls, the colour swatches and wallpaper samples taped all over, the folded dust-sheets and stepladders stored in the open recess that was once going to be a walk-in larder before the contractor my husband had hired for the renovation went bust. It's the same throughout the house, a literal downing of tools. Drills and chargers, shovels and crowbars, spirit levels... I even have a cement mixer in the basement. I'd give it all away if there was anybody left in my life who could find a use for it. The contractor sent a couple of lads round to collect it, just a week after he'd told my husband he'd gone into liquidation and had lost our hundred thousand pound deposit. I wish I'd let them take it, but I was still too angry. Now I've learned to live in this eerie, deserted place. The *Mary Celeste* of houses.

'Water would be good,' he says, coming back to me, and then, more to himself: 'For some reason I thought you were renovating a good while ago.'

And more to myself: 'Still can't decide on the finishes.'

I notice he's thinned out a little, both in the waist and in the hairline of his salt and pepper crop, and despite the season, his skin is quite pale, and I wonder if he's been ill recently.

He coughs into his fist to break eye contact with me. Yes, Detective Wallace remembers me very well. It'd be nice to think it's my timeless beauty that has jogged his memory and not the lack of décor in the house, but eighteen months ago it would have been blotchy skin and chestnut roots betraying the vanilla blonde I was struggling to maintain. And of course the scar across my right eyelid. It's healed to a gossamer thread now, and I doubt anybody would notice it, but I do. Every time I look in the mirror I see it, and it always drags me back to the day that drunken monster—

'Grant Chapman is going to be released in two weeks,' Detective Wallace says.

I hand him his glass of water. 'He's not due out until December. How can that be?'

'Can we sit?' He offers me a seat at my own kitchen table, which I don't take. I'm thinking about the bottle of vodka I keep in the freezer.

*Break glass in case of emergency.*

'How can that be?'

'Compassionate leave,' he says.

'Compassionate leave? Is that supposed to be funny? That drunk killed my daughter, where's my compassionate leave?'

'I understand that this is—'

'Compassionate leave for what?'

'He...' Detective Wallace clears his throat. 'His father has been diagnosed with terminal canc—'

'Fuck him and his terminal father—' I clamp a hand over my mouth. 'I'm sorry, that's an awful thing to say.'

Detective Wallace walks around the table and pulls a chair out for me. 'Sit for a moment, Mrs Young.' I do as he suggests, and while I sit, my face cupped in my hands, I can see Grant Chapman stood in the dock just after the judge pronounced his pathetic two-year sentence, and I can see him turn to me as he's being led away, and the malicious wink he gave me, the wink that hollows me out every time I look in the mirror and see the scar on my eyelid.

Detective Wallace places his untouched glass of water on the table in front of me and I wish for all the world that it's vodka.

'I know how you must feel, Mrs Young...'

He has no idea how I feel, because there are no words that can describe it, only colours, and they range from Blood Red to Midnight and all the shades between. How can he possibly know what it's like to grow a child inside of you, to give painful and bloody birth to her, to listen at her cot in the dark every night, your breath held for so long that your heart begins to pulse in your throat but you can't inhale until you hear her tiny breaths, steady and even. Steady and even. How can he possibly know what it's like to never hear that child breathe again.

'...and I know how justice can seem a little unjust sometimes, but the judge has ruled on it and there's nothing we can do and so I wanted to come and tell you in person...'

As soon as Detective Wallace leaves I'm going to drink the vodka and never stop. People might say it's reckless for a recovering alcoholic to keep booze in the house, but for me I find it empowering. To remove yourself from temptation doesn't mean a thing, it just means you can't, when it should mean you won't. There have been days when I've nearly poured the bottle away, days when I can't stop seeing Becky around the house, days when I find a stray item of her clothing – a sock maybe, or a school cardigan. Days when I can't trust myself. But as soon as I pour it away I've lost, and he's won, and that *fucking* wink becomes a guillotine, severing my last thread of sanity.

'...because if you didn't know and you bumped into him on the street, well, that could be traumatic, to say the least.'

'You mean I might try and scratch his eyes from his face.'

'Well, hopefully you wouldn't try to do that, Mrs Young,

and now that you're aware he'll be out soon you'll have time to...
adjust your emotions.'

'Adjust my emotions...' The only emotion I've felt in the last
eighteen months is despair. 'Thank you for letting me know,
Detective Wallace.'

I show him to the door, neglecting the niceties of goodbyes,
and shut it as soon as he steps outside. His ghost lingers in the
frosted glass, his arm momentarily raised to ring the doorbell
again before thinking better of it. I wouldn't have answered it
anyway.

A minute later and the vodka bottle smokes from the neck
when I twist off the cap – Alpine-clean, pre-avalanche – and
when I empty the glass of water and refill it with the icy poison
(*antidote?*), I can already feel the cold heat searing a path to my
stomach. The brutal ecstasy of the first mouthful, the cotton
wool that will gather behind my eyes with every measure
thereafter, before the white wave crashes over me and I'm
entombed in the dreamless oblivion of a satin-lined coffin.

'No,' I say, as I pour both the glass and the bottle down the
sink. 'I won't let him take me too.'

2

The local community centre has been running an Alcoholics Anonymous meeting there for years, but it had been invisible to me, in the same way you can become blind to a TV ad that doesn't apply to you. I can't think of a single brand name of incontinence pad, for those discreet little "lady slips", or a supermarket own-brand of vodka, because I only ever drank Smirnoff and to drink cheap booze is something an alcoholic would do. And I'm obviously not one of those because I live at a leafy address in a four-bedroom detached house along a wooded country road. Likewise I'd walked past the community centre hundreds of times, oblivious to the "Is Alcohol Costing You More Than Money?" posters. But once the blinkers are removed, and you realise it wasn't all invisible to you, it becomes overwhelmingly sad. Of course I've drunk cheap vodka from a plastic bottle, and I've lost count of how many times I've woken up sore from sleeping in wet knickers. "Denial Is The Alcoholic's First Drink Of The Day!" I see the community centre very clearly now, as I walk in through the main doors, and realise I've always seen it clearly.

I loiter in the small entranceway for a time, feigning interest in the noticeboard while I wait for Justin—

'Dina?'

A young man leans into my field of vision, distracting me from the noticeboard I wasn't really looking at. Fresh-faced and bright-eyed, coarse strawberry-blonde hair parted clinically with a matching swatch of stubble, and a check shirt buttoned all the way to his throat. More a Bible salesman than a recovering alcoholic only one drink away from tumbling back into oblivion.

'Justin Campbell.' He offers me a timid hand, which is softer than mine. 'I'm glad you could be with us today, Dina,' he says. 'Is it okay if I call you Dina? We only use Christian names in the meetings.'

He must take my shrug for consent, because he smiles and invites me along the corridor towards the two doors at the end.

'Can you tell me a little bit about what you do here?' I ask him as we walk.

'Of course,' he says. 'We have a few new faces with us today, so I'll give a brief run-through of what the programme involves at the top of the meeting, and I'm always available at the end if there's anything else you'd like to know. But in essence, Dina, we're just a support group – a fellowship of brothers and sisters who share a common illness and a desire to be free of its hold.'

We reach the end of the corridor and Justin takes the handle to the door on the left, but he must sense my fear as he doesn't enter. 'You're among friends here, Dina,' he lullabies me, and invites me inside.

For some reason I'm expecting a circle of chairs, inhabited by a small group of cagey nail-biters, all dark around the eyes and malnourished, wearing week-old clothes and on the verge of mental collapse. But not this. Not so many of them. Thirty or more "normal"-looking people, seated in chairs which are arranged in rows, all facing a whiteboard that has written on it in looping green cursive the familiar Serenity Prayer:

*God, grant me the serenity to accept the things I cannot change,*

*Courage to change the things I can,*

*And wisdom to know the difference.*

Many of the people here are chatting too, as though they've come to support their child in a cheery school play, and I'm struck by a sick swell in my stomach because I don't have a child of my own to bring to this fantasy production. And suddenly I need to leave, the overwhelming fear of losing myself to the grief of it and breaking down in this room full of strangers, but then a middle-aged woman in the back row smiles up at me and pats the empty seat beside her. She's plump, attractive, good bag and great shoes, hair long and in lustrous layers of Mocha and Pecan. I can't picture her head in the toilet, her beautiful hair dipping the acidic vomit scumming the pan water, and as I glance over the rest of the attendees, I can't see a single person that I could imagine in such a sorry state, but they all must have been, at some point. Just as they all must have been terrified coming here for the first time. Ashamed.

I take the seat next to the woman as Justin takes centre stage in front of the whiteboard, where he prays his hands together, smiling like he's about to lead us into a folksy *Kumbaya, My Lord*, but instead leads us into a group recital of the prayer.

The woman next to me bangs out the prayer a beat or two ahead of the rest of the congregation, tagging a *blah, blah, blah* to the end of it. Is this what I'll be like in a few months, while Chapman enjoys the garden bar at his local pub?

'Welcome, everyone,' Justin says once the room falls silent. 'And especially to the new friends we have joining us. The first step you've taken by coming here today is nothing short of courageous.'

Justin is searching for me in the crowd and I want to die. I lower my head, clutching my bag, hoping he'll locate another one of the "new friends" to give his sermon to because this is utterly, excruciatingly, humiliating.

'We've all joined this fellowship because we share a common illness,' Justin continues, 'an illness that cannot be cured or reversed, but can be managed very effectively through the collective support and strength that comes from sharing our stories of courage and fallibility, of desperation and hope. And as our strength grows, so does it diminish our physical compulsion to drink, and our mental obsession with alcohol loosens its hold over us...'

I still don't dare look up, but I notice in my periphery the door opening to my right and a pair of turquoise Converse All Stars squeak into the room. At first I think it's a kid who's stepped in by mistake because the foot size seems too small for an adult, but as I scan upwards, beyond the Chalk White corduroy dungarees and the Electric Purple long-sleeve T-shirt that jags so heinously against the turquoise, I see a young woman barely into her mid-twenties. She's clearly come through the wrong door, her Walnut hair of unknowable length bundled into a messy bun, a pale rose complexion and the energised bounce of a children's TV presenter. A dancer, not a drunk.

But then I notice she's holding a jar of coffee, which she waggles in Justin's direction before making her way around to the back of the room, to a table laid out with teacups and plates of biscuits, and when I return my attention to the front, Justin captures me with his gaze, the sneak.

'So, now that you've an idea of what we do here, would anyone like to start us off?'

Justin tortures me with another few seconds of his questioning eyes, and then I'm saved. A man stands up in the front row and turns to the rest of us, a limp denim jacket and a packet of cigarettes peeking out of the breast pocket.

'Hi, guys,' he opens with a sniff and a raking glance around the group. 'I'm Ben, for those who don't know me—'

'*Hi, Ben,*' the group returns.

'And umm, yeah, still an alcoholic.'

I glance behind me to get another look at the young woman, but the coffee station is unattended, the semi-commercial tea urn huffing steam as though it's miffed at being left alone. I face front again, thinking that she must work for the community centre – I mean, there's no way she's one of "us" – and then I spot her scruffy bun in the seat next to Justin and I'm startled to find her eyes on me. Pear Green.

'So, yeah,' the denim guy continues, 'it's been a rough week, and if it hadn't been for my daughter, you know, depending on me, I don't know if I'da got through it sober – and this place, of course.' He looks up for the first time, apologetically, and the woman sitting next to him grips his arm and someone else administers a *Stay strong, Ben,* which is echoed by everyone and I want to leave so badly my head feels like it's steaming along with the urn.

Justin stands and thanks Ben, and offers the slot for somebody else to share. There's a round of head tennis from the group, each of them looking back and forth along their row for the next person to stand and bare all, and I even notice the woman sitting next to me dipping her face to meet mine, as if I would dare speak to these strangers, to let them sip my grief like a stiff gin at happy hour.

I sense the woman is about to speak to me, but all eyes turn to the back row, towards the decaying black gentleman who's taken his cap off to talk. I'll be gone from here before he finishes. My mind is made.

'Hello, everyone...'

'*Hello, Walter.*'

Walter's cap threads through his bony fingers as he recounts his week, and when I sense he's coming to the end, I choose my moment to leave.

'Dina, welcome,' Justin says, and it's as clear in the silence as breaking glass. I'm stood, frozen before my seat.

'Hello, Dina,' says the woman sitting next to me, with her good bag and great shoes, and then the group cements my feet to the spot with a *Hello, Dina.*

I look back at Walter, who's seated again, and return my gaze to Justin, and to the young woman in the colour-crime ensemble, her Pear Green eyes like headlights on a startled rabbit, trapping me in the path of the oncoming car. The oncoming car... *The oncoming car... Grant Chapman, you murdering bastard!*

'My daughter was murdered,' I say, surprising myself, even more so when I realise I must continue. To unbottle the words I have never uttered to a single person. 'It was... It was...'

3

It was the December before last, a Friday, and I was late picking Becky up from school. She was a good girl, though, and knew not to leave the premises until either me or Roy arrived.

When I got there Becky was standing at the gates with her Special Needs teacher Ms Dunbar (a young woman barely out of popsocks herself), and I knew she was upset because Becky would always run to me and try to swing on my arm, but on that day she stayed fixed at Ms Dunbar's side, even though I knew she'd seen me. I gave my apologies first to Ms Dunbar, who shamed me by ignoring it to say goodbye to Becky, and then to Becky, who also shamed me by flashing her teacher a bright smile and a wave, only for her face to re-shadow to acknowledge me.

We walked side by side for a minute or two, me waiting for Becky's opening negotiations as to which unhealthy snack she could have before dinner. But as the silence stretched out, and the winter sun began to sink below the houses and treetops in the distance, highlighting just how late I had been, I felt I should do away with the usual gambits on this occasion and cut shamelessly to a sugary bribe.

'As it's Friday, why don't we pick up a tub of Ben and Jerry's on the way home?' I suggested. 'We can get the cookie dough one you like?'

I was met with a shrug, and I knew I'd have to up my game.

'And takeaway pizza, obviously,' I added.

Another shrug. 'I'm not really hungry.'

Oh. I was in real trouble if Becky was turning down pizza. It was something Roy would never dream of feeding us, and so whenever he was away on business it would be our treat. A girls' night in with a twelve-inch stuffed crust and no olives, yuk!

Three shrugs and I'm out. I grabbed Becky by the arm and spun her around theatrically. 'Oh my God, I just saved you,' I told her.

'*Mum...*'

I flattened my brow for intensity. 'You almost stepped on a crack.'

'Mum, I don't want to play,' she said, her head sagging to the side, her beautiful Cerulean eyes overcast beneath her bored lids. 'I just want to go home, it's cold.' And as if to prove it, Becky's sigh produced a dissipating white cloud to go along with my chances of salvaging her disappointment with me.

I grabbed her hand without breaking character. Warned her it was a life and death situation and started to drag her in zigzags across the paving slabs, avoiding the cracked ones as though they were landmines, a game we would often play when she was younger and impervious to embarrassment. I could feel the passersby looking at us. At me. But with every jump and skip, I could hear Becky's reluctant giggle bubble out of her, filling my heart with rapture and banishing the terrible thought that I might be the kind of shitty mother that could forget to pick up her child from school.

Then I heard the scream. Felt Becky's hand leave mine. And for the briefest of moments thought I had won her back and she was deep in the game with me, branching out to find her own path through the minefield, the scream a venting of her joy. But then came the seeping of reality, a surreal landscape that existed somewhere between dreaming and waking. I saw the car first, angled across the pavement, paint matted with age, the bonnet concertinaed against the school railings, a young man folded over the steering wheel, the relentless pitch of the horn a needle in my ear. I felt the pavement cold beneath my palm and only then realised I was sitting on the ground, and a second later realised Becky was nowhere to be seen.

I screamed for her as I blundered to my feet, and was caught by a middle-aged man when I started towards the car.

'Don't go over there, my love,' he said. 'Wait for the police.'

I looked past him, to the crowd that had gathered on the other side of the crumpled car. The crowd that could see what I couldn't. I shoved the man aside and focused on one woman in particular, the hand covering her mouth making my stomach slip and slide. The shock in her eyes telling me everything I didn't want to know or believe.

I made my way around the car, stalling to rest against the boot, my skin sickly chilled and the incessant horn drilling into my ears, making me blink. I doubled over, unsure if I was going to vomit, and through the rear window I could see the driver stir from the steering wheel. The horn cut off. The gasps and whimpers coming from the crowd filled the void.

And then I saw her. A tuft of her golden hair sprouting from behind the twisted metal of the bonnet. Gold streaked with red. I wailed, couldn't move fast enough to be with her, and in my haste I slipped. My eye struck the bumper before my head struck the pavement, and as I lay there, blood trickling warmly down my cheek, the world went dark.

I fled the AA meeting with tears trembling in my eyes. I was never going back there again. Shouldn't have gone there in the first place and shouldn't have poured away my only bottle of vodka. It's all I can think of now, being swaddled in the warm blanket of booze, reality shut out like a toxic fog and me safe inside my self-induced coma. Alcoholism is fine if you're doing it for the right reason, and my reason couldn't be more right. My daughter is dead and I haven't the courage to join her, but I can still be away from this world, the same world that I have to share with the living and breathing and soon-to-be-walking-free, Grant Chapman, who had, sickeningly, escaped that drunken crash without a scratch.

By the time I come out of the off-licence with my vodka, the taxi I called is waiting for me. I'll be home in less than five minutes. Be off the wagon in less than ten.

'Hope you don't mind the windows open, the AC's down,' the taxi driver says as I climb in the back. He must think my face is damp because of the heat.

4

As soon as I get through the door I shuck off my bag and head for the kitchen, dump the vodka into the same freezer drawer where I'd kept the last bottle. It's not because I need it cold, it's because I need to give myself a final few minutes of sober thought. I need to consider what I'm about to do and why I'm about to do it.

I pace the kitchen, clenching and unclenching my jaw, my hands. Grant Chapman is going free, while I am trapped inside this house, a house I cannot sell, a house that every day reminds me of my dead daughter. If this is to be my cell, then why wouldn't I make it just the tiniest bit more bearable? In fact, it isn't even a question. I can't stay in this house without alcohol. I just can't.

I set a tall glass on the kitchen table. Fetch the vodka. Some ice. If this is to be my life, it doesn't have to be... uncivilised. I've often wondered how the high-functioning alcoholics manage it. Work, daily life, family, the continuous hum of alcohol never taking them down, but never allowing them to come up for air, either. I could do that. Especially in the absence of work, daily life, and a family. How lucky I am.

A twist of the cap and the vodka is free to breathe. A twist of the ice tray and the glittering cubes chip and spin on the tabletop. I gather a few, unsticking them from my fingers to plink them into the glass. The rest of the ice cubes are already melting in the heat, weeping at my pitiful breakdown. Even the chrome wall clock seems to stare past me, its second hand tutting its disapproval. I reach for the bottle anyway, needing to be gone from this place, but the doorbell jars me like a cold hand on my shoulder. I rise slowly with no intention of answering it, but the closer I edge, the more the silhouette beyond the frosted pane takes on shape and colour. Colour...

It's her, the young woman from the AA meeting. Her abstract portrait framed within the glass. The Electric Purple of her long-sleeve T-shirt and the Chalk White braces of her dungarees. She stands there, unmoving, as I peer around the doorway, her face aimed straight ahead as if she can see me watching her. Thirty seconds go by. A minute. The clock still tutting and her still unmoving, like a real painting. I retreat into the kitchen and see the evidence on the table piled against me. I can't open the door to her. She'll have to leave eventually.

I take another peek into the entrance hall and she's still standing there, too long for her not to have rang the doorbell again, and too long for her to have waited without answer. I'm caught in a lie. I'm home and she knows it. I don't bother to hide the vodka before answering the door.

Her face is bright, her rose-apple cheeks round and smooth and youthful as she smiles at me, as though she hasn't waited any time at all.

'Hi, Dina,' she says. 'I was at the meeting earlier, you know, *the AA*?' She mouths this last part and cringes ever so slightly, eyes flickering beyond me into the entrance hall.

'It's okay,' I tell her. 'I live alone.' Drink alone.

'That's what I was worried about,' she says. 'Being alone is hard, especially when the sober part of your brain is like' – she claws her hands up in parenthesis around her head and mutes a tortured scream – 'you know, in battle with the other part.' She drops her hands and smiles again. 'Can I come in, Dina?'

For the life of me I cannot picture this pretty young thing in the grip of it. Maybe her daddy had sent her to the meeting because of the three bottles of WKD he found under her bed, or maybe she'd suffered a heart palpitation after drinking a prosecco too quickly at her uni bar. But I'm curious as to what she's got to say to me. Curious to see what she's got to say about the vodka set-up I've staged on my kitchen table.

I step aside and she practically bounces by me, and as she turns into the kitchen I realise she's the first person who's been inside this house in the last six months, if you don't count Detective Wallace and the periodic trickle of estate agents.

I linger by the front door, listening for the gasps and sorry sighs, but all I hear are the birds in the trees that canopy this road of wealthy homeowners, neighbours so far apart we hardly ever acknowledge each other, let alone share our troubles and heartaches.

When I enter the kitchen, I find her twisting the cap back on the vodka bottle. 'Sorry,' she says, wafting her fingers in front of her face, 'the smell makes me bilious – ha! Bilious is such a great word, don't you think? It's one of those onomatopoeia words, words that sound like the thing they're describing – unlike onomatopoeia, which sounds like an Italian taking a whizz on a rug.' She grins, but it soon fades when she realises I'm not seeing the funny side.

'Is there something you wanted to speak to me about...?'

'Rosie. Rosie Rey.'

'Well, Rosie-Ray—'

'Just Rosie, with an *I E*. Rey's my surname, with an *E Y*. I just like saying it all together – makes me sound like I might have special powers, you know, like Lois Lane.'

'I don't think Lois Lane had special powers,' I say.

'She has Superman in her pocket, Dina. I think that gives her some pretty special powers.'

I don't know what's disturbing me more, the fact that I'm caught in this surreal conversation, or that this young woman, this *Rosie with an I E*, is talking about a comic book character like she's a real person. Either way...

'How can I help you, Rosie?' I ask her, and bizarrely go and put the kettle on.

'Well, obviously I was concerned when you got so upset, I mean, it's rare for new group members to speak at their first meeting, but for someone to share that their child was murdered and then run out like that – I just had to make sure you were okay.'

'So you followed me home. Tea?'

'God, no, Dina!' Rosie covers her mouth, her brow creased in shock or shame. 'I would never do something so creepy, but when I came out of the centre I couldn't find you and I was so worried, you know, after what you said, and...'

'And then you saw me coming out of the off-licence with that.' I gesture at the vodka, then fetch two mugs down from the cupboard. 'I'm going with tea,' I say.

'Sorry, yes. Tea's good.' She pulls out a chair.

The kettle belches steam and clicks off. 'I shouldn't have gone to the meeting,' I say, dropping a teabag into each mug, 'and I shouldn't have blurted that out about my daughter.'

'Losing anybody is horrific,' Rosie says, 'but murder... I can't imagine—'

'Technically it was manslaughter,' I say, and place a mug of tea on the table in front of her. Tears had swelled in her eyes but I'm cold to them. 'There's sugar if you want it.'

'Manslaughter?' Rosie says.

'Drunk driver.' And just like that I'm done talking about it. I couldn't finish the story at the meeting and I'm not going over it here with this... girl, as sweet as she might be. Sharing isn't therapy, it's torture. 'I won't be returning to the meetings, Rosie,' I say, sipping at my tea as I lean back against the kitchen worktop. 'Would you let Justin know – thank him – but it isn't for me.'

Rosie gives me a sad smile, her tears dried a little. 'It's not for everyone, Dina, but this isn't the answer.'

I follow her eyes to the vodka, to the glass of melting ice. 'Yeah, I know. I just had some upsetting news, that's all. I think I'm over it now, so I guess I should thank you for that.'

She moons at her tea, her slender fingers laced around the mug. 'Did you want to talk about it?'

'Listen, Rosie, I appreciate your concern, I do, but the last thing I need or want is to talk about my problems with—'

'A stranger,' she says, looking up. 'I get it, Dina.'

'I was going to say *anyone*.' I pour my tea down the sink. 'I thought that's what I needed, some outside help, but nobody can help me except me. This was just a blip. I've had a bottle in the freezer for months without drinking.'

'So how come you bought another bottle?'

I give her a flat smile. 'Like I said, I had some upsetting news. Now if you don't mind, Rosie, I've got things I need to do today, so...'

'Yeah, of course.' She sips her tea and stands, eyes darting all around as though she's only just noticed the place. 'This is a big house, Dina. For one person, I mean.'

'Yeah, I know,' I say. 'Thanks for stopping by, Rosie.'

She wrinkles her nose and gives me a little nod, and I follow her to the front door, open it for her.

'You know what,' she says before stepping outside,

'everybody thinks they can deal with this stuff on their own, Dina, and I really hope you can, but mostly people can't. There's no shame in that.' Rosie hunts through the pockets of her dungarees. 'I know the meetings aren't for everyone – God knows Justin can get a little socks and sandals – but knowing there's somebody out there you can turn to when things get rough can be a real help. So look...' She takes my hand, and with the pen she's found, starts to write on my palm.

'Rosie, I...'

'This is a non-obligatory offer, Dina,' she says, and lets my hand go. 'You don't have to use it if you don't want to, but I'd like to be there for you if you do – and besides, I haven't got anyone under my wing at the moment, so I'll be all yours.' She gives me a bright smile and steps outside.

'Rosie, I'm probably not—'

She holds up her hands to stop me. 'I'm only a phone call away, Dina. If you ever need me.'

I watch her skip down the front steps and along the drive, climb into a battered-looking Beetle with flower-power stickers pasted on the back, then I close the door. When I go into the kitchen I tighten the lid on the vodka and lay it in the freezer drawer where the last bottle used to sleep. Toss the melting ice cubes into the sink and place the glass in the dishwasher.

I can do this, I tell myself. It was just a blip. But I can't help taking a look at my palm.

Rosie has written her mobile number, followed by her name, and something else after that, but with the heat my sweaty skin is already trying to erase it. I step over to the window and spread my palm to get a better look. After her name she's written: *AA SPONSOR*

5

The vodka has remained untouched in the freezer for the past two days, but it's been on a constant carousel in my mind, a jumping horse in a looping race between Grant Chapman and Rosie Rey. I copied Rosie's number into my mobile under the name Lois Lane. I don't know why I entered her under that name. Maybe it's because, like Lois, Rosie is unreal to me, a fictional character I invented in a moment of stress. I won't be calling her anyway, despite keeping her number. What could someone so young offer me by way of worldly advice? How would she counsel a grieving mother who has reached beneath her bed for a lost sock and instead pulled out a dusty finger painting, with the daddy-assisted *Happy Birthday Mummy* crayoned above her two-year-old's chubby handprints. Or talk said grieving mother down from the proverbial cliff edge after she's buttered toast and called *breakfast* up the stairs to her ten-year-old daughter who's been dead for over a week. I wouldn't know what to say to that mother, and I *am* her.

When I answer the door, the estate agent queries me with a

stilted smile and semi-suspicious eyes. Young, black, and a light-grey suit (Seal Grey?) that hugs his lean physique. The stilted smile is no doubt disbelief and optimism both, that a way-down-the-list estate agency has got to step over the threshold of a house that should fetch offers in the region of one point two million, even in this market. The semi-suspicious eyes are probably down to the fact that the cleaner has answered the door.

'Mrs Young?'

Bless him. He could have just stated his business and let me solve the riddle of the woman who looks as though she's slept in her clothes, but he went all out (tentatively, yes) and generously assumed I might be the owner of the biggest house his agency will have listed to date. And I've checked their website, it will be.

'Darryl,' I say. 'Thank you for coming out.'

We start in the kitchen, where I've set up a jug of iced water jazzed with a corkscrew of lemon and lime peel, and he lays out his folder on the table.

'You have a lovely home, Mrs Young,' he lies, as if he hasn't noticed the scaffold tower that dominates the entrance hall, the bare plaster walls and concrete floors. And it's worse even than that. I used to make an effort before an agent arrived – dress the rooms to make it look as though a family lived here, despite the upheaval of being midway through a renovation – to make it look as though it hasn't been this way for the past two years and I am living alone. We're onto jugs of iced water now, but in the winter it was a pot of tea under a cosy and a plate of Gingernuts. I don't bother with the biscuits anymore, and so I'm certainly not going to bother with tidying. Myself included.

With the niceties out of the way, Darryl walks me through the usual agent patter, and I nod politely as though I haven't heard it a hundred times, when all I want to do is throw him one of the dozen mock-up brochures I've been collecting and tell him to get to the pricing. He'll already have a ballpark figure in his head. He'll have researched the area, especially because he's not a local agent, and he'll know that the art deco property opposite was on the market a few years ago asking for offers in the region of three million, and the Huf Haus a few doors down has been listed again for offers in the region of two million. Even the run-down little cottage next to mine has been valued at close to a mill, and that was ten years ago.

But no, Darryl has his job to do, and I'll just have to endure it. And you never know, he might have something different to say. At least he hasn't mentioned the crack yet.

'So, now you have an idea of what we do,' Darryl says, standing up with his folder, 'I'll take some details and measurements. Go from there.' He smiles at me, but I can see he's only seeing the elephant in the room, that there must be two dozen higher-up-the-food-chain agencies more local than his, and why haven't I called them. I feel for him. He must be itching to know.

He starts at the front door, and I'm thrilled that he's using a Dictaphone. I find the younger agents do, and I'm always intrigued by how differently they describe the same rooms, given that they're all gathering the same details. The measurements never change, of course, although the house feels to me like it's getting smaller by the month. I linger just out of sight and eavesdrop on Darryl's take on the place.

'Entrance hall: a spacious, double-height area with high arch window in apex of the vaulted ceiling, providing plenty of light. Exposed oak beams...'

We removed the fifth bedroom and the loft space above it to achieve the generous double-height entrance hall and reveal the beams and the arch window. I commissioned a local stained-glass artist to reglaze the arch, depicting Saint Urban of Langres – a sort of mini-reproduction of a window I'd seen in a little church in France. It was on a school trip, and we had to sketch the window while Mrs Bean gave us a brief history of the saint. I wanted to recreate the same feeling of peace I felt back then, with whitewashed walls and limestone flagstones painted in the rainbow colours of the stained glass, but once our builder folded and Roy died of a heart attack, creating a churchlike feeling suddenly didn't seem as important, even if I'd had the money or the creative energy to do it. All I have now is a concrete floor and bare plaster walls, a vintage coat stand that looks out of time rather than timeless, and a scaffold tower I don't know how to dismantle, which obstructs the lounge door. A long way from the feeling of peace I was hoping for, but I at least have somewhere to dry the bath towels and bed linen, when I can be bothered to wash them.

'...and principal staircase leading to a galleried landing and the first floor...'

I let Darryl climb the stairs, then follow him up, hang around on the landing and look out of the arch window while he measures the first of the two guest bedrooms. Not much to describe in them, both stripped back and awaiting my decisions on colours, fabrics and theme. I was leaning towards a fusion of Transitional and Bohemian, something peaceful and playful at the same time – "*A haven for the artistic and the laissez-faire types...*" Roy would tease whenever I tried to explain the concept to him. And then I'd feign discouragement, sulk at his lack of faith in me, but only because I knew he'd kiss my neck and whisper how wonderful it would look once I'd finished. How wonderful our home was going to be.

Darryl moves along the "principal landing" towards the master bedroom, poking his head into the family bathroom first and listing the roll-top bath, WC with high-level flush and pedestal washbasin. He doesn't mention the limescaled taps or the fungussy smell of mould though, so I don't have to blame the builders for the state it's been left in, or joke about it being the new Shabby Chic – lines I've used several times before. It used to be clean, used to smell of Becky's hair after I'd rinsed out the shampoo, of the fresh towels I would bundle her in, scrubbing her plumped skin in my fingers and hearing her giggle and squeal.

He pushes open the door to my bedroom, revealing the unmade bed and the clothes that litter the floor, ignoring the mess like it's a ghost he cannot see.

'Master bedroom: a generous double bedroom with two large casement windows on the front and rear elevations providing views of the back garden...'

I don't think I'd call it a garden anymore, although somewhere out there, buried in the overgrowth, is a rusting swing-set and a sandbox. The garden was Roy's domain, and he had heady plans to grow organic vegetables and pickle things in his old age, until I persuaded him to dig half of it up to provide access to the basement so my exclusive list of discerning clients wouldn't have to come in through the house. Such plans, such... Oh. I think Darryl has spotted the crack.

He turns to me, gestures at the dark line in the wall that runs diagonally from the top corner of the room to the floor, where it actually splits the skirting board like a lightning strike.

'Do you have a structural report on this, Mrs Young?' he asks.

'Not as such,' I tell him. 'Our builder appraised it and gave us a price to deal with it, which we paid. He then went belly-up, taking all our money with him into bankruptcy. And you know how it is, the taxman gets his share first. We lost everything.'

'I'm sorry to hear that,' Darryl says, and then, 'So this is...'

'Subsidence, yes.'

'And it still needs...'

'You tell me what it needs, Darryl. The crack goes all the way down to the basement. Let me show you.' I walk him back out onto the "principal landing" and past Becky's room. I doubt Darryl will want to see it now anyway.

6

I take Darryl through the kitchen, to the basement door that would've been discreetly hidden within the walk-in larder if the door had been hung, but instead the door stands against the wall, still sheathed in its protective polythene, suffocating in its own body bag.

'The main crack runs from the bedroom and through the snug,' I tell him as I open the basement door and flick the light on. 'And there's also damage in the kitchen, but the units mostly hide it.' I take the narrow stairs to the basement floor and make my way over to where the crack emerges from the ceiling and strikes a path through the brickwork to the bottom corner of what was one day going to be my design studio and office.

Once Darryl has joined me on the cold concrete floor, among the dozen or so bags of sand and cement and the mute concrete mixer that squats beside them, he notices the two gaping holes that have been excavated. One in the corner where the crack disappears, and one in the centre of this large – if not low – space. Both holes are around four-by-four feet wide and about half as deep, revealing the dark earth that slumbers below this house.

'Is it safe to be in here?' he asks, having to hunch to stop his head from touching the boarded ceiling.

'Well, it's been like this for over two years now,' I say, but I can see by Darryl's wide eyes that I haven't reassured him, and so I change the subject. 'We were going to take out this wall here, to create a separate entrance to what was going to be my studio and office. These holes were excavated to see how far we could lower the floor, to give us the headspace, but...'

'But the subsidence needed addressing first.'

That and the debt my husband and builder left me in. And Becky... There are dark holes everywhere in my life, not just in the basement floor.

We go back up into the kitchen, which has a tropical climate compared to the basement.

'Can I get you some more iced water, Darryl?' I ask.

'I'll finish upstairs first, Mrs Young,' he says, 'and then—'

'Darryl, look, I know there's a process you have to go through, and I really don't want to waste any more of your time, but you've already got a figure in mind and I just want to know that we're on the same page.'

He lowers his gaze, tapping a knuckle gently against the kitchen table. 'I know how much you purchased the property for, Mrs Young, and the market has crawled since then—'

'But it hasn't lost value,' I say. 'You should have seen the state of the place when we bought it – the old lady who owned it had lived here all her life before she passed away, I mean, if you'd seen the amount of woodchip we had to—'

'In its present state – taking into consideration the subsidence – we could only list it as a renovation opportunity, and I'm afraid, with the best will in the world, it wouldn't attract interest over the million mark. Now I know that's not what you want to h—'

'But we've improved so much on the house since we've been here,' I say, as I've said to all of the agents who've come here.

'I'm not saying you couldn't achieve one point two – or even exceed that – but you would have to complete the renovation to a very high spec, resolve the subsidence issue – and I think a basement studio would be a fantastic addition.'

I can't do any of those things, and this house has just grown a little smaller around me.

*"I think every room should have colour in it and black."*

~ Ray Staples

7

I've been feverish for the past week, drifting between shivering chills and suffocating night sweats. Sleep has come in hallucinogenic waves, and I've woken several times to find myself standing in Becky's room, the duvet wrapped around my shoulders and sucking to my skin, my eyes wringing out tears from the newly-minted loss of my child. The daylight colour of this loss I have named Sirocco. It's curiously colourless in my mind, like the wind, but has a heat and a low pressure to it. The night-time loss I feel when I wake from a dream, expecting to find Becky in my bed, I've yet to name, but it's neon white and searing, like staring into a winter sun.

I shower for the first time in days and will myself to eat. Toast with a scraping of butter. I only manage one slice. I can't stop thinking about the vodka, or Grant Chapman. He'll be out in six days, ready to join the world again. Anew. I wonder how often he thinks about what he's done, how his actions have wiped two lives from this earth (yes, I blame him for Roy) and destroyed another. If there's one thing I could hope for, one thing that could give me a grain of comfort, is that he looks in the mirror every day and is reminded of what he's done, in the same way the scar on my eyelid sends my mind rushing back to the scene of the crash. To the image of Becky's golden hair streaked with blood. That would be something.

The mid-morning heat is already unbearable, and more so as I'm sitting on the driveway in my car. A silver Saab. It's not flashy, not a new or expensive model I don't think. Roy bought it for me, thought it was time I stopped relying on taxis, considering I'd been legal to drive since I was nineteen years old but had never bothered to buy myself a car after I passed the test. I sit out here quite often, to get a break from the house and to turn the engine over. I can't remember the last time I drove it, and I don't know if I'd have the confidence now, but the leather smells nice against the cigarette smoke, and I don't dare smoke in the house. Roy would be too disappointed in me. When I look in the rear-view the house is flipped around and I can imagine an alternate universe where Becky is alive and Roy and me are still together. And from here I can imagine the house is finished inside – this beautiful old Suffolk red-brick, with its arched, hardwood sashes, and the rose window set within the apex of the roof, which provides natural light to what's left of the loft space. It was going to be so wonderful, our lives together.

I'm smoking with the windows down, hoping to glimpse the comings and goings of my nameless neighbours, but it isn't one of those roads. You'll never catch anybody putting out their bins, or watering their front lawn in their bathrobe and slippers – the houses are just too far apart. Our house sits on the high side of the road, semi-shielded by skeletal evergreens. The houses on the other side of the road sit way back, half-buried in their sunken drives, the woodland behind them blotting out the view of the town. The art deco house, with its white-washed walls and curves, rises like a cruise ship. I've yet to see the captain, and I wonder if any of my neighbours would recognise me in the street, as I wouldn't recognise them. I blast the car horn for thirty seconds, to see who might stir, but nobody does. They never do. I wonder what would happen if I screamed.

8

Grant Chapman will be out in four days, and I'll still be trapped in this cell. *My hell.* I found one of Becky's colouring pencils down the back of the sofa this morning while I was digging around for change. I wanted to walk into town and buy a newspaper, or a carton of milk, anything to give me a reason to get out of this house that meant I didn't have to draw money from the bank and see how close I am to plummeting into my overdraft, as Roy's pension money doesn't go in for another week. But no. I found a colouring pencil instead. Pastel green. Chartreuse.

I've been rolling the pencil around on the kitchen table for some time now, wondering whether I should put it in the bin or return it to Becky's room, to her craft drawer. Both choices are torture. Discarding anything of Becky's feels crushingly disloyal, but equally, venturing into her room always ends the same way. Daytime bleeding into night-time and an emptying of myself, and when I close the door it's as if I don't know where I am, stood in the dark on the landing, the scaffold tower surging up beyond the balustrade, into the vaulted ceiling like some mystical tower in a fantastical land. Oh how I would love to climb that tower and escape this place.

I return the pencil to the depths of the sofa, and take a walk down by the river.

Three days. That murdering bastard will be out in three days. The view of his cell walls will become blue skies and countryside, if he so chooses, as will alcohol be back on his menu.

I wonder if he'll celebrate his freedom. Wonder if his family and friends will organise a party for him. *Pop! A toast! We've missed you, son! Welcome home!* Or maybe shame will drive him far away from here. That would be the right thing to do, wouldn't it? Start his new life somewhere else, somewhere not near me.

No. Detective Wallace seemed to think there'd be a chance we might cross paths, so I bet Detective Wallace knows the details of Grant Chapman's immediate plans for release. I remember something mentioned in court about Chapman being a bartender. Does that mean he'll walk straight back into his old job? Don't convicted murderers have to have a job lined up before they leave prison? Have a place to stay? Maybe, maybe not. But Detective Wallace knows, and even scum like Chapman wouldn't skip town if his father had terminal cancer – *especially* if he had terminal cancer. Might be some inheritance money in it for him. Just think about that for a second. Chapman strolls out of prison and has his dying father's house to look forward to, and a nice little nest egg I imagine. You couldn't make it up.

The vodka sings to me, and I need something to occupy my mind, my hands. If Chapman's view is about to change, then so should mine. This house, *my* cell, has been telling the same story over and over for the past eighteen months, a continuous looping reel of the same stagnating frame. Time to change the narrative. And who knows, throwing myself into a design project might reboot my creativity (haven't my colour charts been calling to me lately?), and provide me with an empowering *fuck you* to Grant Chapman, and a glimmer of hope that he hadn't decimated every last thing in my life but left me with an artistic seed that I could nurture.

The workmen's tools have to go. There's equipment here that must have value for somebody, I just have to be bothered to research what I have and put a price on it, eBay the lot. And if I can scrape together enough money to buy some paint, a roll of wallpaper for the chimney-breast in the snug – doesn't have to be Edmond Petit or Thibaut – Laura Ashley will do in a pinch. Imagine, a refuge within this house, a single room that doesn't remind me of what I've lost. Even the Saab has its ghosts.

10

I spent the following day cataloguing and photographing every single item the contractor had left behind, leaving off a few bits that I thought might come in handy for when I tackled the decorating of the snug. The remainder of the list was long, and took me several hours to upload the pictures to eBay and cut and paste the details I'd found for identical tools, or close enough, to give me a rough estimate for what I was looking for moneywise. The offers started rolling in before I'd finished listing them all, and by early evening I had six different people arrive at my door to collect various items, from belt sanders and buckets to cordless drills and chargers. I got peanuts for the buckets, but the power tools netted me over a hundred and forty pounds, and I still had plenty more to sell. The cement mixer and the scaffold tower included.

Both the vodka and Grant Chapman remained in my thoughts, but not nearly as fresh and bright, and Becky only came to me when I finally collapsed into bed, my mind nicely numbed by the menial tasks of the day. She was doing her homework at the kitchen table while I was sitting on the counter waiting for the frozen pizza to cook. She had this way of hunching when she wrote or drew, the tip of her pink little tongue peeking from the corner of her mouth, which seemed to highlight the fact she had learning difficulties, a result of her birth being premature by three weeks and causing her brain to be underdeveloped. It was this level of concentration that she had to apply to even the simplest of tasks, that made it appear like she'd escaped to a different world, hiding there. I remembered thinking, while I waited for the pizza, that I didn't blame her for trying to get away from me.

11

'Grant Chapman will be free tomorrow, and there is nothing I can do about it.' There. It's said. And I'm surprised at how calm I feel about it, or is it hopelessness I feel? Either way it's out of my control and the only thing I can do is carry on.

Apart from the cement mixer and the scaffold tower (no enquiries on the mixer, and only one for the tower, who went dark when I told them they would have to dismantle), I have the last of the tools being collected this afternoon – something called a "skill saw". It's a vicious-looking thing that I imagine could dismember a body quite neatly, if a person had a mind, but I'll be glad when it's gone. The temptation's too great, especially as it's cordless and surprisingly light. I'm kidding myself, of course. I'm way too squeamish around blood, and besides, if I was going to do anything like that to Grant Chapman I would have kept the nail gun I sold this morning. Far less messy, if perhaps less fun.

The doorbell. Thank God they're here early, I was starting to think of places to hide a body. With the thirty pounds I'm getting for the saw I'll have over four hundred to spend on the snug, and more importantly, a creative project to distract me. Murder, even fantasyland murder, is a grotesque preoccupation for an artistic mind. Especially when I think I'd be rather good at it. Again, kidding.

'Detective Wallace?' He tucks away the handkerchief he's presumably just dragged across his brow, but with his jacket and tie buttoned and cinched, in this heat, I don't sympathise.

'Hello, Mrs Young.' He stares at the skill saw I'm holding and I can't help thinking of that Tom Cruise movie where you can be arrested for just thinking about a crime. 'Doing a bit of DIY?'

'No, umm, just getting rid of some stuff. Is there something wrong?'

'No, I was in the area and I thought I'd swing by, to see how you were doing. I wasn't sure if you were okay when I left you last time.'

'That's kind of you,' I say, 'but I'm fine – will be fine.'

'Good.' He offers me a tight smile, which I suppose is to reflect sympathy, or maybe his own unease, but only serves to highlight the darkness around his eyes. Poor sleeper, I imagine. 'And I didn't mention it before, but I was sorry to hear about your husband, you know, so close to your daughter...'

Two days. That's how long it took for Grant Chapman to fell my entire family. 'He had an underlying heart issue,' I say, 'but I'm sure it didn't help that he'd just lost his only daughter to a drunk driver. And at least he wasn't around to witness Chapman's corrupt solicitor magic up a two-year joke of a sentence – and who no doubt had a hand in that murderer's imminent release tomorrow – because that would have killed him for sure.'

'Actually, Mrs Young, it was yesterday.'

'What was yesterday?' The saw tightens in my grip.

'Chapman's release. His father took a turn for the worse and so—'

'And so the judge thought he'd better have an early release from his early release. Naturally.' I want to double over from the pain, a pain that can only be lessened by the medicine in my freezer drawer.

'Could I step inside for a moment, Mrs Young?' he says, reaching for something in his jacket pocket. 'I've some numbers for you – counsellors and support groups that could help—'

I look over Detective Wallace's shoulder and he follows my gaze, towards the young man in shorts and sandals walking up my driveway.

'I'm here for the saw?' the young man says sheepishly when he reaches us. We make the exchange, and when I return my attention to Detective Wallace he's holding a piece of folded paper.

'It really can help,' he tells me.

I accept his offering, but only to get him off my doorstep.

12

The taxi drops me home a couple of hours later, the driver sitting idle as I struggle to my front door with the paint and rolls of wallpaper. I'd phoned for a cab the moment Detective Wallace left, and waited for it in the Saab to get out of the house, reading over the list of support groups he'd suggested I might find useful: three different bereavement counsellors, for the loss of a child, the loss of a spouse, and a widow support group. The last group Detective Wallace had suggested irked me more than a little. It was for the local AA meeting I'd already been to and crashed out of, and irked me because my alcoholism is visible even in sobriety and I'm blind to it. When I look in the mirror, apart from the scar on my eyelid, I only see a tired, ill-kept woman in her early forties staring back. Depressed perhaps, yes, but no neon sign lighting me up as a recovering soak. Maybe the AA is a standard-issue handout in cases like mine. Preventative as much as anything else. But for some reason I didn't think so, hence the irksomeness.

When I step inside my echo chamber of an entrance hall – the entrance hall that was once going to be a peaceful and semi-religious embrace upon entering – I dump down the paint and the wallpaper and fold to the returning pain in my stomach. The sheer will it's taken for me to go outside and function in public, knowing I might bump into Grant Chapman, has bent me before the scaffold tower, which has become day by day a mocking monument to my life. I've been naïve to think that a newly decorated snug is going to resuscitate the stillbirth that is my interior design career. Chapman put paid to that with a single wink, and I'd toasted the event with a double vodka and tonic. If I have ever felt sadder in my whole life...

A dry sob escapes me. I have no fight left. Chapman can claim his third and final victim of the Young family, as if he hadn't already.

I go to the freezer drawer and take out the vodka, but this time there's no ceremony. Civilised alcoholism is still alcoholism, and either way will lay you low. I drink deeply from the icy bottle and my eyes begin to stream, the vodka near tasteless at this temperature but no less potent. I feel the burn and I feel the burn. My poor Becky. Please forgive me.

13

I wake in near darkness, but it's the sliver of moon that allows me to see my hand in front of my face. And that sliver seems odd to me. Oddly close. A cloud drifts across the moon and it makes my stomach lurch, as though the house is floating, as though it has uprooted in the night and I'm miles away, over a foreign sea or ocean. I roll onto my side and vomit, the familiar acidic vapour stinging my eyes and nostrils as I laugh and cry at the same time. Silly bitch. So weak...

*Becky...*

When I'm done retching I try to sit up, but it feels all wrong. I'm not in bed or on the floor, and my feet seem to be floating. I think maybe I've passed out on the kitchen table – a first. *"Congratulations, Dina, you always fancied yourself the bohemian,"* I imagine Roy saying, but not in a teasing tone.

The crescent moon zooms in again when the cloud passes, and with my eyes more adjusted I can see it framed within the arch window, but the window is impossibly close. I scooch forward until my knees hinge and my feet dangle over the tabletop, and then I feel the subtle sway that I know isn't my seasick stomach, because I know how solid my kitchen table is. And from my kitchen table I wouldn't be able to see the arch window, which is set within the apex of the vaulted ceiling, the ceiling that's in the entrance hall…

I'm suddenly and utterly frozen with fear as I realise I'm sitting on top of the scaffold tower platform, almost ten metres from the concrete floor below.

I sit here for some time, unable to move and unable to remember how on earth I managed to get up here. There's no ladder attached to the tower, because the safety rails had yet to be erected, so did that mean I scaled the criss-crossing braces? I feel sick again but know I have nothing left to bring up. Why would I do such a thing, such a dangerous thing? I often fantasised about this tower being a magical gateway to another place, but in the state I was in, had I thought it the stage for my suicide? Was I going to jump?

I venture forward and peek over the edge, can barely see the floor in the darkness. My head swims. I grope for my phone and thankfully it's slid into the back of my jeans, start to dial nine-nine-nine but stop before the final nine. I can't be seen like this. Can't have my neighbours woken by sirens and flashing lights on my drive. Can't have them know that I've become a danger to myself. Instead I scroll through my contacts, past the names of old student pals and school friends I've long since lost touch with, people from Roy's social circle who soon showed their loyalty towards me once he died. Past Mum and Dad, who I rarely ever speak to anymore, and finally I highlight the only possible name I can call, a complete stranger to me, a fiction. Lois Lane. The phone rings twice before she picks up.

'Rosie…' My voice is weak, pathetic to my ears.

'Dina,' Rosie answers without question. 'I'll be right over.'

I sat under the critical eye of the moon for what felt like an hour or more, but it's only fifteen minutes when I check what time I'd called Rosie. Bless her, it was gone midnight, and whether or not I'd got her out of bed, I had no right.

The headlights of her car sweep a beacon of light through the front door, and a few seconds later the engine dies and the entrance hall sinks back into shadow. Then Rosie rings the doorbell.

'It's open!' I shout, hugging my knees. The silhouette at the door steps inside.

'Dina?'

'I'm up here. There's a light switch on your right.'

'Shit!'

'You okay?'

'Yeah,' Rosie says, and the entrance hall lights come on. 'Just kicked over a pot of paint – don't worry, the lid stayed on, it's just the skin on my shin that came off. Fuck, that hurts... Where are you?'

I peer down at her. She's hopping around, gripping her leg above the laces of her turquoise All-Stars, only this time she's paired them with a funky, animal-print pyjama set. I *have* gotten her out of bed. I also notice the vodka bottle, which lies in glittering shards beneath the scaffold tower, a darkened bloom soaked into the concrete that I could optimistically gauge at no more than a quarter of a bottle – the rest shared between me and the puddle of vomit that sits beside me. Had I really tried to climb up here with it? It frightens me that it could so easily be my blood staining the concrete. My bones in shards.

Rosie scrubs her shin a final time and follows my embarrassed cough. 'How the freaking hell did you get up there, Dina?' she says.

'I'm guessing I climbed, but I can't get down, not on my own.'

Rosie limps to the foot of the tower, surveys me with her hands on her slim hips, then to the crime scene of booze on the floor. 'Well, okay,' she says, blowing a few strands of hair from her eyes. 'You did the right thing calling me.'

14

The scaffold tower is on wheels, and as I couldn't possibly climb down the way I'd apparently climbed up, Rosie thought if she rolled the tower against the balustrade I might be able to get a foothold onto the handrail, and from there she could help me to the safety of the landing.

I yelp inside when the tower begins to move, and again when it bumps into the gallery rail, then Rosie trots upstairs to meet me.

'Okay, Dina,' she says, as I peer over the platform. 'You need to get a toe on this strut here first, then it's just a little step down onto the handrail. Just like when you were a kid at the park. Fearless, remember?'

*As fearless as I was when I climbed up here*, I think, and notice all of my courage shattered on the concrete below. I roll onto my stomach and lower my legs over the edge of the platform, crane a foot towards the first strut.

'A touch to the right, Dina, your toe is almost there.'

I feel the strut beneath my foot and risk sliding my body from the platform, relieved that I can now see where to place my hands and my other foot.

'Keep coming,' Rosie says, and grabs my ankle and plants it on the gallery rail. 'There you go, now give me your hand.'

It's a curious feeling, the calm that washes over me when I take Rosie's hand and transfer my weight from the tower to her, the trust I transfer too, to this young woman. This stranger. I hop down from the rail, and with her help, land softly on the landing. A shuddering sigh escapes me.

'Let's get you some coffee,' Rosie says.

She sits me at the kitchen table and fetches me a glass of water while she makes the coffee, asks me where I keep the paracetamol. She's done this before, I think. Both sides. She sets the pills and the coffee down in front of me and asks where I keep the dustpan and brush, the mop and bucket. I tell her not to bother, I'll do it in the morning, but she reminds me that the smell of vodka makes her bilious and she can't get rid of the smell until she's got rid of the glass. I haven't the will to argue, and so I take the paracetamol with the water and sip the coffee until my head stops throbbing, which doesn't take long, as this isn't a real hangover. There are parts of me that are unaffected by this lapse, like it's only the partially laid pieces of the jigsaw puzzle that are suffering, and the pieces still in the box remain untouched. It's only when you've been drinking for uninterrupted weeks and months that all the pieces become woolly, and it doesn't matter whether the puzzle is complete or there are still pieces in the box, the overall picture is blurred.

Once Rosie has put away the mop and bucket, she joins me at the kitchen table with a coffee of her own. Mine's gone cold, but I can't stomach another one.

'So...' Rosie hangs the word out there like a baton I'm supposed to pick up, when all I want to do is go to bed. But how can I? I've dragged this poor girl from her own bed, to come save a woman who's as much a stranger to her as she is to me. And maybe it's time, time to have somebody shake me by the shoulders and tell me to get on with it – that obsessing about this... *man*, will only drive me deeper into insanity.

'It was the winter before last when my daughter died,' I say, hugging my cold mug of coffee. 'I was walking Becky home from school, and we were playing *Don't step on the cracks* when a car mounted the pavement and crushed her dead against the school railings.' I pinch my eyes shut. 'I can still feel her hand in mine sometimes, before it was ripped away.'

Rosie touches her mouth. 'I'm so sorry, Dina.'

'The driver, Grant Chapman, was three times over the legal limit, and for killing my daughter the judge gave him two years. *Two years*. But the worst thing, the thing that really tortures me, is that when they were about to take him down, he winked at me.' I pinch my eyes again, and see that wink fresh in my mind.

Rosie sucks in a sharp breath.

'Then a couple of weeks ago a detective came to see me, to tell me that Chapman was going to be released early, and I just – I just wasn't prepared, and so...'

'Nothing can prepare you for that, Dina,' Rosie says. 'And nobody said you needed to be. There's no rule book.'

'I suppose.'

'And give yourself some credit while you're at it. You reached out, and that tells me you're stronger than you think. Forget about tonight, it's done.'

'But I'm not strong,' I say. 'I hate what I've become.'

'Do not let alcoholism define you, Dina.'

'I'm not talking about the drinking, Rosie. I've become mean-spirited – have horrible thoughts about that man. Vengeful thoughts.'

Rosie lowers her gaze from mine and I see I've frightened her, told her too much. She may have experience of the ravages of alcohol, way beyond her years, but the poison of hatred is something she cannot know, because in this area she *is* too young. Her brightness screams of unbreakable optimism. She is orange, luminescent in her outlook. Tangerine against the toxic bruise of my Indigo.

'Colour me curious,' Rosie says, as though disagreeing with the shades of us I've chosen in my mind, 'but what would you want to do to this man?'

I laugh. It's nervous. 'What do you mean?' I ask her.

'I mean, if you could even the score somehow, what would you do?'

'Hypothetically?'

She shrugs. Sips her coffee.

'I'm being melodramatic,' I say. 'Of course I wouldn't do anything, it's just...'

'Just?'

My turn to shrug. 'It's just that he walked away without a scratch and I find it sickening that he did so much damage and has nothing to show for it. Even I was scarred that day.'

'You were hit too?'

'No, I stupidly slipped and fell trying to get to Becky. Cut my eyelid open on the back of his car.' I stretch the lid down with a finger. Rosie leaves her chair and comes over to me, holds my head still at the temples, so close I can feel her coffee breath on my face. When I open my eye again she stays there for a beat, and I can pick out the different flecks and shards of green in her irises.

'Well, if you hadn't told me it was there I wouldn't have noticed,' she says. 'But *you* see it, don't you?'

I nod, and she lets go of me but doesn't return to her seat. Instead, she crouches and takes my hands.

'Every time I look in the mirror,' I say, 'it brings it all back so fresh. I suppose that's what I want him to feel. I would want him to look in the mirror every day and be reminded of what he's done to me. Hypothetically, of course.'

'Hypothetically, maybe karma will get somebody to throw acid in his face.' Rosie suddenly squeezes my hands, and almost to herself, says, 'Actually, Dina, you should totally throw acid in his face.'

15

The one thing I used to love about Roy, and the thing that used to infuriate him about me, was that I could always tell when he was bluffing. Like the time he threatened to leave me because of my smoking. I'd fallen asleep in the snug again with a cigarette on the go and could have burned the house down if he hadn't been there. Even then, despite his apocalyptic tones, I knew he wasn't serious. But I did feel mean that I could see through him so easily, and so I compromised with a promise to only smoke in the Saab.

I've got no such read on Rosie Rey, who has just suggested I throw acid in Grant Chapman's face. And as I sit here waiting for her expression to change from the picture of calm it is at the moment, for her mouth to widen in a gotcha-grin, my mind is fifty-fifty split as to whether she is being serious or not.

I cave. 'Are you being serious, Rosie?'

Rosie takes the chair next to me. 'I'm not suggesting you disfigure the man, Dina, but we've all heard the stories about the jilted lover flicking acid—'

'Oh my God, Rosie, you *are* serious.' I laugh, and the craziness I hear in it disturbs me, that for the briefest of moments I imagine Grant Chapman screaming, smoke pouring from his burning skin...

Rosie holds her hands up. 'Hypothetically, Dina, you have to agree that a couple of drops of hydrochloric acid flicked at him would be poetic justice.'

I think even hypothetically that's a bridge too far, but I'm too tired to get into it with her. 'Rosie, if you don't mind, I really need to sleep.'

She drums the tabletop and points at me. 'You gonna be okay?'

'I'll be fine, thank you for coming out.'

'That's what sponsors do.' She springs up and heads for the kitchen doorway. 'I'll pop back in a couple of days to see how you're doing. No arguments.'

I concede with a flat smile and show her to the front door.

'When does he get out?' Rosie asks when she steps into the night.

'He's already out,' I say. 'Nite, Rosie, and thank you again.'

She gives me a girly wave as she skips to her car in her animal-print pyjamas and turquoise All Stars, and I lock the door.

16

The following day I desperately need distraction, and so despite the weather forecast predicting we're going to hit a skin-blistering ninety-one degrees, I make a start on the snug. I've always been good with a brush, both as an artist and a decorator, and I had to be. Roy had neither the time nor the inclination for DIY, and in the early days we didn't have the money to pay professionals to do the work, so I did it – the painting at least. And it paid off too. My early (so-called) clients seemed to appreciate me getting hands-on with my design projects – onsite through concept to completion. But today it feels like I don't know which end of the brush to hold, so it's a welcome break to race to the kitchen to answer the phone, and especially nice to find it isn't Rosie Rey or Detective Wallace.

'Hello, Mrs Young, it's Darryl from Hatcher & Lake. How are you this morning?'

Awful. 'Fine,' I say, a little confused as to which estate agent I'm speaking to, there's been so many.

'Excellent,' he says, and the lustre of his voice sparks an image in my mind. It's the young black man from the other

57

week. 'I just wanted to let you know that we're listing the property.'

'Listing it? But I thought... At what price, Darryl?'

'At the price you suggested, Mrs Young. I'm going to pop over this afternoon to take some internals, if that's okay? I've only got the façade on the website at the moment.'

'I thought you were reluctant at that price?'

'I was, and am, but like you said, a house like yours will look good on our list.'

'Even if it never sells...'

'Let's not write it off straight away,' Darryl chirps. 'I did have some interest this morning just from the external picture alone, from a woman looking to relocate back to England from the United States. Might come to nothing as she needs to speak to her husband first, but I'd be very surprised if she doesn't call back to at least arrange a viewing. Would twelve o'clock be convenient?'

'For a viewing?' I picture the mess in every room.

'For the internals.'

Again, I picture the mess in every room. 'Can we say two?'

A few hours later, Darryl appears in the Saab's rear-view mirror, hopping down my front steps with his camera held up like a gold medal for his proud parents to inspect. I lean my head out of the window and blow smoke.

'All done, Mrs Young,' he calls, not coming over. 'I'll upload to the website tomorrow and email you a link.'

'Thanks, Darryl,' I say. 'Any news from the lady about viewing the house?'

'Not yet,' he says. 'But I'll call you as soon as she gets back in touch.'

When Darryl has gone, I notice a spider busily constructing a web across the windshield, and I think of another reason to miss Roy. He opened windows for glass-bumping flies, cupped moths and freed them in the garden, and always used humane mouse traps, releasing them each time in the exact same place in the woods behind the house, believing they would catch the scent of the previously liberated mouse and be reunited with its kin. He was sweet like that.

'Sorry, Roy,' I say, as I flick the ignition key and light up the Saab's dash. The wiper blade swipes, but instead of harmlessly casting the spider aside, as I'd hoped, it spreads it in a muddy arc, as I'd feared. I feel terrible, but with Roy gone I am reduced to such callous methods of disposal as I'm the classic cringer when it comes to anything that scurries, creeps or crawls, making the very notion of throwing acid in someone's face almost unbearable to think about. *Almost.* At least I did cringe when I thought about it, in that brief moment in the night before sleep dragged me elsewhere.

And now I'm thinking about it again, and I can feel Roy's eyes on the back of my head, judging me. 'I'm sorry,' I repeat, and activate the screenwash but only hear the whirr of dry jets, the wiper blade spreading the spider like Marmite over hot toast and flashing an image of Grant Chapman's acid-burned face in my mind. I suppose I'll have to endure the spider's remains until the next downpour, though Chapman's burning face might be harder to dislodge. I'm sure Roy would say I got what I deserved, for even thinking about something so awful.

I decide to get back to work on the snug, if only to brighten one room before the possible viewing of Darryl's interested party. It probably won't come to anything, but you never know. The universe has to balance out eventually.

With my limited palette and funds, I'd no choice but to paint the ceiling white, instead of the copper leaf it was crying out for, which would have married the Jewel Teal I'd chosen for the walls and the Turmeric and white Moroccan trellis I'd chosen to paper the chimney-breast. I know I can't finish the room to the spec I want, but I can see the finished space in my mind, the chenille throws and sumptuous floor cushions, the teak ottoman and side table inlayed in gold and mother-of-pearl quatrefoil, the tea lights and handcrafted candle lanterns scenting the air with sandalwood. Opulent and atmospheric, but only achievable in the mood board of my imagination. So whether the house sells or not, my vision of the snug will remain in my head, and the best I can hope for is that I stop seeing Becky lounging bored on the sofa, her little chin resting in her hands while she watches her after-school shows and waits for whatever culinary delight I have rotating in the microwave.

The other feature I'd decided not to tackle is the subsidence crack, which angles down from the top corner of the fireplace to the corner of the basement below. To fill it would be a cosmetic waste of time and feel deceitful. If I'm still here a year from now, I might style it into a flowering vine. The Italian designer Massimo Vignelli once said: *"The life of a designer is a life of fight: fight against the ugliness."* A noble battle for both a designer and an alcoholic.

I haven't wallpapered for some time, and I'm nervous about the first drop – a simple four feet from the cornice to the mantelpiece – but it goes up well. Rounding the corner of the chimney-breast is a different beast altogether, and the full ceiling-to-floor drop has peeled from the wall and draped over my head twice before I can cut it in. When it happens a third time, the doorbell chimes as though to save me, and so I take my cue to step away for a moment and breathe. The drop rolls down the wall to the floor and I know exactly how it feels.

After I grab the extension cable from the kitchen, I go to answer the front door. The man who's buying it knocked me down to a miserly ten pounds, but I'd been short on offers so had to accept. To my surprise it's a female silhouette I see in the frosted pane, and guess the man is waiting in the car. I'm more surprised when I open the door and find Rosie standing there.

'Hey, Dina,' Rosie says, removing her sunglasses and slipping them onto her head. She's more conventionally dressed today, wearing faded jeans and a plain white T-shirt, but I can make out a burgundy bra beneath, which predictably clashes with the lime-zest scrunchy that tames her messy bun, and of course, her turquoise All Stars. Her eyes drop to the extension cable. 'Watcha doing?'

'I...'

'I really have to pee, do you mind?' Rosie knocks her knees together, her eyes wide and hopeful.

I point. 'It's the door beneath the stairs, there.'

She pigeon-steps by me and I catch the scent of her skin, hot from the sun and mixed with a cocoa lotion of some kind. I can't remember the last time I'd put anything feminine on my skin except for the habitual jet of deodorant under my arms, to camouflage the evidence of not showering.

I leave the front door open and keep my post. Rosie is not staying. I hear the flush, watch her emerge and shimmy by the scaffold tower that semi-blocks the loo door.

'Is it just me or is it the hottest day so far this year?' she says, fanning her throat with her T-shirt.

'It is hot, yes.' I put the extension cable down beside the coat stand.

'But I suppose that's one good thing about having concrete floors,' Rosie says, looking around the entrance hall. 'Keeps the place cool – could I get a glass of water or something, Dina? Feel like I'm gonna pass out.' Another flap of her T-shirt and I'm closing the door and heading for the kitchen.

'Was there something I could do for you, Rosie?' I ask, handing her a glass of water. No ice.

'Not as such,' she says, making me wait for the rest while she drinks. 'I said I'd pop by, remember? To see how you were holding up?' She palms her brow and drinks again.

'I appreciate that, and thank you, I'm doing okay. And I have your number, just in case.' I edge back towards the entrance hall, but Rosie waggles her empty glass at me.

'Sorry,' she says, 'didn't touch the sides.'

I refill her glass at the sink and hand it to her. 'Was there anything else, Rosie? I'm sort of in the middle of something.'

'Oh, God, I'm so sorry, Dina.' Rosie sets the glass down on the kitchen table, taps her temple. 'Sometimes I just don't pick up on the social cues, you know – of course you have ice, duh! I'll get out of your hair.'

'Oh, no, it isn't that, Rosie,' I say as I follow her into the entrance hall, feeling now like a prize bitch. 'It's just that I'm wallpapering at the moment and I really want to get it finished today—'

'Well, why didn't you say, I'm great with that stuff. Do you know I decorated my whole flat on my own?'

'I didn't, no.' Again, I try to encourage her toward the front door, but again she doesn't take the hint.

'If you need a hand, Dina, just say. These old things...' She dusts her thighs. 'Doesn't matter if they get paint on 'em.'

'That's kind of you, Rosie, but the painting's all done. Just a bit of wallpapering left to do.' I reach the front door and open it, see a middle-aged man walking up my driveway. He raises a ten-pound note. I grab the extension cable and make the exchange, fold the note into the back pocket of my jeans. When I turn to face Rosie, she isn't there. 'Rosie?'

I step into the kitchen and call her again, but with no answer. I close the front door and check the loo. It's empty. I squeeze by the scaffold tower and go into the lounge, and through there down the short flight of steps that lead to the snug, which is where I find Rosie.

'Oh, Dina, it's gorgeous,' she says when she turns to me. 'I could smell the paint and couldn't resist a peek. I hope you don't mind?'

I hang back on the final step, mildly fuming. 'Well, actually, Rosie, I—'

'I saw Grant Chapman yesterday,' she says, stroking the one length of wallpaper I've hung so far, and gestures at the walls. 'What colour is that?'

'What...?'

'The wall colour. It matches my sneaks, look.' Rosie twists a foot onto its toe, and I step down into the snug.

'Those are turquoise, the walls are teal. What do you mean you saw Grant Chapman?'

Rosie tries on a wounded look. 'I mean I saw him at the pub he used to work at, then I followed him home.'

I'm sideswiped, can barely gather a coherent thought or question, but I know I must. I point towards the snug's steps. 'Kitchen.'

'You've got great taste, Dina,' Rosie says, gazing around the snug a final time before she heads for the steps. 'Shame about that crack.'

18

I place an iced water in front of Rosie and take the chair opposite her at the kitchen table. 'How did you find him?' I say, and my own iced water trembles at my lips and so I have to set it down.

Rosie bites the tip of her tongue and says, 'I googled the accident.'

'And?'

'And I wasn't snooping on you, Dina, I promise. I just wanted to get a fix on that murdering fucktard, and I found a piece that mentioned he was a bartender, and from there I started ringing around all the pubs in the area, close to the, you know, *accident*.'

'And what, you asked them if he was there?'

'Oh, no. I asked whoever picked up if Grant Chapman was coming back to work this week.' Rosie shrugs. 'All of them said they didn't know a Grant Chapman, except for one. A bloke at the Red Lion said that he didn't know if he was coming back to work, so I went there and sat at the bar for a while.'

'And he just walked in?'

'Bold. As. Brass.' Rosie sips her water.

'And you're sure it was him?'

Rosie brings out her phone. 'He's a little chubbier than his picture, but...' She slides her phone across the table and I shrink away from it. The picture's upside down, but I can see a face, and when Rosie flips it around, I see him. Grant Chapman. With a pint of beer at his lips.

'Was he... Did he look happy?'

Rosie takes her phone back and her thumbs work the screen in a blur. 'You tell me, Dina. I've been to the pub a few nights now, and it didn't take him long to come sniffing around me. He's super chatty when he's drunk, and he is always drunk.'

'You... you spoke to him?'

Rosie hands me her phone again. 'Just hit play.'

I swallow at the sight of Chapman's face in profile, as he reanimates when my trembling finger touches the play button. Rosie must have set her phone up to record him, as they sat opposite each other at a table near the bustling bar:

'You sure you don't wanna drink, Jenny?' Chapman asks, quaffing down the last of his pint.

'I'm good,' Rosie says, and then, 'Hey, somebody told me that you'd just got out of jail, is that true?'

'Brandon!' Chapman calls to someone stood at the bar, ignoring Rosie's question. 'Beer me, motherfucker!'

Rosie reaches across the table and touches Chapman's hand. It makes me feel sick. 'So, is it true? You just got out?'

Chapman sniffs. Seems to notice Rosie for the first time. 'Might have.'

'Drink driving, wasn't it?'

His jaw grows slack. 'Complete bollocks,' he says. 'I've driven home that route a million times, and waaaay drunker than that, but wham' – he claps his hands together – 'wrong place, wrong time. Bye-bye, freedom – Brandon, beer me!'

Rosie glances into the camera, then says, 'But didn't a girl die or something?'

'What?'

'Somebody mentioned a girl dying?'

'If ya like,' Chapman scoffs, his head unsteady. 'But if she hadn't been stood there I wouldn't have hit her, would I? And the joke is, I coulda got a lot more than two years – where the fuck is my beer...? Brandon!'

'You got two years for killing a girl?'

'I know, right?' Chapman says, thinking he's got a sympathetic ear, and I want to stop watching, but I can't. 'The girl's crazy-bitch mother was pushing for like ten fucking years – and if it hadn't been for my solicitor pulling something out of the bag, I don't know what – I could still be in there now!'

'So your brief got you off with a shorter sentence?'

'Said I was very lucky,' Chapman says, standing up with his empty pint glass. 'Though I didn't feel very lucky at the time. You sure you don't wanna drink, Jenny? I'm flush since my old man kicked.'

'Actually,' Rosie says, 'I have to go.'

'Suit yourself.'

Chapman dives into a space at the bar, waving his glass for service, and Rosie switches off her phone.

I rush to the sink and vomit, and it comes harsher than any hangover sickness I've ever experienced. Rosie rubs my back and I want to shrug her off, but on a deeper level I crave the comfort. And her voice in my ear is almost mothering.

'Get it all out, Dina,' she soothes. 'All the hate, the anger...'

I rinse my mouth and reach for a tea towel, smother my face and suppress a sob. I refuse to cry. Not because of *him*. When I lower the towel, Rosie is standing in front of me. 'You said you followed him home?'

'He doesn't live far from the pub,' Rosie says. 'He left at

around ten and cut through Dreydon Park, then went into one of the bungalows in Richmond Road.'

Richmond Road. Not even ten minutes' walk from here. I sit back at the table, my legs weak. I wonder if it's his father's house. *Was* his father's house. Those bungalows rarely come up for sale, and when they do I'll bet they fetch a high price. A lovely cushion to soften the blow of his miniscule stint in prison.

'Let's sit down,' Rosie says, and guides me to a chair. Drags another one close to me and takes my hands in hers. 'This man winked at you, Dina, after killing your daughter. Did you think two years of prison was going to reform that kind of behaviour?'

'I don't know,' I say, feeling the tears come. 'I don't know anything anymore.'

'I can't believe I'm saying this, Dina, but after meeting that scumbag in the flesh, I think we can ditch the hypotheticals.'

'This is crazy, Rosie, what you're suggesting.'

'A few jets of hydrochloric acid from a squeezy bottle and he'll be marked forever – see those little scars every time he looks in the mirror. And you'll know why they're there, Dina, even if he doesn't. You'll know it's for Becky. That's what you want, isn't it?'

'No. *No.*'

Rosie rubs my hands. 'And as ugly as it is, I think it's what you need, Dina. Closure.'

I blink tears, but they keep coming. 'And I'll be looking at the bars of a prison cell, and I'd deserve it.'

'You deserve some justice for what that man took from you, and you wouldn't have to worry about prison, Dina, because I would be your airtight alibi.'

19

As a show of strength, I replaced the vodka, and the next three days drifted by in a feverish heat – days I mostly spent hiding beneath my sheets whenever I felt myself being drawn into Becky's room. For whatever good that did. With the sun streaming in through the window, I remembered the afternoons when I would take Becky into our bed, her little round face iridescent as I swam her above me. And when I swept her close she would dock her pretty pink gums on the tip of my nose and leave behind a shimmering string of saliva, angelic in its purity then, but now only serving to amplify the loss of our umbilical connection.

And there was of course the occasional trip to the Saab to be near Roy. I don't know why, but I feel closer to him when I'm sitting in the Saab, and I so needed that contact, even if it was only in my mind. The rake of his fingers down my back... the saline taste of his neck... all fictions of my imagination, I know, but the physical sensations I get through remembering are real. Even if they are painful.

And Roy's a great listener, too. I've told him every day what I plan to do to Grant Chapman and he hasn't tried to talk me

69

out of it once, despite the fact that he would never do something so… I want to say vicious, because that's what it is, no question, but it's also, as Rosie says, what I need. Both for justice and my own sanity.

My phone warbles on the dash. It's Lois Lane.

'Hey, Dina,' Rosie says. 'We still on for movie night?'

'Movie night?' I ask, and Rosie sighs. 'Oh, movie night. Yeah. Yes.'

'Great. See you at seven.' Rosie hangs up, and I light another cigarette.

'Last chance, Roy. If you don't think I should go through with it, now's the time to say.'

Before Roy has the chance to protest, I notice a little white van pull up on the grass verge outside my driveway and a silver-haired gentleman climb out. He goes to the back of his van and removes the FOR SALE sign Darryl said would be arriving today, and I can't help but wonder if the universe is balancing out after all.

20

'We have to assume the police are going to be thorough,' Rosie says when I open the door to her. No hellos, she just slips by me into the kitchen and places the rucksack she's brought with her on the table. 'I doubt they'll be anything like thorough, but we've got to assume. Dummies if we don't.'

'I think that's sensible,' I say. 'So what's the plan?'

'Well, I followed Chapman the past three nights,' she says, 'and he's gone to the Red Lion on all three occasions, and also walked home the same way through Dreydon Park, and always alone, and always, always staggeringly drunk. The only thing that differed was the time he left the pub, which varied between nine and eleven thirty. Do you know the bench, the one beneath the streetlamp?'

'In the park? I think so,' I say. 'The bench nearest the far exit?'

'That one, yeah. You'll hide in the bushes opposite the bench, which'll be outside of the lamplight, and when Chapman leaves the pub, I'll call and send you a picture of what he's wearing, just so you don't go for the wrong man—'

'That man's face is seared into my mind's eye, Rosie, so—'

'I will send you his picture, Dina, just in case.' Rosie goes to her rucksack. 'When he walks beneath the lamplight – which'll be approximately three minutes from my call, I timed it – you step out from behind the bush and in passing you—'

'What if he retaliates?' I ask.

'Trust me, he'll be so drunk he probably won't even notice you got him until he gets home. He'll think it's bird shit or something.'

'And what if he recognises me?'

'He won't.' Rosie starts unloading the rucksack, hands me a baseball cap, a lightweight bomber jacket and a pair of glasses. 'The specs are clear lenses, and you'll tie your hair up beneath the cap, get it?'

I try on the jacket, the glasses. They fit fine.

'And the peak of the cap will leave your face in shadow,' Rosie says. 'Because of the streetlamp shining downward. He will not recognise you, Dina.'

'As long as he doesn't leave the pub at nine, when it'll still be light.' I hold my hair up and slip the cap on. Rosie takes out her phone and shows me what I look like. My neck is slender with my hair up, my eyes (which are normally a mix of Brushed Nickel and Meridian Blue) are nondescript behind the narrow black frames of the glasses. I look younger. Feel empowered. And so what if he recognises me? A part of me wants him to.

'Then what?' I ask when Rosie lowers her phone.

She dives into the rucksack again, brings out a plastic carrier bag and a pair of latex gloves. She snaps on the gloves, goes back into the rucksack and removes two catering-style squeezy bottles of ketchup, the second of which she holds up to me.

'This, Dina, is filled with hydrochloric acid.' She places it on the table and tosses me the other ketchup bottle. I screech and bat it away to the floor. Rosie laughs. 'It's empty, Dina!'

'Why on earth...' I blow out a deep breath, remove the cap

and glasses and toss them on the table. 'Jesus, Rosie, that wasn't funny.'

'Sorry,' she says, her laugh still visible in her shoulders. 'Now come on, fill that bottle up with water, we need to check your aim. Tomorrow night's the night, Dina, and there's still a lot we need to go over.'

21

My stomach is all over the place the next morning, and the last thing I want is breakfast, especially not the chips and dips Rosie brought with her yesterday. But she had put a lot of time and effort into constructing this intricate plan, and as I didn't think justice would be properly served if I got caught for attacking Grant Chapman, I thought I should follow her instructions to the letter. Rosie doubted very much that Chapman would even report the attack, but if he did, it was a safe bet that the police would place me at the top of the list of suspects. Especially as Detective Wallace had warned me of Chapman's release.

I set the scene in the lounge. Watched the DVD Rosie had brought (*Titanic*), and munched my way through the Thai-flavoured tortilla chips and the sickly-sweet chilli dip that went with them, leaving plenty of crumbs on both sides of the sofa, and a few chips left in the bowl that had sat between us during the film. I also placed a tumbler on each of the side tables that flanked the sofa, and splashed them with the adult soft drink we'd shared – an acidic tropical cordial that tasted of wine gums. Non-alcoholic, of course, as Rosie and I had met at the AA meeting I no longer felt I could attend, though we'd kept in touch, as friendly support for one another. Keep it simple, Rosie had said. Don't mention anything about her being my sponsor, Rosie had said.

I dug out an old jigsaw puzzle, too, and partially assembled it on the kitchen table, separated the edge pieces from the middle pieces of the seaside vista. The picture isn't important, but the picture I'm painting is. As with the scones I baked this morning that now sit cooled on the wire rack by the microwave, and with the snug I'm in the process of decorating. It's the picture of a woman with no preoccupations other than of passing her time soberly, and not the picture of a woman who could flick acid in a man's face out of revenge for killing her daughter.

By early evening I am starting to get anxious, so I decide to have a cigarette in the Saab to calm my nerves while I wait for Rosie's taxi to arrive. She brought a pushbike with her yesterday, in the boot of her car, and it now stands in my entrance hall propped against the scaffold tower. It's a silver racer. Old-school looking. Rosie will use it later to go into town and get back again. The idea is to get a taxi here and a taxi home – two separate time stamps, she said. Both corroborating our whereabouts. I know that still leaves a few hours in between those times that our whereabouts can't be accounted for, but as Rosie said, that's what she's for. The airtight alibi from a casual friend and fellow alcoholic, who had known nothing of the tragic death of my daughter, or of the man that had caused it. All Rosie knows is that her friend never left her side all night, and that Leonardo DiCaprio is sex on a hickory stick. Her phrasing, not mine.

I look up as Rosie's taxi pulls onto my drive, and I climb out of the Saab and greet her with an over-the-top embrace. We giggle and remark on our hilarious movie-night attire, for the benefit of the driver. Me in my Candyfloss Pink pyjamas, and Rosie in her animal-print set – minus the turquoise All Stars, which are no doubt in the rucksack she's carrying, along with the change of clothes she'll be wearing in a moment or two, when she rides into town to find Chapman.

'It may not happen tonight,' Rosie says as the taxi pulls away. 'But if he doesn't turn up, we should do a dry run, you know, practice makes perfect, and all that jism.'

'Yeah, okay,' I tell her, but I can already feel it in my bones that something is going to happen tonight, something huge, and my life is going to change forever.

And I'm proved right, as only an hour after Rosie rode off on her bike, I receive a text from her, along with a photo. The text tells me: *We're on*. The picture shows me Grant Chapman stood in the beer garden of the Red Lion pub.

I zip up the jacket despite the heat of the evening, and slip on the glasses and the baseball cap – the ketchup bottle of acid safely concealed within the carrier bag, a familiar weight to me now, thanks to all the practice I'd had with the water-filled version. When I close my front door, all I hear is birdsong. My distant neighbours reliably non-existent. I wonder if I'll see a face or two if the police show up tomorrow. I doubt it very much. Not one of them came to pay their condolences when Becky died, or showed any concern when the ambulance arrived and tried to save Roy, who lay dying in my arms across the driver seat of the Saab.

22

I remember the first time Roy suffered severe chest pains and I had to rush him his tablets. We'd been arguing over the takeaway pizza box he found crushed into the recycle bin. I'd fed our daughter nothing but junk food since he'd been away on business, and that apparently equated to me not caring about her. I'd owned up to the odd pizza, to the odd tub of Ben and Jerry's, but how dare he insinuate I didn't care for our daughter, the daughter he didn't seem to care about while he was off all over the world trying to make his fake meat fortune.

And around and around we danced... until Roy started clutching his chest. He went to the sofa, half sitting on the edge and half kneeling on the floor. It's a horrid thing to admit, but I thought he was faking it, trying to hammer home his anguish at my pitiful mothering skills, and so I did nothing. But when he rolled back into the cushions, his right hand crabbing from his chest to his left arm, I realised he wasn't faking, and I rushed to his briefcase for his pills.

I couldn't imagine the kind of pain Roy had gone through, to stop him cold in the tracks of our argument. Not until now.

Rosie called me a minute ago. 'He's on his way,' she said.

'Orange T-shirt.' And from that moment my chest has not stopped pounding.

I collapse against the brick wall that surrounds the park, where an hour ago I had secreted myself behind the bush that faces the bench. The streetlamp had only come on twenty minutes ago as daylight seemed never to want to leave, and neither did the two teenaged boys who'd been sitting on the bench in front of me, smoking and swearing and causing me to shallow-breathe for fear of giving myself away.

I suck in a sharp breath and my chest eases a little, but I'm so hot in this jacket that I've become light-headed and my hands are so sweaty inside the gloves the ketchup bottle of acid feels slippy in my fingers. I try to stand, have to inch up the wall to stop my legs from folding again. I put the glasses on when I hear his approaching footsteps, and just as he walks into the light of the streetlamp, I edge my way out from behind the bush and stumble. He stops. My cheeks burn with the fire of embarrassment. Of shame.

'What the fuck,' Chapman says. 'Scared the shit out of me.'

'I'm sorry,' I blurt, feeling so utterly foolish, to think I could go through with something so malicious. It would make me no better than him. I go to leave.

'Wait, do I know you?' He squints as he sways towards me.

'No, we've never—' I'm frozen to the spot. Why on earth did I think a stupid pair of glasses would hide my identity? Because Lois Lane can't tell Superman from Clark Kent? Where's Rosie? I need Rosie.

'You're the mother.' He stops a few paces away from me, drifting on his feet.

'Look, I don't want any trouble. I shouldn't have come...'

'Then why did—' His head tilts, eyes lowering to my hands. 'Why the fuck are you wearing gloves...?' And then he sees the bottle.

'I'm sorry,' I say, holding up my free hand. 'I'm going to leave now.' But it's too late. Somehow this drunken lowlife has put it all together, and he has no intention of letting me walk away.

Chapman rushes me and shoves me so hard I spill to the ground, but I manage to keep hold of the acid bottle.

'Fucking bitch!' he yells, and takes a swing at me with his foot, trying to kick the bottle from my hand, but he misses completely, and the momentum of the air shot brings him down next to me. I try to roll away but I feel his fist gathering up my jacket, pulling me towards him.

'Get off me!' I cry, but the rising panic in my throat cuts off my supply of oxygen when I feel his hand envelop mine. The hand that holds the acid bottle. Then he climbs on top of me and I cannot move for the weight of him.

'You'd dare throw acid in my face, would ya?' he spits at me, his breath rank with beer and cigarettes. 'Well let's see how you like it, shall we?'

His hand tightens around mine, the bottle cap popping off with the pressure. The bottle rises into view at the side of my head. 'No!' I scream.

'Yes,' he says, and laughs.

I force my other hand across my chest to reach for the bottle and he bats it away, but in that brief scrap I feel his grip loosen and I manage to tear free, and do the only thing I can think of. I squeeze.

Chapman immediately rolls off me, clutching his face, and as soon as I've scrambled to my feet, the screaming starts, as only men can scream.

A quick look up and I can see a silhouette heading this way. I need to leave. I snap the lid shut on the ketchup bottle and walk calmly but quickly out of the park, Chapman's wailing growing more distant with every electrified step. I follow the main road until I reach the entrance to the boatyard, passing several couples but keeping my head down and the acid hidden behind my leg. Through the boatyard and over the railway track, and by the time I make it onto the dirt path that runs along the river, my jacket and gloves, cap and ketchup bottle are stowed in the carrier bag, and I am just a panting shadow in the darkness.

It takes me twenty minutes to make it home via the river, my sweat-drenched skin cooled and dry, my hair scrubbed free from its bun. I key open my front door and close it behind me, leaving it unlocked while I strip out of my clothes and back into my pyjamas. Rosie arrives a few minutes later.

'Taxi's on its way,' she says as she slides her bike in through the front door. 'Your buttons, Dina.'

I look down and see I've buttoned up my pyjama top wrong. I fix it while Rosie sheds her clothes and puts on her animal-print set, then stuffs what she was wearing into her rucksack. I hand her my bag as headlights pan the driveway.

'Taxi,' I say, barely able to breathe.

'Is this everything?' Rosie asks, looking into the bag I've just given her.

'Yes, everything.'

She quizzes me with raised eyebrows. 'The other ketchup bottle?'

'God, sorry.' I dash into the kitchen and retrieve the other bottle from the sink, where I'd been testing my aim this afternoon. I offer it to her and Rosie opens the carrier bag. I drop in the bottle and she stuffs it all into her rucksack.

'What shall I do with the bike?' I ask.

'Put it out of sight somewhere and I'll collect it whenever.'

'And the... acid? What will you do with all that stuff?'

Rosie comes over to me and rubs my shoulders. 'Did you get him?'

'I...' I nod.

'Then all we have to do now is stick to the story, Dina, because we are gold plated.' Rosie gives me a wide smile, like we're just a couple of friends who *have* spent an enjoyable evening together watching a movie. 'Now see me out.'

I wave the taxi off from my driveway, then go inside and lock the door. '*What have I done?*' I whisper, and fall to my knees on the cold concrete and sob before the scaffold tower.

23

I didn't sleep well last night, which thankfully saved me from the inevitable nightmares that would surely have come, but it did mean I had to endure the waking fever dream of the unfolding events that led me to jet acid in a man's face. I know if Rosie and I stick to our story, I can't see any way for us (*me*) to get caught, but I have no idea how Chapman is going to react to being permanently scarred, let alone facially scarred. If he doesn't get his justice through the courts, then he is certainly malicious enough to want revenge. And he'd deserve it.

Oh, the irony. If I don't sell this place, have I just made myself a prisoner of it? Terrified to go outside for fear of him, and seeing his mutilated face lurking in every darkened corner of the house when I turn out the lights to go to bed. I'll go mad.

Perhaps when the police tell him that I was at home and have a witness to prove it, he'll doubt his drunken eyes. I never, after all, confirmed who I was.

*Why couldn't I have just let it go...*

I mix up a fresh bucket of wallpaper paste, but have no intention of finishing the snug today, even though I'm wearing my painting clothes. I add a few pieces to the jigsaw puzzle, eat a stale scone for brunch and wash the stinking sheets I stripped from my bed. Three cigarettes in the Saab. No sirens. No doorbell. No calls from the police. Is it too soon to feel safe? Is it possible I won't even be suspected of such a hateful crime? Yes, let it be that.

By four o'clock I've finished the puzzle and broken it up again. Baked fresh scones and tossed the stale ones in the bin. If I don't hear anything by the end of today I'll hoover up the tortilla chip crumbs in the lounge and wash the glasses, like any normal person would.

Night-time falls and I climb in between cool, clean sheets. It's strange how the passing of only a few hours can lessen the feeling of dread, and allow a flicker of hope to ignite into something... I don't know. I've been tinkering with the idea that perhaps I didn't get Chapman as badly as I'd thought – that most of the acid just flew by his face, as I'd suffered no residual splashback whatsoever. And I'm sure I'd closed my eyes at that moment, so how could I possibly know? I'm just assuming the worst, based upon the writhing and screaming of a drunk, when in reality I could've caused no more damage than what I'd set out to cause. A mark, and nothing more. That's it. That's why the police haven't come. Chapman hasn't even bothered to call them, and he probably never will.

I settle into my pillow, my shoulders releasing some of the tension that had been steadily building. Tomorrow I'll find another puzzle to do. Maybe even hang that tricky drop on the corner of the chimney-breast. I found baking the scones to be surprisingly therapeutic, so perhaps I'll try baking some bread. On that thought, I start to drift, the cooling breeze at the open window combing my skin and holding sleep just out of reach, but not so far that I can't see the colours of Morocco already forming on the palette of my dreams.

*So this is what peace feels like...*

"*I am going to make everything around me beautiful – that will be my life.*"

~ Elsie de Wolfe

24

The droning of my phone wakes me, but by the time I stir enough to realise it's my phone, I've missed the call. I gather the bed-sheet towards me, feel around until my fingertips sweep across the screen, not daring to open my eyes and instead try to decipher the non-existent Braille. Would the police still have my mobile number? Would they call me over something so serious? Detective Wallace came to see me, to share the potentially disturbing news that Grant Chapman was getting out of prison early. I'm guessing an acid attack ranks higher in seriousness than that.

Or maybe it was Rosie, making a totally understandable call to her friend, to say what a lovely evening she'd had the other night. We'd already deleted our correspondence of what took place before, during and immediately after Grant Chapman's... comeuppance? Yes, comeuppance! I'm not going to mention acid again. If he'd let me walk away like I wanted to, he'd have suffered nothing more than a well-deserved hangover.

I open my eyes and check my phone. It's neither the police nor Rosie. I return the call.

'Hello, Mrs Young,' Darryl answers. 'How are you this morning?'

'I'm very well, Darryl,' I say. 'Sorry I missed your call.'

'I was just calling to see if it would be okay if I brought somebody out to the property today, for a viewing?'

I sit up in bed. 'More interest?'

'Well, more interest from the same woman I spoke to you about, yes.'

'Right. Great.' I cover my mouth. I almost smiled. 'What time were you thinking?'

'She's renting a local holiday let, so I suppose whenever suits you best.'

I glance at the alarm clock. Only ten. 'I can be ready in an hour.'

'Excellent,' Darryl says. 'I'll speak with her and get back to you, but I'm sure that'll be fine.'

I toss my legs over the side of the bed, stand and stretch. Today, I can feel, is going to be a great day.

## 25

Mrs Delevingne is an elegantly-dressed early to mid-seventy-something, hard-faced and with a soft American accent. But I liked her before she spoke a word, and more so when she finally did.

She'd arrived in Darryl's car, and waited for him to get the door, and from there Darryl walked her to my front steps, she holding his arm while I watched from the kitchen window. She didn't have a walking stick, but I could see she was in some pain as her gait was wary. When I opened the door to greet her, she smiled up at me with what seemed like her whole face, and silently begged my patience while Darryl helped her up the steps. Then she reached for my hands, but still didn't speak, her eyes raking up towards what I thought was the scaffold tower.

'Apologies about the tower,' I said.

She patted my hands, still agape. 'Not at all, young lady. I was looking at the window.' She turned to me, her old face childish with joy. 'I've never seen it from here.'

'Of course,' I said. 'We removed the ceiling, but it's easy enough to reinstate.'

'Oh, no, dear, it's wonderful,' she said. 'Truly wonderful.'

Darryl is now showing Mrs Delevingne around inside while I sit and smoke in the Saab.

'Don't hate me for this,' I say, glimpsing into the rear-view. Roy, of course, doesn't reply.

I'd closed my eyes briefly, enjoying the rare breeze coming through the Saab's open windows, imagining myself elsewhere, near the sea, perhaps. But judging by the dashboard clock I must have dozed off, as twenty minutes have ticked by. I curse, hoping Darryl hasn't been and gone by now, as I so wanted to speak with Mrs Delevingne again, to get a sense of how interested she is after looking around. Thankfully, Darryl steps out of the front door and trots over to me. I snap off the radio.

'Everything okay?' I ask, leaning out of the window.

'Fine, Mrs Young,' he says, hands on his knees to meet me at eye level. 'I was just wondering how you were doing for time?'

'Oh, don't worry about me, Darryl, take as long as you need.'

'Well, Mrs Delevingne would like to look around the outside of the property, if that's okay?'

'Of course.' I snap the radio back on and Darryl gnaws his lower lip.

'Thing is, Mrs Young, she'd like you to give her the tour?'

'Oh, okay.'

A minute later Darryl helps Mrs Delevingne down my front steps and I offer her my arm.

'I feel so silly being fussed upon like some decrepit senior citizen,' Mrs Delevingne says, taking my arm and mouthing thanks to Darryl.

'It really is no problem at all,' I say. 'My dad had arthritis in his early fifties—'

'Oh, no, dear,' Mrs Delevingne says, looking up at me. 'I could best you over a hundred yards, no doubt, if I hadn't broken my toe yesterday morning.'

'Ouch,' I say, and we set off along the front of the house.

'Ouch, indeed,' she says. 'I was doing my Zumba class in front of the TV when Joe called – that's my husband, dear – and I was so feeling the rhythm that I danced over to pick up the phone and kicked the coffee table on the way. There were expletives.'

'I bet.'

'And it's too insignificant to cast, the doctor said. This was my mother's house, did you know that, dear?'

'Your mother was Mrs Lancaster?'

Mrs Delevingne nods. 'I couldn't persuade her to move to the States, so she was alone when she died. She did love this house.'

'I'm sorry to hear that, Mrs Delevingne – that she died alone, I mean.'

She shushes me with a flap of her hand. 'We all die alone, dear – and call me Dotty. By name and by nature, my husband would say. You married, dear?'

The question startles me, and Dotty sees it. Sees me rub the pale band of skin on my finger, where my wedding ring used to be.

'S'kay,' she says. 'None of my beeswax. But can I ask why you're selling up? Seems as though you were in the process of remodelling.'

'They're both fair questions,' I say, and we turn onto the paved pathway that leads to the back garden. 'But they're both husband questions, really.'

She pats my hand and offers me a warm smile. We continue on.

'We were in the middle of renovating, but then our builder went bust, taking all our money with him, and that was on top of a loss my husband had already made on an investment. Then our...' I swallow deeply, and it pushes a tear to the surface of my eye. 'Then our daughter was killed in an accident.'

Dotty stops me and takes both of my hands in hers. The tear bursts and runs.

'A drunk driver,' I say, determined not to give in to the rising swell of my emotions, but don't quite manage it. I free my hands from hers and laugh as I brush away the oncoming tears. 'And then! And then Roy has a stupid heart attack two days later and I've been stuck here ever since! I can't sell the place for what I need because we gutted it, and then with the – Darryl showed you the crack?' – I cuff my nose as I nod like a crazy woman – 'and then with the subsidence I'm buried in negative equity with a pension that barely covers the mortgage on a house that in every room I see my dead daughter...'

I cover my face and turn away from Dotty to hide my pathetic sobs.

'It's okay, Darryl,' I hear Dotty say. 'Just having ourselves a girly chat, is all.'

'Mrs Young?' I hear Darryl ask.

'I'm fine, Darryl, thank you,' I muffle from behind my hands, and feel Dotty stroke my back and a final sob lurches out of me like I've been exorcised. 'I'm so sorry.'

'You have nothing to apologise for, dear,' she says. 'Losing a daughter is not the natural order of things. Here.' She pushes a tissue into my hand and gives me the moment I need to collect myself.

'It seems we've been brought together,' Dotty says, jazzing her hands and smiling at the endless blue of the sky. 'Either by the Good Lord Himself or the divine comedy that is life.' This time she offers me *her* arm. I take it and we move on.

'I grew up in this house,' Dotty continues, 'and I would very much like to live out the rest of my days here. If you think this is hot, then you need to spend a summer in Arizona, where I have now spent thirty-five of them.'

She brings a smile to my lips, and I switch our hands around so I can take her weight again.

'I know the price is a little on the strong side – and be assured my husband will try to bend you on it – but you will tell him no! The price is the price! God knows he can afford it.' Dotty squeezes my arm. 'Eventually he'll succumb and do as I ask, and if not he'll do as I say. I've given that man four healthy children, he can certainly give me a little old house.'

'You mean you want to buy the house?'

'That's what I mean,' Dotty says. 'Now my husband will have to see it, naturally, before we make an official offer, and naturally, you'll be all surprised when he does. But yes, I'd like to buy your house, dear – I haven't even asked you your name, how thoroughly rude of me.'

'It's Dina,' I say as we reach the back of the house. 'And I should've mentioned it, Dotty, but the garden is not as beautiful as your mother left it.'

Dotty smiles and pats my arm. 'I paid for her gardener the last ten years of her life. My husband can pay for the next one.'

When I close the door to Darryl and Mrs Delevingne, I start to cry again. Pure guilt this time, for the glimmer of joy I'm feeling, which can't be unpicked from the fact I will soon be leaving my daughter and my husband behind, to linger in this cursed house without me. What a selfish and utterly awful human being I've become, that I've dared to dream of a different life for myself, a life where I might no longer be haunted by their ghosts, and instead have the chance of remembering them lovingly, without the accompanying pain.

I go into the kitchen and splash my face with cold water at the sink. I'm not going to cry again. I'm done with tears.

While I'm drying my face, the doorbell chimes. Could it be Darryl? Has Mrs Delevingne decided not to wait for her husband's approval and made an offer already? I go to the front door and open it, ready to cry all over again, but it isn't either Darryl or Mrs Delevingne.

'Hello, Mrs Young,' Detective Wallace says. 'May we come in for a moment?'

26

I let them in. Detective Wallace and a young Asian woman he introduces as Detective Anand. She is boyishly beautiful and with eyes so large she looks almost surprised to be here. Wallace, on the other hand, does not look surprised at all, and the sympathetic disposition he arrived with last week is long gone, replaced by an underlying something I can't grasp. It's like we haven't met before.

I offer them tea, keenly aware that I haven't asked them why they are here, something I should have done at the door. I can't afford anymore slip-ups. Just stick to the story.

'You don't need to keep checking up on me, Detective Wallace,' I say, setting a tea down on the kitchen table for each of them, puzzle pieces everywhere. Detective Anand looks across at him, silently asking him with those big eyes what I'm talking about.

'I came by the other week,' he tells her. 'To let Mrs Young know that Grant Chapman was being released early.'

Detective Anand forms an O with her mouth, then sips her tea.

94

'And actually, Mrs Young, we are here to check up on you,' Detective Wallace says.

'There's really no need,' I say, sitting down at the table with my tea. 'I'm fine. Would anyone like a scone?'

They both decline, thankfully. The scones are as hard as pebbles they've been sat on the side for so long.

'Could you tell us where you were the night before last?' Detective Anand asks, with not a trace of an accent, neither Suffolk nor Indian.

'What day is it today?' I ask, as Detective Wallace takes out a notebook and pen.

'Thursday,' he says.

'So Tuesday night?' They each nod. 'Can I ask why?'

Detective Wallace lays down his pen. 'Grant Chapman was the victim of an attack on Tuesday night.'

'Oh,' I say. 'Nothing trivial, I hope.'

'It was an acid attack, Mrs Young,' he says. 'So no, it wasn't trivial.'

I set down my tea and cover my mouth. Sigh. 'I'm sorry, that was a callous thing to say. Is he... okay?'

'Tuesday evening, Mrs Young,' Detective Anand says. 'From eight o'clock onwards. Can you remember where you were?'

I lean back in my chair and sigh again, feigning my forgetfulness, my disgust at wishing Grant Chapman ill will. 'Tuesday, Tuesday – yes, Tuesday! I had a movie night with a friend.'

'Your friend's name?' Detective Wallace asks, pen poised.

'Rosie. Rosie Rey. Rosie with an *I E*. Rey with an *E Y*.' I'm starting to ramble.

Detective Wallace jots, and Detective Anand asks, 'What film did you watch?'

'*Titanic*. DiCaprio is sex on a hickory stick, don't you think?' *Calm down, Dina*, I can hear Rosie saying. *Calm down.*

'Do you have an address?' Detective Wallace asks. 'Phone number?'

'I have her number, but I'm not actually sure where she lives. She mentioned a flat, I think.' I get up to fetch my phone from the side.

'You don't know where your friend lives?' Detective Anand asks.

'She's a newish friend,' I say, returning with my phone. 'But I don't think she lives far.'

'How do you know that?' she asks.

How do I know that? Is it because I called Rosie in the middle of the night and she turned up in her pyjamas in fifteen minutes? I can't tell them that. Rosie said we shouldn't mention her being my sponsor.

'We met at the local AA meeting,' I say, 'so I guess she lives *locally.*'

'And how new is newish?' Detective Wallace asks.

'A few weeks,' I say, realising I've just told my first checkable lie. *Please don't ask how many meetings, please don't ask how many meetings...*

'So would it be fair to say,' Detective Wallace says, picking up a puzzle piece to examine it, 'that you don't know Rosie that well?'

The heat of the kitchen suddenly hits me, and a bead of sweat traces down my spine. 'I'm not sure what you're implying,' I say.

Detective Wallace leans back from the table and holds his hands up. 'Mrs Young, I'm not implying anything, I'm just trying to understand the situation.'

'What situation?'

'I think what Detective Wallace is trying to understand...'

Detective Anand sips her tea, making me wait for the second part of her assessment. 'Is how you came to be having a movie night with somebody who you've essentially only just met.'

Detective Wallace inserts the puzzle piece into *my puzzle*, and says, 'Who chose the film?'

'She did.' I stand from my chair. 'I feel like I'm being interrogated here. Do you actually believe I had something to do with this... attack?'

The detectives look at each other, then Detective Wallace says, 'You're right, Mrs Young. We got a little off topic there, my apologies.'

I take a calming breath, tuck my hair behind my ears. 'That's fine. I just started to feel quite intimidated, that's all.'

Detective Anand sits mute, her big brown eyes unreadable as she looks up at me.

'If we could get your friend's number.' Detective Wallace gestures at my phone and clicks his pen a couple of times.

I recite the number and show them to the front door.

'I shouldn't say this,' Detective Anand says as she steps outside, and my stomach flips. 'But we could really do with some rain.'

I ease out a sigh of relief. 'I completely agree.'

'Well, thank you for your time, Mrs Young,' Detective Wallace says, and pats his breast pocket, where he's just stowed his notebook. 'We'll give Ms Rey a call, and I'm sure we'll be able to draw a line through this avenue of our investigation. Enjoy the rest of your day.'

He follows Detective Anand down my front steps, but stops when I call his name.

'I'm sorry for what I said about Grant Chapman,' I say. 'I'm not usually that mean-spirited. It's just... well, you know.'

'It's understandable, Mrs Young. I think I would feel the same way.'

'Yes, well, I hope he recovers okay.'

Detective Wallace bats his head a little. 'He didn't make it, I'm afraid.'

'What do you mean?'

He glances towards their car, to where Detective Anand is laying her suit jacket onto the back seat. 'Whoever threw the acid into Grant Chapman's face, he unfortunately ingested some, resulting in his throat swelling. He suffocated before the ambulance arrived.'

'Oh my God, he's dead?' I think I'm going to be sick.

'I'm afraid so,' he says, bunching his mouth. 'Thank you again, Mrs Young. We'll be in touch if we need anything further.'

27

I close the front door, the insides of my cheeks sour with bile. I rush to the kitchen sink, but the only thing that comes out is a guttural wail. I swipe the cooling rack of scones to the floor, whirl and do the same with the jigsaw puzzle, the mugs of half-drunken tea. I dig my fingernails into my temples but don't have the courage to scratch myself down to my collarbones. He's dead! I've wished it for so long, and now that he is, I am sick with revulsion, sick with the woman I have become.

The vodka screams to me and I see it as the only answer. I open the freezer and snatch out the new bottle, rip the screw cap around, put the bottle to my trembling lips, which peel back against my gritted teeth. The guttural wail pours out of me again. I throw the bottle to the concrete floor and it shatters.

I hobble through the broken glass, through the rising stench of alcohol and into the entrance hall, the space that was one day going to be my spiritual embrace. I look up at the swatch of blue sky set within the arch window, and my eyes settle on the scaffold tower and I get a vague sense of having climbed it. A vague sense of why.

I snap out of my trance. I need to call Rosie. Before Detective Wallace does.

'Hey, you,' Rosie says when she answers. 'How's it hanging?'

'The police have just been here, and—'

'Well, we knew that was going to happen sooner or later. How'd it go?'

'I told them that we'd been friends for a few weeks, and—'

'Why'd you do that?'

'Because having a movie night with someone you've only recently met is...'

'Totally nobody's business but ours. Stick to the story, Dina, jeez...'

'There's something else—'

'Wait up, Dina, incoming on the other line.'

'That'll be them, listen—'

'A few weeks, got it. Wait, you didn't tell them I was your sponsor did you?'

'You said not to so I didn't. Look, Rosie, Chapman—'

'Gotta take this now. Call ya back.'

'Rosie, wait! Chapman's dead—' She cut me off. Fuck!

No, wait. It might be better if she doesn't know. They probably won't even mention Chapman at all, just confirm my whereabouts. Draw a line through this avenue of enquiry. It is going to be okay. Rosie's alibi is granite. It has to be.

28

Rosie didn't call back. She called round. At seven o'clock. With Chinese food.

'Jeez, Dina. It smells like a distillery in here,' she says as soon as she goes into the kitchen.

I'd cleaned up all the debris from earlier. The scones, puzzle pieces, the broken glass and mugs. But I hadn't done anything about the smell of vodka, which had soaked into the concrete and I just didn't have the mental or physical energy to get down on my hands and knees to scrub it out.

'Can we eat this in the living room?' she says. 'You know how the smell of vodka makes me bilious. And I hope you didn't drink any of it. It'd be a dick move to reprise that ole habit at a time like this – you got any soy sauce?'

'I don't know how you can think about food at a time like this,' I say.

'Girl's gotta eat. You should eat, too, Dina. Plates?'

'I'm not even nearly hungry,' I say, and then test how hungry Rosie really is. 'Grant Chapman's dead.'

'Say what?' Rosie doesn't even stop hunting through my cupboards.

'I said, Grant Chapman is dead.'

She turns to me, crinkles her nose with a goofy smile. 'That's what I thought you said. I can't find the soy.' She goes back to nosing in my cupboards until she finds a plate, a fork, then walks by me and heads into the lounge. I follow.

'Did you not hear what I just said?' I ask her once I've negotiated the scaffold tower and reached the lounge doorway.

'Why is everything covered in dust sheets in here,' Rosie says as she plates up her food.

'Grant Chapman is fucking dead, Rosie. Please can you acknowledge that fact with a response.'

Rosie stops plating her food and lets out a sulky sigh. 'So he's dead. That doesn't change anything, Dina, just makes it more important to stick to the story. You do want to do that, don't you?'

'What kind of a question is that?' I ask.

Rosie shrugs. 'Sometimes guilt makes people do crazy things. So, do you?'

'What, do I want to stick to the story?'

'No. Do you feel guilty?'

'Of course I feel bloody guilty, I've just killed a man!'

Rosie walks over to me, but I can't look at her. 'And there's precious little you can do about that now. And let's not forget what he did to you – what he did to Becky.' She touches my arm. 'This is still justice, Dina. Harsh, yeah, but justice should be harsh, and you should not feel guilty about that.'

I look up, and for the first time since I met Rosie I see an older soul in her eyes, those Pear Green eyes, and I know there is a woman hiding in there somewhere, and I wonder how many people get to see her.

'Come eat with me,' she says, squeezing my arm and searching my face. And I must give something away, because she smiles and says, 'I'll get you a plate.'

When she returns I watch her portion out the food, listen to her as she recommends all the different dishes I have to try. The spicy and the sweet. My stomach grumbles at the memory of something that isn't toast.

'So what did the police ask you?' I say a while later, once I've managed a few mouthfuls of chow mein.

Rosie sets her empty plate down beside her and rocks back into the sofa holding her flat stomach. 'I think I'm going to have a food baby.'

'Rosie? Questions?'

'Oh, you know, the kinds of questions we expected them to ask.' She streaks a line across her plate and sucks her finger. 'They asked me how long we'd known each other – how we'd met and all that. I kept it vague, few weeks, no deets – and then they asked about times, and I told them what time the taxi dropped me off and what time it picked me up.' Rosie winks at me. 'They'll follow that up, *if* they can be bothered, but it really doesn't make any difference as long as we keep singing the same song.'

I have to admit, I can't see how they can break our story down. Even if they found out I've only been to one meeting, it only brings into question how fast me and Rosie became friends. It may seem odd to have someone over for a movie night so soon, but that's all it is, odd. You can't prosecute odd.

'So that was it? No mention of Grant Chapman?'

'Nope. Just said they were looking into an "incident". Not even serious.'

'And no other questions?'

'No intelligent questions, anyway. Are you going to finish that?'

'No,' I say, and hand her my plate. 'What do you mean by intelligent questions?'

Rosie sucks up a noodle and cuffs her chin. 'I mean, I told

them we met at an AA meeting, and he asks me if I'd had anything alcoholic to drink that night.' She scoffs. 'I'm like, mate, I just told you we'd met at an AA meeting, we're in recovery?'

'Hmm, maybe they were just trying to see if you were conscious for the entire time, that maybe I could've slipped out while you were asleep or something.'

'Well, I shut that shit down. No alcohol.' Rosie holds her stomach again, gives me a sideways glance. 'Twins now. Dina, take the plate away before I split.' She gas-burps into her fist as though she's thinking about vomiting, but then says, 'One last bite.'

29

I felt better for having seen Rosie, as she'd put my mind at ease – at least about our chances of getting caught – if not about how I should deal with the knowledge that I was responsible for the death of another human being.

I also felt better about not seeing or hearing from Rosie over the next few days. Or the police. And with every cigarette I smoked in the Saab, cooking in the leather seats, the sun baking down through the windshield and sticking my clothes to my skin, I could easily imagine that I had been forgotten. The lone survivor of a shipwreck, washed up on a four-bed detached property surrounded by wispy evergreens that shielded me from the rest of the world, and the rest of the world from me. Not so great that I hadn't heard anything from Darryl, and I started to wonder if I'd dreamed up Mrs Delevingne. Dotty. The more I played it over in my mind, the more I doubted she existed, and perhaps she was a mirage. It's easy to go mad in this heat. In this isolation.

Roy's pension money went in yesterday, so I decide to walk into town to buy some cigarettes and a paper, to see if there'd been any mention of Grant Chapman or any comments from the police. I take the river route, which is longer but cooler, and after buying some essentials from the Co-op, head home via Dreydon Park, or as I will refer to it from this point on, the Ripper trail.

They say a criminal always returns to the scene of their crime. Out of morbid curiosity, I suspect, or bravado at not being caught. My reasons are different. I want to know how I'm going to feel, in the light of day, knowing what I have done by the cover of night. Will I be able to live with myself? It's an important question.

I enter the park via the same entrance, pushing open the unwelcoming iron gates, waiting to see if my palms become sweaty. Waiting to see if my heart skips a sickly beat. But I feel nothing, and so I continue along the path, getting closer to the scene of my crime.

When I reach the spot on the path, the last place I saw Grant Chapman alive, I stop to adjust my shoes. I don't see any evidence of his death. No stains from coughed up blood or acid burns on the tarmac. And that's good. I didn't come here looking for that. I came here to face what I'd done and to see if I could deal with it. Live with it.

I sit on the nearby bench and wait for some kind of emotion to take over me, but I'm less than numb to it. A man walks by with his dog, a freshly-clipped bichon. The dog doesn't sniff a thing, just happily trots ahead of its master, oblivious to Chapman's scent and his passing. Then I realise there's something else missing from this scene.

The day after Becky's death, and for the weeks to come, the school railings became a floral memorial. What started as the odd bouquet, soon grew into a forest of flowers that stretched twenty metres or more. She was loved and missed and mourned by everyone who knew her, from the children and the teachers to the mothers who had never spoken a word to me in all the times I'd collected Becky. Grant Chapman had nothing to mark his passing, or anyone to mourn it.

As I walk away, I'm relieved to learn that I *can* live with this burden. I'll just put it with the others I have to carry. What option do I have? I head back along the river, my heart a little lighter, but when I reach my house, Detective Wallace is waiting for me, and a heaviness returns.

He has nothing, I tell myself, but the weight of my heart tells me it doesn't share my head's belief.

30

Detective Wallace is sitting on my front steps as I walk up, sweating heavily in the face, and not just because it's over eighty degrees already. He's still wearing his jacket. Tie as tight as ever.

'I hope you haven't been waiting long?' I say as I squeeze by him on the steps.

'No, no, just a few minutes.' He groans as he stands. 'It's over a hundred degrees in the car, so I thought I'd treat us both to a few minutes in the shade.'

I glance over to where he's parked in the shadow of the evergreens. 'Perhaps it'd help if you took off your jacket? Loosen the tie?'

'I'm sure it would.'

I unlock my door. 'Is there something...'

'Yes. I thought I should let you know that we've spoken to Ms Rey, and she's confirmed what you told us about your whereabouts. So... no further action, I would expect.'

'That's good to hear,' I say. 'Thank you for letting me know.'

He pinches his lips in a flat smile and palms sweat from his forehead. Examines his glistening hand.

'Can I get you a glass of water or something?' I ask.

He puffs out a breath as he looks at his car. 'Actually, Mrs Young, that would be good.'

I dump my shopping on the kitchen table and fetch a glass, fill it with ice, jolt when I turn to the tap.

'Sorry.' Detective Wallace holds up a hand. 'I was supposed to wait outside, wasn't I?'

'That's fine,' I say, and fill his glass with tap water. 'Thanks to the concrete floors it's usually a lot cooler in here.' I hand him the glass and also a sheet of kitchen paper. 'For your face.'

'Thank you.' He mops his brow with the kitchen paper and takes a drink.

'Do they make you wear a jacket and tie, even in this heat?' I ask, and start to put the shopping away.

'No, I can take them off if I want.' He mops his brow again and pockets the kitchen paper.

'Which begs the next question...?'

'Why am I sweating like a pig? No pun intended.'

'Well, yeah.'

Detective Wallace takes a drink, then says, 'My wife always said I looked handsome in a jacket and tie, so I tend never to take them off in office hours.'

'Oh, I'm sorry.'

'What for?'

'Your late wife.'

'How did you arrive at that?' he asks, and drinks again, crunching an ice cube this time.

'Well, you said your wife *said* – past tense – and as you're still wearing a wedding ring, I guessed the past tense wasn't because you weren't married anymore, so it must have been because she'd died.' I stall as I'm putting the loaf of bread in the cupboard. 'I'm sorry, I shouldn't have said anything.'

'Not at all,' he says. 'You'd make a good detective. Thanks

for the water.' He goes to leave, but then says, 'Is it me or can I smell vodka?'

'Vodka?'

'Sort of, in the air.' He wafts a hand towards his face.

'Ah.' Of course, the bottle I smashed. 'A little accident a couple of days ago.'

'But aren't you – I mean, weren't you...?'

'An alcoholic, yes, but it isn't what you think. I always keep a bottle in the freezer, and the act of not drinking it gives me strength. The bottle slipped out of the freezer drawer when I was getting some peas, that's all.'

'Well,' he says. 'Whatever gets you through.'

'Yes,' I say, tugging at my imaginary tie. 'Whatever gets you through.'

I show Detective Wallace to the front door and he pauses before he steps outside. 'That's a beautiful window,' he says, looking up at the arch window in the roof space.

'It was going to be,' I say. 'I'd commissioned a stained-glass artist to refurbish it, but then... you know.'

He nods. 'And now you're selling up.'

'Hopefully. It's too big for one person, and the memories...' My gaze drops away.

'Well, I'm sure you'll have your pick of buyers,' he says, and steps outside.

'Thanks again,' I say. 'I hope you find who did it.'

Detective Wallace turns at the bottom of the steps. 'I doubt it very much. Chapman was unsavoury at best, and would've had more than a few people who had issues with him. Drug-related, maybe, or an unpaid debt. We'll likely never know. Thanks for the water.'

'Bye,' I say, and go to shut my door.

'Oh, I nearly forgot to ask.' Detective Wallace raises a finger.

I hold the door half open, raise a brow.

'Did Ms Rey consume any alcohol when she came over for your movie night?'

The same stupid question he asked Rosie. 'No, why?'

'Not even a glass of wine or two?'

'We're both in recovery. So no alcohol.'

'Right.' He taps his temple. 'Of course.'

I go to shut the door again.

'And the meeting you both attend, is that the one at the community centre, in town?'

'Yes. I've really got to put some stuff in the freezer.'

He raises his finger again. 'Who runs that meeting?'

I sigh. 'Justin... Justin Campbell.'

Detective Wallace gives me two raised palms in thanks and backs towards his car. I close the door, a slip-slidy feeling in my stomach. A bead of sweat breaks and runs down my neck.

*"Design is defined by light and shade."*

~ Albert Hadley

31

Since we removed the ceiling in the entrance hall, the builders put in a temporary loft hatch to access the remaining loft space. The hatch is in the little walk-in wardrobe in the smallest of the two spare bedrooms, and has a drop-down ladder that you can only drop down when the wardrobe door is open. It's awkward and tight, and was never meant to be permanent, but the ceiling in the "principal landing" (the hatch's intended position) was heaving above with old trunks, tea chests, and cardboard boxes, which were frankly more of a hassle to move than installing a temporary hatch.

Apart from the furniture, everything else I own is stored in the loft, and as far as I'm concerned, can stay up here. But since the dream of selling the house is becoming a possible reality, and the Grant Chapman situation could very well be behind me, I can't help looking to the future.

There's a torch just inside the hatch, even though the rose window at the front of the house lets in enough dusty shafts of sunlight to see by. The trouble is, where there is light there is shadow, and so the sun also converts this still generous loft into an American-style attic cut straight out of a haunted house movie. Which I suppose, it is – haunted, I mean.

I step up onto the floorboards and immediately break out in a sweat, the air a heated syrup to breathe and already suffocating. I hopscotch the torchlight across the many trunks and chests, but I can't remember in which I stored all of my design stuff. Roy had told me to label everything, and I'd mocked him for being a fusspot. I wish I'd listened to him now, as there are boxes in here that I do not wish to open, and so it's going to be an emotional minefield, one of my own creation.

The first box I try is filled with toys from when Becky was small, and I have to stop myself from lifting out a bathroom ducky that used to cause her to giggle and splash, her chubby little legs kicking with excitement and soaking my top. I shift the box aside and shine the torch into the tea chest it's sitting on, find a stack of vinyl we'd inherited from Roy's parents, and dozens of old mix tapes I'd compiled when I was a teenager. It would be nice to go through them, but now is not the time.

Chests filled with old Christmas cards, wrapping paper and tinsel. Boxes filled with dusty board games. A trunk filled with snorkelling gear, fancy dress costumes, Halloween masks and hats. And the glassware... God, did we really ever need this much? At one time I suppose we did, when people still came to the house.

Then I step on the first mine. A trunk full of photographs. The urge to slam down the lid is strong, but not as strong as the urge to lift out the framed picture of Roy and me standing with Becky as she blows out the candles on her birthday cake. I count seven candles, and many friends in the background whose faces I've long forgotten. It's funny how memories can disappear, and how a photograph can bring them all rushing back. It's like that with the second picture I lift from the trunk, of Roy and me dancing on our wedding day – the haunting piano opening to

'The Power of Love' by Frankie Goes to Hollywood that dragged a fingernail along my spine and was doing the same thing now as I see myself back there in his arms. How I ached for him that night. I replace both the pictures and gently close the lid.

Finally, as the loft begins to feel like a furnace, I find my design stuff. It's in a tea chest, which I *had*, despite my ribbing of Roy's suggestion, marked with a pencil drawing of what I had one day hoped would be my company logo: a flowering vine that spelled out *Dina Young*. I remove the two boxes that sit on top of the chest, but before I get the chance to look inside, I hear tyres splash onto the gravel driveway.

I cross the dusty floorboards to the rose window, look down to see Rosie Rey climbing out of her Beetle. Denim shorts and a blousy sleeveless top, her hair streaming from beneath a khaki baseball cap. The doorbell drifts in through the loft hatch, and I wonder how long I will have to wait in this oven before she gives up and leaves.

Apparently not long.

Rosie calls out my name. From inside my bloody house!

'Dina, you home?' she calls again.

I can hardly breathe, partly because of the heat, but mostly because I'm so furious at Rosie for having let herself in uninvited. I dive my hand into the tea chest and grab the first thing I can find, which turns out to be the sketch folder I use for my wallpaper designs. Then I replace the torch and climb down out of the loft.

'Dina, it's me, Rosie. You around?' She's getting closer.

I catch her just as she's about to come upstairs. 'Rosie, what are you doing here?' I say, and head downstairs to stop her from coming up, which I know she would have.

'Oh, hi, Dina,' she says with a big smile, and takes off her sunglasses. 'I was looking for you.'

'What I mean is, Rosie, what are you doing in my house?'

'Told you, Dina. I was looking for y—'

'Shall we?' I direct her to the front door, my palm in her back. She seems confused, but she complies.

'Have I done something wrong?' she asks.

'You mean apart from letting yourself into my house?'

'Oh, that.' She stops with a shrug, even though I'm still *encouraging* her to the front door. 'I only let myself in because I knew you couldn't hear me.'

'You rang the doorbell once, Rosie, and I could have been out. Do you make a habit of entering people's houses when they're out?' I open the front door for her.

'Course not, but you were in, Dina – by the way, I love this coat stand, is it an antique or something?'

'You couldn't possibly know I was in, Rosie.'

'The door was unlocked. You would never go out and leave the door unlocked, would you?'

'No, but that has nothing—'

'So I knew you had to be in when I tried the door and it was unlocked, and then I heard you banging around upstairs and I called out to you.' Rosie steps outside. 'God, Dina, it's ninety degrees out here, and what, you think I'd rob you or something? None taken.'

'It isn't that, Rosie, it's – you know what, it doesn't matter.' I sigh. 'Was there anything specific you came round for?'

'Yeah, my bike. What's that?' Rosie points at my sketch folder with her sunglasses.

'This is my... um... Just some designs I was working on.'

'Cool,' she says. 'Like an artist or something? I wish I was more artistic, I mean, I write poetry sometimes, but that isn't like real art, is it?'

'Well, actually...'

'Anyhoo. Bike?'

I feel like I've been twirled around and let go. 'It's in the basement, I'll get it for you.'

Rosie mouths *okay* and fans her face, squinting into the sun. I ponder closing the door on her. As if I could.

'Come in, Rosie.'

She steps back inside and I leave her at the front door. I place my sketch folder on the kitchen table on my way to the larder and go down into the basement where I left Rosie's bike leaning against the cement mixer. As I wheel it around, I jump at Rosie's voice on the stairs.

'This house seems to get bigger and bigger, Dina,' she says, staring open-mouthed around the basement.

'I was bringing the bike up to you, Rosie,' I say, more to myself as she really doesn't seem to get the implied *anything*, or understand the social etiquette of being invited or not invited into someone's home. She would make a terrible vampire.

'I can see why you're selling up, Dina,' Rosie says, slipping her sunglasses onto the peak of her baseball cap. 'Must get spooky here at night on your own.'

'Here's your bike,' I say, offering it to her, but she steps around me and goes over to the excavation hole in the corner, glances at the one in the centre of the basement floor. Grins. 'You could bury a body down here.'

'Who says I haven't?' I lift the bike and start my way up the stairs.

'You're not the type, Dina,' she says, and follows me up.

I wheel Rosie's bike through the kitchen and into the entrance hall, then out the front door, where I stand with it in earnest. After a minute of waiting I lean the bike against the house and go back inside. Rosie is sitting at the kitchen table flicking through my sketch folder.

'You drew all these?' she asks.

I should scream, but instead I control a frustrated sigh. It's not often I get to talk about my design work with anyone. Not anyone who's interested.

'They're wallpaper designs,' I tell her, and take the seat opposite. 'One day I want to have my own range, paint colours, fabrics... The basement was going to be my studio, but then...'

'But then that fucktard blew up your family, and your creativity.' Rosie says this as though to herself, without even looking up from my designs. 'It's all possible now, Dina.'

'I'd like to think so.'

'These are so beautiful.' Rosie strokes the pages as she turns them. 'I wish I had done more with my life.'

'Rosie, you're still so young. You've got your whole life ahead of you.'

She gently closes the folder. 'What life? There's nothing in it.'

'Don't say that.'

Rosie looks up, but not at me. 'It's true. I've got no ambition, no plans for the future. In fact, the only thing I've done lately that's made me feel anything like good about myself is helping you.'

'Well, if ever I can repay the favour...' God, why did I just say that? All I want now is to be as far removed from Rosie as I can get.

Rosie half smiles. 'Thanks, Dina, that means a lot.'

I rise from the table. 'But in the meantime, I think it would be a good idea if we maybe didn't see each other for a while.'

Her half smile evaporates. 'What do you mean?'

'It's still a very serious matter we're tied up in. I think we'd be wise to cool the situation down – at least until we're ruled out completely from the investigation.'

'But we have been,' she says. 'That comedy duo haven't got a single scrap on you.'

*On me?* 'I still think we should distance ourselves for a while. Let it all blow over.'

'And then what?'

And then I'll freeze you out of my life and put this all behind me, sell the house, move away, forget that this whole mess ever happened. 'Then we'll see.'

I head to the front door, and to my relief, Rosie follows.

'We'll keep in touch by phone though, won't we?' she says once she's stepped outside.

'Let's fully distance for the time being,' I say, hand on the door, ready to close it.

Rosie looks towards her car, nodding a little to herself, then she picks her sunglasses from the peak of her cap and slips them on.

'Take care, Rosie.'

She grabs her bike, looks at me with no emotion. 'In a while, crocodile,' she says.

I offer a weak smile and close the door, with the intention of locking it as soon as Rosie leaves. But she doesn't. I back away toward the kitchen and watch her frosted silhouette through the glass. A minute ticks by and makes me swallow – not because she hasn't moved a single muscle, but because I can still picture the emotionless look she gave me. It seemed to be the first time she'd understood the implied. Or perhaps, the first time she'd allowed me to see she'd acknowledged it. Either way, this would be the last time Rosie Rey set foot inside my house, and God willing, I think she understood that too.

A minute later and I hear her car leave my driveway. I lock the door and bolt it.

32

The following week, sweet release. The temperature has dropped five degrees and it feels like it's broken the fever I've been suffering for so long now. I'm showering every morning, deodorant and a spritz of cologne, and I've been washing my clothes too – steadily going through the rails and rails of unworn outfits that I used to cherish but which I've allowed to become stale. Bringing them in from the garden, smelling them clean again, it's tempting to try them on, but they're all going to the charity shop. I don't need fancy outfits and designer clothes where I'm going. I don't need material ties to my past.

I finished the wallpapering in the snug too, and dragged the sofa and coffee table in there to give me a neutral space to work. I brought down a basic kit from the loft – coloured pencils and chalks, a few sketch pads, some filled out with finished design briefs and some half-filled with ideas and colour-matching suggestions for one potential client who had yet to finalise the spec. They probably moved on with another designer a long time ago, someone with more experience, and I don't blame them, but I'm not going to let that hold me back. There had to come a time when it was right for me to move on, and I know at first it will be tinged with a sense of guilt, but push on I must. It's what Becky and Roy would have wanted.

All of my designs begin with an analogue sketch, a freeform expression of an idea that isn't clear to me until I have something to look at, something to compare it to. At this stage I have no style in mind, no colours or fabrics, no textures, and working this way there is the inevitable half-dozen false starts. But the amorphous idea is eventually given life, through either a controlled stroke of the pencil or a blind-luck gaff, and then I am away, and it's as if the idea has always been fully formed within my mind and I only had to remove the dust sheet to reveal it. Once the house is sold, and I'm set up proper, I'll invest in the digital tech of a professional designer who has a client portfolio and a blessed studio. iMac Pro, Wacom tablet, Pantone Matching System... The works. For now though, and thus shall ever be, the birthing of ideas will always come from paper and pencil, just like Da Vinci.

With no current clients, the only thing I can work on is my wallpaper designs. I go through all of the half-finished sketches, to try and tap into a thought or feeling that had once moved me to begin the concept in the first place, but jump-starting my creativity is like pushing a boulder up a hill. I just can't get it moving. To make matters worse, I hear the letterbox clap, and the slap of the local paper hitting the cold concrete, and when I get up to retrieve it, the first thing I see on the front page is a picture of Grant Chapman, below the headline: WE MISS YOU, DADDY.

Chapman had a daughter. Six years old. Her name is Erin.

In profile Erin is not unlike Becky at that age. There is a picture of her, below that of her dad's, and she is laying a bouquet of flowers on the ground before a plaque. I read the article three times, my mind, stomach and heart sharing between them feelings of shame, anger and apathy. My mind only tasting the memory of vodka.

From what I can glean, Chapman hadn't been in contact with his ex-partner (Lauren Spence, Ipswich) or daughter since well before he went to prison, but they had been thrown together at Chapman's father's funeral, as Erin and her mother had maintained a relationship with Lionel Chapman despite their estrangement with his son. From here, Chapman is portrayed as nothing less than a born-again Christian, and his death a tragic loss to the community. After he'd inherited his father's estate, he had vowed to be a part of Erin's life again, promising her a trip to Disneyland, Paris, until of course, his life and plans had been horrifically and brutally cut short after the violent acid attack, which the police were still investigating. I screw up the paper and stuff it into the kitchen bin.

Why is nothing straightforward? Why must I be constantly clawed backward? I didn't mean to kill him, or want to. I just wanted to scar him, leave an indelible mark on his face that, even if *he* didn't know what it meant, *I* would. Something to link him to his crime and my loss. But now I've taken away a child's father, all because I couldn't move on with my life. If I hadn't let Rosie persuade me into doing it, I would have met Dotty and I could have moved away from here, leaving this house and its memories behind, but no. Rosie brought out the malice in me, and it wasn't even hard.

I grab my purse and bag. I'm walking into town and I'm going to buy vodka for the freezer drawer. I've had it too easy of late and I need to test myself again. If I can see out the week without drinking, without the thoughts of Erin crying herself to sleep at night – if I can do that, then I know I can live with what I have done to her. I can't take it back so I'll have to take it forward with me.

I'm about to open the front door when my phone drones in

my bag. I hope it's Darryl, but it isn't. It's Lois Lane. I cut her off, and a minute later it rings again. I cut her off again. I know exactly why she's calling me. She's seen the paper and is going to offer me her support as my sponsor. She thinks I'm going to come off the rails, and she may be right, but the last person I ever want to see again is Rosie *fucking* Rey! I fumble about in the settings, wondering how I can block her. I've never blocked a caller in my life. Never needed to. The phone rings again in my hand and I scream at it, but it's Darryl. I take a breath to compose myself.

'Hi, Darryl,' I say calmly, though I can still hear the angry tremble in my voice.

'Hello, Mrs Young,' he replies. 'Will you be at the house today?'

'I've got to pop into town quickly, but I'll be free all day after that, why?'

'Mr and Mrs Delevingne would like to come and look at the house together, if that's okay?'

'Of course, Darryl,' I say, taking another silent breath. 'That would be perfect.'

33

The vodka is barely a minute inside the freezer drawer when the Delevingnes arrive. I blot my face with a tea towel and dry my sweaty hands, then open the door to them.

Darryl begins to introduce the couple, but Dotty waves him away. She squeezes my arm hello and reminds her husband in a semi-jovial tone that he's still wearing his hat. Joe Delevingne is as big a man as I have ever seen, both in height and breadth. He peels off his fedora with a hand the size of a pitcher's mitt, revealing a thicket of dense white hair, and engulfs my hand in his other mitt.

'Ms Young,' he says in a soft, southern tongue, and bows to meet my eye. 'Delighted.'

'Mr Delevingne,' I say, fighting the urge to giggle and curtsy. 'I'll be in my office. Take as much time as you need.'

I leave Darryl to take the Delevingnes on the tour of the house and I retreat to the Saab. I haven't been out here much over the past week as I've been preoccupied with my design work – which means I haven't been thinking about alcohol, and therefore haven't needed cigarettes to distract me. Not the case now though. I have a bottle chilling in the freezer and a mind burdened with guilt. A chat with Roy is what I need.

The dashboard lighter pops and I take the pack of cigarettes down from behind the sun visor. The temperature is creeping back daily. My fever with it. The leather seats are cooking and releasing their oils, and for the first time I catch the chemical undercurrent. Something to do with the curing of the cow skins, I morbidly assume. I inhale a deep one and blow the smoke into the back of the Saab to mask this new smell, but it's too late. I can taste it now as well.

'Erin,' I say, looking into the rear-view, but Roy doesn't answer. 'Chapman had a daughter—'

I start at the ringing of my phone. Lois Lane. I let it ring out, to see if she leaves a message. She doesn't. *Rosie* will get the message eventually, I try to convince myself, but then remember how long she stood at my front door while I hid in the kitchen. She did not move, and I broke. I will not break again. I switch off my phone and toss it into the passenger seat. Now where was I...

'I didn't know he had a daughter, Roy. You know I wouldn't have even contemplated it if I'd known he had a daughter—'

There. Cycling past my bloody drive on that silver racer of hers. Rosie. She's wearing a baseball cap and sunglasses, but it's clearly her. Those turquoise All Stars a beacon even at this distance. I toss my cigarette out the window and grab my phone. Switch it back on. I'm going to ring her, tell her to leave me alone or else. Or else what? Or else *what?*

I toss my phone back into the passenger seat. I don't have an *Or else.*

For the next twenty minutes I sit here smouldering in the heat until Darryl comes out of my front door, alone.

'How's it going in there?' I ask when he comes over.

'Mr Delevingne is no fool,' Darryl says with a frown. 'He

spotted the crack immediately and estimated how much off the asking price he would cut to make it good. Amongst other things.'

'Other things?'

'American houses come with hardwood floors and landscaped gardens with water features.'

I reach for my cigarettes. 'And he has an estimate for that too, I bet.' I jab in the dashboard lighter.

'Yes, but...' Darryl crouches at the Saab door and we both look toward the house. 'Mr Delevingne also has a Mrs Delevingne.' Darryl turns to me, smiling, and in a pretty decent southern accent says, 'And I don't get the impression she is taking advice from her husband at this time, but don't hold me to that, *Mizz* Young.'

As the lighter pops, the Delevingnes emerge from the front door and Darryl walks back over to greet them. Dotty blows me a kiss and waves before taking Darryl's arm so he can help her down the steps, and her husband replaces his fedora and surveys the façade of the house with his mighty hands fisted at his hips. He then joins his wife and Darryl at their huge whatever-it-is of a vehicle.

I stay in the Saab and smoke for a while, once they are all gone, and just as I'm about to go back into the house, my phone pings with a message. I blow out a sigh, expecting something from Lois Lane, but it's Darryl.

*Mrs D's lawyer will be in touch within the week with an offer... of the FULL ASKING PRICE!!!*

I scream and blast the horn in celebration, realising now that I do not need an *Or else* for Rosie. I'll be gone from this place soon enough, and she will be a distant memory, along with all the other things I've tried so hard to forget.

*"I'm an interior designer from the soul. It's not about just putting things in a room. It's much deeper and broader. It's about self-discovery."*

~ Alexandra Stoddard

## 34

Over the next two days I begin to see the house a little differently. Can feel a distance growing between us. I've been in Becky's room twice without crying – the second time filling up a cardboard box with her stuffed animals and taping it shut. When I'm ready I'll contact the local charity shop to come and collect as much as they want, it's time to let go. It's just stuff. Just a house. It isn't Becky or Roy. They will be with me always.

I list the scaffold tower again on eBay, but with no takers. I expect I'll have to leave it here for the Delevingnes. I imagine Joe Delevingne will know what to do with it. He seems that kind of man. Roy was never that kind of man, and felt no shame in hiring people to do the most menial jobs for him. When I say he was going to grow his own vegetables in the garden, I meant he was going to hire a gardener to grow them for him. Roy was not one for getting his hands dirty, that's what solicitors are for, he used to joke. When we learned our builder was going to take us under with him, I screamed at Roy to go round to his house and deal with him, make him give us our money back, but he wouldn't. Of course you won't, I'd said, feeling mean as soon as I'd said it but unable to stop myself. That's why his friends walked all over him – well, one friend. What was his name...? God, I can never remember his name.

Detective Wallace for some reason springs from my memory. He's driving me home, the day of Becky's accident, my eyelid bulky with gauze and tape from the medics who'd arrived on the scene. I'm crying, ranting about something, and all he does is listen. But it is a strange comfort. He doesn't offer me any condolences for what has happened, or any assurances that justice will be served. He just listens, and the only thing I can remember of anything passing between us is the soft tick-tocking of the indicators as he navigates the back roads, like a faulty metronome is trying to keep time with my jumbled mind. I wonder if it's in their training, that they're not allowed to offer advice or make promises, to keep a professional distance from the victims. He did come inside, though. I remember that much. He was the one who made the call to Roy, to bring him home from his business trip. I certainly wasn't in any state to make that call.

My phone rumbles on the kitchen table. A message. I grab it, hoping it's an update from Darryl about the Delevingnes' solicitor, a date that I can start looking forward to. But no. It's from Lois Lane: *Hi, Dina. I'm outside.*

My first instinct is to ignore her. She cannot know that I am home, and why didn't I hear her ring the doorbell? I jerk my head towards the kitchen window, sneak a peek at the front door but don't see anyone standing there, so I creep upstairs. The smallest of the spare bedrooms overlooks the driveway, and so I go to the window and look down. I don't see Rosie's car or any other sign of her. Perhaps she's waiting by the road, respecting my wishes as best she can. I crack the window open and peer out, but again I don't see any sign of her. I go downstairs and unlock the front door.

There is no one outside, and when I walk down to the road it's as desolate in both directions as it always is, apart from the distant whirr of a lawnmower. I head back, rereading Rosie's message and wondering if I should reply or just ignore it. She is clearly playing games. But then I look up.

Rosie is sitting in the passenger seat of the Saab. She gives me a short wave and reaches for the driver side door and opens it. I ponder the invitation for a moment, knowing without doubt I should go back into the house and lock the door, but also know that our little friendship has to end, messily or otherwise.

'Rosie,' I say, bending to look inside the Saab. 'What are you doing in my car?'

She leans over to look up at me. Very little make-up today, and the sun has brought out a spray of freckles across her nose and cheeks, giving the impression of "girl next door" innocence, if you hadn't met her. 'I know how you don't like me coming in the house,' she says, 'so I thought you'd prefer to sit and talk somewhere neutral. You getting in?'

'Neutral? This is my car, Rosie.'

'Well, yeah, that's why I didn't get in the driver's seat.'

Rosie's logic defies logic, and frustrates more than I can put into words. 'Get out, Rosie.' I slam the door.

She climbs out of the Saab and snicks the door closed. 'Sweet car, by the way. Shame about the fender-bender at the rear. Is that why you don't drive it anymore?'

'What? Who says I don't?'

Rosie shrugs. 'The arches are full of cobwebs and the back right's half flat, so...'

'Why are you here, Rosie?'

She picks something from the roof of the Saab and dusts it from her fingers. 'I needed to talk to you.'

'Rosie...'

'I know, I know, we shouldn't be seen together, but that's what I wanted to talk to you about.'

I step closer to the Saab, put my hand on the roof but it's baking hot so I snatch it away, angry that I've burned myself. 'We need to stop this,' I say, and it's a relief to get the words out, tear the plaster off. I should have had the guts to say it as soon as I found out that Grant Chapman had died. 'I'm sorry, Rosie, but I need you to—'

'I'm going to go to the police, Dina.'

'You're going to do what?'

'It's all my fault what I've put you through, this anguish, so

I'm going to go to the police and tell them what I've done. Tell them what I made you do and that it's all my fault that he's dead.'

'Wait, you can't do that, Rosie.' I march around to the other side of the car, can see her eyes filling up. 'Let's think about this.'

'I have, Dina. I've put you through so much, and for what? I thought I was helping you heal, but all I ever do is cause people pain, and now a man's dead because of me. The least I can do is own up to what I've done, and—'

'And I'll go down for manslaughter, at best, and you'll probably get community service or some trivial amount of time—'

Rosie starts to cry. 'But I supplied you with the acid, Dina. You, you couldn't have done anything to that man if I hadn't got you the acid, so it's on me, not you.'

'The police won't see it like that, Rosie, and look...' I rub her shoulders, search out her eyes, which she has dragged away from me. 'Let's not forget what he did. He wasn't a good man.'

Her eyes come back to me. 'He had a daughter, did you know that?' she says.

'And so did I until he took her from me.'

Rosie sniffs, seems to gather herself. 'I should go.'

'Not like this you shouldn't. I'll get you some water.'

'Listen, you don't have to worry, Dina,' she says when I reach my front steps. 'I won't say anything if you don't want me to.'

'We can't take it back, Rosie, so we'll just have to live with it.'

Another sniff. 'But I don't know if I can. I thought I could, but then I saw his daughter in the paper and I, I became so sick of myself.'

I go back to her, take her by the shoulders again and make sure this time she's looking me in the eyes. 'You didn't force me to do anything I didn't want to do. I wanted to hurt that man—'

'But not kill him.'

'No, not kill him, but he's dead and I can't take it back. I wish I could. I wish I could have my daughter and husband back too, but that can't happen either, and so I just have to move on, and I can't do that until I know you are going to be okay, okay?'

Rosie gives a little shuddery nod and a tear runs off her chin.

'So will you be okay?' I ask.

'I'll try,' she says.

'That's not good enough, Rosie,' I surprise myself by saying. 'I think I might have sold the house, and I'm going to move away from here and start anew, but I can't keep looking over my shoulder worrying about you going to the police, worrying that my future could end at any moment, because whether you like it or not, this will all come down on my head, not yours, so I need to know that you're going to be okay.'

'I'll try – I mean, I will be. I'll think of a way to make it right between us.'

'You haven't got to make it right between us, Rosie. I just need to be reassured that you're not going to go to the police.'

Rosie cuffs her nose, palms her cheeks dry. 'I get it, Dina. It's on you, not me. I get it.'

'The worst is over. Detective Wallace is looking for thugs, and thanks to you my alibi is unbreakable—'

'That's it!' Rosie suddenly beams, eyes wide and energised.

'What's what?'

'How I can reassure you that I won't ever go to the police!' She takes me by the shoulders now, and my stomach begins to knot.

'What are you talking about, Rosie?'

She gives me a squeeze. She's almost trembling with excitement. 'You, Dina, are going to give *me* an alibi.'

36

In the distance, the lawnmower cuts off, and it's like every house along this road has hushed to hear the next words come out of Rosie's mouth. I've stopped breathing myself, praying she will lose her train of thought in this beat of silence, praying she will jump to some obscure observation that has nothing to do with me giving her an alibi. And for what, I am too terrified to ask.

'I'll get you that water,' I say, turning for the house, but it's a weak distraction and I know Rosie won't fall for it. And of course, she doesn't.

'It makes total sense if you think about it, Dina,' she says, following me to the front door. 'If you give me an alibi, then together we'd have built a house of cards that will come down on both our heads if one of us goes to the police, you know?'

I stop, close my eyes. 'I don't know, Rosie, no.'

She steps around in front of me. 'It isn't fair that I've got this thing held over you, Dina, and I don't want you to feel for one second that I might crack and go to the police' – she flaps her hands and flutters her eyelashes – 'even though I almost did just now, but anyway... What I mean is, we'll both have something on the other, so if one goes down, we both go down. Kinda perfect, ain't it?'

In whose twisted version of reality is that "kinda perfect" I want to scream at her, but instead hear myself asking, out of some morbid curiosity: 'An alibi for what?'

'I've been seeing this guy for a while now, and I really thought it was going somewhere, but then, you know, I found out the cheating fucktard had a wife, and all he wanted from me was sex.'

'Right... So...?'

'So anyway, he's got a little love pad in Ipswich – God, I'm so stupid – and I thought, to teach him a lesson and to stop any other young women from getting used the way he used me, I thought I'd burn it down.'

'You want to what?'

'Teach him a lesson and stop him from—'

'By burning down his house? My God, Rosie, just tell his wife!'

'I did tell his wife, and she didn't seem to care. And I wouldn't burn down their home, Dina, jeez... Just his little love pad.'

I'm stunned – no, actually, I'm a tiny bit terrified. 'Count. Me. Out,' I say, and stomp up my front steps and close and lock the door behind me. As I'm heading for the kitchen I hear the letterbox creak open.

'Dina, if you do this one thing for me, I promise you'll never have to see me again and you'll know I'll never go to the police. You can get on with your life, that's want you want, isn't it? That's all I wanted for you.'

The letterbox slaps shut, then opens again.

'I'll give you a couple of days to think about it. If you don't want to repay the alibi, Dina, that's fine, no hard feelings. I'll get rid of the acid bottle either way.'

*What?*

The letterbox slaps shut again, and by the time I get to the front door and unlock it, Rosie is already on the road heading right on foot, towards the river. I do not go after her.

37

That night I can't sleep. There is not a breath of wind at my window, and only the pale light of a half-moon seeping in, accompanied by the chirrup of crickets. I kick the sheets down the bed and roll to a dry spot, my skin dewy with sweat.

Why had Rosie not yet disposed of the acid bottle? It's the one thing that could shatter our alibi and open us up to deeper investigation. Where and why did she purchase the acid? Why did we lie about being friends when we'd only just met? At least I had a modicum of deniability. I'd worn gloves. Any fingerprints on the bottle would be Rosie's, so I could lie. If she forced my hand I could lie, say that she had threatened me with the acid if I didn't give her an alibi. *I had no idea she was targeting Grant Chapman. You have to believe me, Detective Wallace, by the time I found out what she'd done it was too late. What could I do?*

I reach for my water glass, but find it empty. I climb out of bed and take the glass down to the kitchen and refill it. Drink deeply. Refill.

The entrance hall is semi-shadowed and eerie, but the bright half of the moon is hypnotic enough to stall me here within its gaze. I stare back at it through the arch window. My skin cooling and drying. The house breathing and sighing. The scaffold tower looking on, indifferent to my torment, which doubles when I notice the glass in my hand.

'No...' A whisper escapes me. *'There were two bottles...'*

Rosie had given me a second bottle to practise with, and I'd filled it with water at the sink.

'No...'

And I'd given it back to her, at her request. Dropped it into the carrier bag with the bottle filled with acid, which Rosie then placed in her rucksack.

Rosie has my fingerprints. All she has to do is pour the acid into the other bottle and I'm screwed. If Rosie wants me to be screwed.

The question is, does she?

## 38

The following morning I almost feel hungover, even though the bottle of vodka remains untouched, sleeping soundly in the cradle of the freezer drawer. I did not sleep soundly, if at all.

I shower, drink coffee. Spend the morning sitting at the kitchen table listening to the ticking of the chrome clock, thinking about what I'm going to do. About Rosie. About the alibi she wants from me and what she might do if I don't give it to her. I'm staring at Lois Lane's number when my phone rings in my hand and makes me jolt in my chair. It's Darryl.

'Good morning, Mrs Young,' he says with a bounce in his voice.

'Morning, Darryl. Any news?'

'The best news,' he says. 'The Delevingnes' solicitor has just been in touch with the official offer of the full asking price, and they want to move ahead as soon as possible.'

I close my eyes and swallow. My hand reaches up to stop a sob escaping.

'Mrs Young?'

'Sorry, Darryl, that's wonderful news.'

'Do you have a solicitor?'

'Not yet.'

'Well, I can recommend one if need be,' Darryl says. 'Rachel Beatty, of Soames and Beatty. Very efficient.'

'Let's do that,' I say.

'Excellent. I'll have her contact you. Have a great day, Mrs Young, I'll be in touch.'

I murmur something and Darryl hangs up. I head out to the Saab, smoke a cigarette in a semi-trance, one leg draped out of the open door. Zero breeze.

'I think this is goodbye, Roy,' I say, and in a whisper, *'Don't hate me...'*

I bring up Lois Lane's number and dial.

'Oh, hi, Dina,' Rosie answers, as if I'm the last person on earth she's expecting to hear from.

'If I do this, if I give you your alibi, I want two things from you in return.'

'Fire away, Kemoshabee.'

It's too early for Rosie-speak, if there's even a good time of day to be speaking with her. 'Firstly, I want the acid bottles.'

'I said I'd get rid of them, Dina—'

'But you didn't, so I will. Bring them to me and I'll deal with it.'

'Fine,' she says, and I can picture her rolling her eyes. 'And the second thing?'

'When this is done, I don't want you to contact me anymore, not ever, and not for anything.'

'Well, I'm not going to pretend that doesn't hurt, Dina, but—'

'There is no *but*, Rosie,' I say. 'I'll be moving away from Suffolk as soon as my house is sold, but until the sale goes through, I don't want you calling me or calling round for any reason, is that clear?'

Silence for a moment, and then, 'I only ever wanted to help you, Dina. I saw how affected you'd been by Grant Chapman and I wanted to help you, and if I'm being honest, I think he's still affecting you. I can sense it in your aura.'

Good grief. I flick my cigarette out onto the driveway. What I wouldn't give right now to have never attended that bloody AA meeting. 'Those are my two stipulations, Rosie. You either want my help or you don't. It's up to you.'

'Wow, you must really want me out of your life.'

'Rosie...' I bury the phone against my chest for a second. She's actually made me feel terrible. 'I just want to move on with my life, that's all. Please don't take it personally.'

Silence.

'Rosie?'

'I'm here.' A light cough. 'Thursday night he plays squash between seven and eight. I was going to do it then.'

'This Thursday? That's two days away.'

'I'll see you at six. I'll bring the acid bottles and the film. You can supply the nibbles.'

'Film?'

'Yeah,' Rosie says. 'I thought we could have another movie night.'

## 39

I spent the rest of yesterday and the best part of this morning worrying about the consequences of helping Rosie, and trying to remind myself why I was doing it. The consequences are simple. Prison. But that was true whether I helped Rosie or not. I was responsible for Grant Chapman's death, and that fact carries a double-figure sentence, even if you threw a little arson into the mix.

The *why* is somewhat more complicated to pin down, but selfishness would broadly cover it. I don't want to go to prison, and I don't believe I deserve to after what I've been through these last couple of years. Do I deserve a brighter future is a better question, especially after I caused the death of another human being. A father. Let me spend a year in a new house, in a different county, or country, maybe. Let me have that time away from these old phantoms and let my conscience answer the question of whether I deserve a brighter future. I'll guess that the answer is yes, and I'll defy any mother that says they would have done things differently.

And it's as if karma agrees with me. From my bedroom

window I notice a little white van pull up on the grass verge outside my driveway and the silver-haired gentleman from Darryl's agency climb out. I wait until he's finished and then walk down to the road. The FOR SALE sign has been changed. It now reads SOLD.

40

Rosie arrives at the pip of six. I'd done as she'd suggested, dragged the coffee table back up from the snug and into the lounge, window-dressed it with nibbles and the same sickly cordial I'd bought for our first fake movie night, though I didn't bother to bake scones this time. I found it mildly ridiculous that Rosie wanted to tell the same lie twice, even though her "if it ain't broke" speech held more than a morsel of logic. I didn't want Detective Wallace thinking we were mocking him in some way, in the event Rosie was implicated and I had to straight-faced lie to him again. In truth, I couldn't see how she would be implicated, given that the only person who could throw her name into the hat of potential suspects was a cheating married man, who I imagine would do everything he could to keep Rosie's name out of it and spare himself the inevitable tricky questions he would certainly invite from his wife. A shame, really. I'd have liked to see Detective Wallace again. There's something about him I find comforting.

Rosie has brought her bike again, and I watch her drag it out of the boot and lean it against the side of her car. She removes her rucksack from the passenger seat and brings it with her to the front door. I let her ring the doorbell before I answer it.

She steps inside and I close the door behind her. No greetings from either of us. I follow her to the kitchen, where she begins to unpack her rucksack on the table. I watch her from the doorway. She's wearing charcoal-grey leggings – and of course her All Stars – and a sleeveless white T-shirt that has been raggedly cut to reveal her taught little tummy. When she turns to me I can see her T-shirt has an image printed on it – a sequined likeness of Elvis Presley singing into a hairbrush. Cute, if I didn't know what Rosie was planning to do this evening.

'Just leave all this set up on the table,' Rosie says. 'When I get back I want to get showered and gone.'

She continues dragging items from the rucksack and placing them on the table next to her animal-print pyjamas and clean set of underwear – mismatched with royal-blue knickers and black bra. Then follows a DVD, a box of matches, a tin of lighter fluid, a takeaway menu...

'You'll be taking the matches and lighter fuel, won't you?' I ask.

'No, I've got that covered,' she says without looking up. 'Those are for you.'

A tube of salt and vinegar Pringles, a bottle of Diet Coke, a couple of magazines...

'Why would I need matches and lighter fuel, Rosie? I'm just the alibi.' I step into the kitchen and stand on the opposite side of the table, cross my arms.

'Absolutely, Dina, for sure.' Shampoo, shower gel, deodorant, bath towel... 'But when I come back here to get showered, I'm gonna need you to dispose of what I'm wearing now.'

'I'm not getting involved, Rosie. I said I'd be your alibi, and that's it.'

She slouches onto a hip. 'Jeez, Dina, think about what I did for you. I got the acid – which I brought, by the way.' She delves into her rucksack and brings out what looks like the same carrier bag from our last movie night, and hands it across the table to me. 'And I mapped out where Grant Chapman would be, and came with you on the night, and came up with the plan so you wouldn't get caught – which you didn't, I might add.' She shakes the carrier. 'It's all in here.'

I glance between Rosie and the carrier bag for a moment, then take the bag. 'But—'

'Look, Dina, I haven't got a garden or even a fireplace at my flat, but you have both. You've got to get rid of the acid bottles anyway, so just burn it all at the same time. It would really help me out.'

I hold the bag away from me at a worrying thought. 'Won't the acid explode or something?'

'I don't know, I've never tried to burn it before.' She hangs her rucksack over the back of a chair. 'My advice, empty the acid bottle into one of those dirt holes you've got in your basement and dig it over a bit. Then burn the bottle, along with my clothes.' Rosie tosses me the magazines she brought.

'What are those for?' I ask.

'To get the fire started.'

Again, Rosie has thought of everything, and I'm just along for the ride. I suppose I could burn her clothes for her, as I am going to burn the acid bottles anyway. Plus, the less evidence that survives this night, the better, and to be honest, I'll sleep easier knowing I was in control of that aspect. I reach across the table for the matches and lighter fluid.

'You might as well take this too.' Rosie hands me the DVD. 'You'll need to watch it tonight.'

I take it. 'What is it?'

'*Revolutionary Road.* I thought we should stick with the DiCaprio/Winslet theme, you know, if Wallace needs a reason for our second movie night.'

And last.

'I'll put it on as soon as you're gone.' I flip the DVD to look at the back. 'What's it about, anyway?'

'Oh, you'll love it. I've seen it about a dozen times. On the surface it's about a marriage that turns toxic, but underneath it's about the lack of bravery to own your future.'

Well, I can't be accused of that anymore. Just look at the things I've done – am doing – to own mine.

41

I watch Rosie leave. Watch her take a bum bag from her car and clip it around her waist, mount her silver racer and push off. I guess the bum bag is for her phone and purse, and something to help set a man's house on fire. The thought makes me shiver.

I ring for a takeaway and ready two plates and two sets of cutlery. No need to time-stamp our movie night with taxis, Rosie said. A delivery from the local Chinese restaurant will do. I open the Pringles and pour myself a glass of the sickly cordial, then put the film on. Not that I'll be able to concentrate on it, and I'll be surprised if I can even manage a bite of food when it arrives. My stomach is all over the place, and not because of the foul cordial.

An hour or so later, and after Kate Winslet has told Leonardo DiCaprio of her ideas of them moving to Paris to start a new life, a young Asian woman arrives with the takeaway. I tip her five pounds in cash, calling back into the house first to see if Rosie has change, but she doesn't seem to hear me. I plate the food and take it through to the lounge, where I resume the film.

I was right, I couldn't eat, but the film did manage to grab my attention and distract me from the anxiety of waiting for Rosie. Ultimately, Kate Winslet doesn't make it to Paris, and she dies giving herself an abortion. That made me cry, not that she'd lost her life, but because she had been prepared to abort her unborn child in order to fulfil her dream of moving to Paris. I wondered how Rosie saw this as a lack of bravery. April Wheeler (Winslet's character in the film) made the ultimate sacrifice in order to realise her dream, her desired future. She took her destiny in her own hands. What could be more courageous than that?

By nine o'clock the sun is beginning to set, and still no sign of Rosie. My mind races. What if she's been caught? Or worse, what if she'd been caught in the fire? The flames raged out of her control somehow, or she'd tripped while making her escape and succumbed to smoke inhalation. I shake the thoughts away and start tearing up the magazines, balling the pages and placing them in the snug's fireplace in preparation for when she does arrive, because of course she will. She must. This has to end tonight.

I'm dousing the balled-up pages in the lighter fluid when the doorbell rings, and when I open the door, Rosie is at her car, humping her bike into the boot, followed by the bum bag. Once she closes the boot, she heads towards me, her face glistening in the night and with sweat stains soaked into her leggings and her Elvis top, which for some reason she has turned inside out.

'What did you think of the film?' she asks as she passes me in the doorway, the faint whiff of smoke in her hair and on her clothes.

'Good,' I say, giving a cursory glance toward the road, listening for sirens that I could never hear from Ipswich. When I shut the door I follow Rosie into the kitchen, where she is unlacing her All Stars, stripping off her clothes and piling them on the table. When she turns to me she is fully naked and sheened in sweat, taut and hairless as a mannequin. 'How did it go?' I ask, straining to keep my eyes on her eyes.

Rosie shrugs, her young breasts unmoving. 'It's done,' she says, and gathers up her bath towel, pyjamas and toiletries, and walks by me and heads for the stairs.

I don't bother telling her where the bathroom is. For some reason I believe she already knows.

I gather Rosie's sweaty clothes and All Stars and take them into the snug, place them down next to the hearth. I won't start the fire until she's gone. Back in the kitchen my mind wanders to the vodka in the freezer drawer. How I wish I was strong enough to just have one glass right now, but I know that can never be. Upstairs, I listen to my hairdryer whirr and think of Becky, of me drying her beautiful hair, marvelling as it turns from Umber to Honey with every stroke of the brush.

When Rosie emerges she is wearing her animal-print pyjamas and her hair is combed back long and straight, making her appear even younger than I know she is, and more innocent.

'I hope you don't mind,' she says, walking over to where I'm sitting at the kitchen table, 'I stole a touch of the Chanel you've got in your bathroom cabinet.' She leans in and offers me her throat.

'That's fine,' I say, avoiding Rosie's offer to smell her with a question: 'Are you sure you want me to burn your shoes? They look new.'

'Nah,' she says, standing back from me. 'Burn 'em.'

'Okay.' I rise from my chair. 'I put your DVD back in your rucksack, and there's plenty of Chinese left if you want to take some with you?'

'You should leave it here for the night, just in case I get a visit from the you-know-who.' Rosie stuffs her bath towel and toiletries into her rucksack, and to my relief she shoulders it.

Could this really be the last time I'll ever see her? Could I finally move on? God, I hope so.

'I'll see you out,' I say, and the crumpled expression that appears on Rosie's face makes me want to hug her, but I won't. Instead, I head for the front door and open it, and when I turn around I'm pleased to see that Rosie has come along with me and she's looking brighter.

'Well, Dina,' she says, stepping outside into the night, 'I guess this is it.'

'I guess so.'

'And at least you got to see *Revolutionary Road.*'

'Yeah, thanks, I enjoyed it.'

'Those Wheelers are a riot, aren't they?' she says, nodding at me with a smile.

I don't want to get into this. I just want her to go. But... I'm curious. 'It certainly was a toxic relationship, but I couldn't see how what April did in the end wasn't brave.'

'You mean aborting her unborn kid so she could move to Paris? You thought that was brave?' Rosie's face is deadpan when she asks me this, and God, I wish I'd kept my bloody mouth shut.

'Don't you?' I ask, cringing inside.

Rosie looks off and I can see her frustration with me in the flare of her nostrils. 'April Wheeler wasn't brave for taking the life of her unborn baby, Dina, because she was only doing it to spite her husband. If she was going to be brave, she would have murdered Frank and moved to Paris with the kids on the insurance money.' Rosie turns back to me, shaking her head. 'April Wheeler liked feeling sorry for herself, and having Frank around to blame for how miserable her life had turned out suited her just fine. Some people are like that, aren't they? It's easier to feel sorry for yourself and blame others for your failures than it is to take responsibility. That's bravery, Dina. Taking responsibility.'

'I... I hadn't thought of it that way.'

'Nobody does,' Rosie says, adjusting her rucksack over her shoulder. 'Bye, Dina.'

And with that, Rosie is gone. No waves or glances back. No pipping of the horn. Just tail-lights disappearing in the distance when she turns out of the road. Hopefully, never to be seen again.

42

The morning after the night before. The night that had not gone as I had planned, and the morning that was so far spiralling into a nightmare, as I stand at the sink washing the dirt from my hands, the erratic thuds coming from the washing machine and jarring my tattered nerves... While I wait for Detective Wallace to tell me why he is here in my kitchen.

I didn't burn Rosie's clothes or the acid bottles in the snug's fireplace. As soon as Rosie had left, I did start to, but the smell from the burning lighter fluid when I lit the magazine pages was so chemically strong that I put out the flames immediately with the glass of water I had standing by. And Rosie's clothes were so damp with sweat, I would've had to douse them with more lighter fluid, and the house would have reeked for days. Which I couldn't allow, just in case Rosie did have to use me as her alibi and I did get a visit from the police. How right I was.

And so I decided to burn it all in the back garden. Roy had bought a metal bin for destroying old bank statements and junk mail, but I didn't want to start a fire in the dark and have any of my anonymous neighbours suddenly grow concerned and call the police or fire service, and so I planned to burn it all the following morning. But I woke to find an email from Rachel Beatty, the solicitor Darryl had recommended to me to oversee the sale of the house. She'd requested certain details about the property, which led to a sweaty hunt in the loft for documents. And boom, another chunk of my morning evaporated, on top of the lateness of my waking thanks to a restless mind that had kept me tossing and turning into the early hours.

And then, as I was loading my sweat-soaked bed-sheets into the washing machine, the phone call:

'Hello, Mrs Young. This is Detective Anand. Could I speak with Detective Wallace, please?'

'Umm... Detective Wallace?'

'Is he not there, yet?'

'Umm, is there any reason he should be?'

'He said he was coming out to you this morning,' Detective Anand said. 'I've been calling him but he isn't answering his phone. I'd hoped he might be with you.'

'Can I ask why?'

'I think it has something to do with his age. He often leaves his phone at home, in the glove box, battery always on ten per cent or less...'

'No, I mean why is he coming out to see me?'

'I'll let him explain when he gets there, Mrs Young. If you could ask him to call me when he does?'

'Umm... yeah, okay.'

Detective Anand hung up, and I began to panic.

At first my mind went beyond blank, and I stood there, by the washing machine, its door gaping open and mirroring what I imagined was the same look of shock on my face. But then I reacted. I had to.

I ran to the kitchen window and checked the driveway. Empty except for the Saab. I'd left Rosie's clothes and the acid bottles by the fireplace. They had to disappear, but where? I ran to the snug and collected all the incriminating evidence in my arms, and literally darted in three different directions, sending an image of Charlie Chaplin cane-twirling into my brain but without the humour.

*Think, think, Dina!*

Rosie's voice suddenly came to me, calm and clear. Her suggestion of pouring the acid into one of the excavation holes in the basement and digging it over. That's it! I could bury it all!

I rushed back to the kitchen, through the larder to the basement door, bundled it open, elbowed the light switch, took a moment to catch my breath. One, two, three, four. Down I went.

I dumped Rosie's clothes by the side of the nearest hole, along with the carrier bag with the acid bottles, lighter fluid, matches and the scraps of balled-up magazine pages I'd cleared from the snug's fireplace. I then took the shovel that was leaning against the cement mixer and started to dig into the soft dark earth.

It didn't take long to make a hole big enough for my needs, but as I was going to dig it up again later, I thought I should place Rosie's clothes inside the carrier bag to keep them dry and free of dirt, to make them easier to burn when I had the chance. First, the leggings went in, then her underwear, but when I reached for her Elvis top, I stalled. When Rosie had come back last night, she'd turned her Elvis top inside out for some reason. I had no time to be curious at that present moment, but I had also come to learn, at a very young age, that I was self-destructive by nature. I turned the Elvis top outside in again.

That's when I saw the blood, and heard the faint chime of the doorbell drift down into the basement.

43

'Had you been knocking for long?' I ask Detective Wallace, drying off my hands with a tea towel.

'Only a minute or two,' he says. 'Are you a keen gardener, Mrs Young?'

He's referring to the fact I answered the door to him with my hands caked in dirt. I said I'd been weeding in the back garden and that's why I hadn't heard the doorbell. 'Not really. I'm just trying to keep it tidy for the new owners.'

'Yes, I saw the sold sign as I drove in.'

I gesture at a chair. 'Can I get you something to drink, Detective Wallace?'

'No, thank you,' he says, taking the chair. 'I'll just get to it, if I may.'

'Sure.' I fix myself an iced water and take the chair opposite him. The washing machine lulls into a sleepy cycle and the thudding dies temporarily. I can't stop thinking of the blood on Rosie's Elvis top.

Detective Wallace ponders over his notebook for a moment, then says, 'Can you tell me where you were last night?'

'Can I ask what this is about?'

'I'm just following up some routine enquiries.'

'About Grant Chapman?'

'About Rolland Childress.' Detective Wallace glances over his shoulder as the washing machine reawakens. 'Does that name ring any bells with you, Mrs Young?'

Yes. A tiny bell, almost imperceptible in the distance. 'No, should it?'

He consults his notebook. 'He's a solicitor. He represented Grant Chapman in the case of your daughter.'

That's him. The thinning young man with the thick lenses and the squint. The man who had Chapman's sentence slashed by (how did Chapman put it in the footage Rosie showed me?) "pulling something out of the bag?".

'What's he up to now?' I ask. 'Trying to overturn Harold Shipman's conviction?'

'Mr Childress died in an arson attack last night.'

'What?'

'Yes, Mrs Young. Somebody set his house on fire, and unfortunately he was still inside.'

*Dear God, Rosie...*

'And you think I had something to do with it? You... You think I could have...' The washing machine gallops into a spin cycle and the *thud-thudding* drills into my head.

'It could be argued that you held him accountable for Chapman's lenient sentencing—' Detective Wallace is distracted by the washing machine. The thudding. 'Which by your own admission is true, Mrs Young. So this line of enquiry has to be investigated, if only for elimination purposes. You understand.'

'I understand that you think I'm on some kind of revenge rampage.'

'Every avenue has to be considered.'

'So how many other *avenues* do you have to investigate, Detective Wallace?' I ask. 'Because if I'm the only person you've contacted over the death of this man, this is borderline harassment.'

'We do have other persons of interest.'

I scoff. 'Not any you're trying to link to Grant Chapman, I bet.'

He faintly bats his head.

'*Really*. So you have a suspect who possibly had it in for both of these men. I don't believe it.'

'We have a description of a young woman we'd like to speak to, who was seen in and around Dreydon Park on the night of Chapman's attack, and in the vicinity of Rolland Childress's address, not long before the fire was called in.'

'Hurrah for being old,' I say.

'We don't know for sure the age of the woman, only the description of her... attire, shall we say – suggests someone on the younger side.'

'You mean like a school uniform?'

'No. But we do have a pushbike – white, maybe silver – and wearing a pair of American-style sneakers/trainers, green or possibly blue.'

*Turquoise.*

My eyes skip beyond Detective Wallace's notebook, to the thudding at the washing machine door behind him. To one of Rosie's All Stars peeking out from between the tangle of my bed-sheets to kick against the glass. I couldn't bring myself to burn them. The thought of the rubber soles gluing up the hearth or metal bin, while the rest reduced to ash and floated into the ether, seemed... unnecessary. I was never going to see Rosie Rey again, and so stupidly, recklessly, in some melancholic bout of madness, I decided to keep them. I would wash them and destroy any evidence that might have lingered, and hide them in one of the tea chests in the loft. I could picture myself finding them years from now, wherever I might be in the world, and looking back on Rosie and our time together with no regret. Less regret. I don't know. Like I said, it was stupid and reckless and now Detective Wallace is going to look round at any moment and see them bobbing in the churning soapy water and we would both go to jail.

'Well,' I say, staring toward the kitchen window, trying to draw his gaze away from the washing machine, which has, thankfully, stopped spinning and started to drain. 'I don't own a pushbike, I'm afraid.'

'No, I don't see the appeal myself, either,' he says. 'So, anyway. Could I ask where you were last night?'

I look back to him. His pen is poised above his notebook. 'I was here.'

'Okay. And was anybody with you? Can anybody confirm—'

'Rosie Rey.'

He nods. Jots. 'And was Rosie with you all night? Some of the night?'

'Between six and around midnight. We had a takeaway.' I glance toward the foil containers on the draining board.

'I thought I could smell Chinese.'

Of course he can. Most of it I emptied into the pedal bin.

'So, just a casual dinner engagement.'

It isn't really a question, but his pen is waiting for an answer, and as much as I don't want to give Detective Wallace more than he's asking for, I have no choice. Rosie will tell him anyway. 'And a movie.' I wish for all the world my iced water was vodka, right now.

'Movie night,' he speak-writes, and I can't unhear the suspicion in his voice as he plots out each syllable. 'Anything good?'

'Umm... *Revolutionary Road*.'

'Great film, I've seen it myself.' He jots it down, aims his pen at me. 'DiCaprio, again.'

'Yes.'

He skips back through his notebook. 'Sex on a hickory stick. That's how you described him in *Titanic*.'

'Did I?'

He taps the page with his pen. 'I wrote it down.'

I shrug. I can't breathe. Why would he write that down?

'It's only because I'd never heard that expression before.'

'Well, you can have it,' I say.

'It only stuck because when we interviewed Rosie Rey, she described DiCaprio in the same way. Exactly.'

'I probably picked it up from Rosie, then.'

Detective Wallace fudges his bottom lip in a pondering pinch. 'It does sound more like something she would say – not that I know either of you.' He closes his notebook.

I stand from my chair, relieved that this is almost over. Relieved that my bed-sheets have concealed Rosie's godforsaken All Stars. I walk Detective Wallace to the front door.

'Thanks for your time, Mrs Young.' He steps outside and I go to close the door. 'One last thing,' he says. 'Did Rosie get a taxi here again last night?'

I open the door fully, along with my expression. 'No, she drove.'

'So she didn't drink last night?'

'We're both in recovery,' I remind him. 'She's my sponsor.'

He slaps his notebook in his palm. 'Of course she is, it's in here. I'll clear this up with Rosie and then I'm sure we can draw a line under it. Good luck with the house, Mrs Young.'

I close the door, and only realise when he has driven away that I've forgotten to tell him to call Detective Anand, because my mind is elsewhere, impaled upon the irony that Rosie Rey is, for the second time, giving *me* an alibi. And I do not think for one moment that irony is lost on Detective Wallace.

<h1 style="text-align:center">44</h1>

An excruciating few days passed, exacerbated by the disappearance of the moon, which blinked out entirely to deepen my feelings of isolation. I didn't hear from Detective Wallace or anyone involved with the sale of the house, and nothing from Rosie. That was the hardest silence to endure, as I had so many questions, whether or not I had the courage to ask them. The hardest being: did Rosie Rey murder Rolland Childress?

I had first hoped that Childress's death might just have been an accident, and completely unrelated to Rosie. I trawled the internet, trying to find another arson attack, but all I did was confirm that Childress lived in Ipswich, which is where Rosie said she was going. And Detective Wallace had definitely said that somebody had set his house on fire. So no accident. It was deliberate. And the reason he came knocking on my door to investigate the now *two* dead men linked to me.

I jab the lighter in on the Saab's dash and slip another cigarette from the pack. I've smoked two already, and chewed my thumbnail down to the raw under-flesh whilst staring at the dried remains of the spider I squished across the windscreen the other day. I can sympathise with it, the feeling of squishedness, and while I focus on the dead spider, I don't notice Rosie's Beetle pull into my driveway until the lighter pops and shocks me back into the present.

Rosie climbs out of her car and skips towards my front door. *Skips!* And suddenly I'm so bloody angry. I blast the Saab's horn and she jumps, giggles, and walks over to the passenger side and climbs in.

'Ooh, can I bum one?' she says, nodding at the unlit cigarette clawed between my fingers, and when I don't answer, she drops my sun visor and catches the pack that falls down. I watch her with incredulity while she lights up, knuckle-raps her window for me to power it down. Eventually I do, keenly aware that it's my car but Rosie's world I'm sitting in.

'What. The. *Fuck*, Rosie,' I spit.

'I know you're angry with me, Dina,' Rosie says, flicking ash out of the window, 'but just hear me out, okay?'

'Oh, oh, sure, I'll hear you out. I'm actually keen to learn how another man is dead and the police are knocking on *my* door to find out if *I* had anything to do with it! You set me up!'

'God, no, Dina!' Rosie pivots in her seat and looks shocked that I could ever think such a thing. 'It wasn't like that at all, you have to believe me. I was just trying to help you.'

'How on earth could you think that killing a man could possibly help me, Rosie?' She opens her mouth to speak but I raise a finger. 'How could you possibly think that having the police turn up at my house—'

'It was an accident, Dina.'

'You fucking planned it!'

'The burning his house part, yeah, but I didn't mean to kill him, I swear.'

'I found blood on your top.'

'Oh, that.' She shifts back in her seat, clicks another tail of ash out the window. 'Just a freak gusher.'

'A what?'

'Nosebleed, what did you think, Dina?'

'That's your blood?'

'I get them sometimes, when it's hot. It's like a pressure valve.' Rosie explodes a hand in front of her face, belches cigarette smoke for effect. 'I was riding home when it happened. I stopped and got it under control, turned my top inside out so I wouldn't draw attention to myself. That's it.'

I stare at her while she smokes. She pushes down the lighter. I realise I still haven't lit my cigarette.

'Rolland Childress represented Grant Chapman, and now he's dead. Can you explain that, Rosie? How did you even know about him?'

She shrugs. 'I told you I looked up Becky's accident, you know, checking on Chapman, and Childress's name popped up.' The lighter pops up too, and Rosie pulls it and offers me a light. I hesitate for a second, and lean in. 'Well, after I showed you Chapman explaining how his solicitor had pulled something shady to get him off with only two years, I could sense a shift in your aura.'

All I can do is look at Rosie while I draw my cigarette alight, then I ask, 'And what did my aura say?'

'That you wouldn't be able to fully recover from your addiction until everyone who'd had a hand in this injustice had paid a price.'

'But death?' I massage my forehead and collapse back in my seat, the cigarette doing nothing for my nerves.

'Dina, Grant Chapman was an accident, and I swear to God I saw Rolland Childress leave his house before I torched it.' Rosie leans over and touches my arm. 'He must've doubled back for something soon after I'd left,' she soothes, 'tried to put the flames out himself and succumbed to the smoke, I don't know, but I did not mean for him to die.'

I pinch my eyes. This is beyond insane.

'Dina, Childress repped some truly horrible people – he basically lies for a living. How'd you think he got Chapman out early?'

It's so stinking hot in the Saab I have to climb out. Rosie climbs out too.

'Don't mourn that man, Dina,' she pleads across the roof of the car. 'You can start your recovery now. They paid for Becky, and you'll find peace again. With my help.'

I laugh to myself, toss my cigarette down and grind it into the gravel. 'I think you've done enough.'

'No, Dina, my work here is not yet done. We both of us have much healing to do.'

'What are you even talking about, Rosie?'

'We're almost at that place...' She spreads her palms on the roof of the Saab, and I know how hot that roof must be. 'We're in each other's hands now. If one of us falls, we both fall.'

'Neither of us is going to fall, Rosie,' I say. 'If we just stick to our stories.'

'It's not just our stories we have to worry about, Dina.'

'No?' I want to test the roof of the Saab, to feel the heat Rosie is bearing.

'When Detective Wallace came to me and told me Childress was dead, I almost spilled my guts, you know, for the sake of sanity, but I knew it wasn't my call because I had to protect you, Dina.'

I test the roof with my fingertips. It's even hotter than I expect, but I try to keep them there. 'I would do the same for you, Rosie,' I say, watching her hands still somehow on the blistering roof.

'And as much as I give it the big bravado, the thought that I'd killed a man, shook me, and I knew how you felt.'

It's no good. My fingers are burning and I have to snatch them from the Saab.

'But there was something else, Dina,' Rosie says, her hands still unmoving. 'Something that really scared me and made me think we're not out of the woods just yet.'

'And what was that?' I ask, rubbing the tips of my fingers.

'It was the first time, in a long time, that I wanted to drink, and it made me understand the torment you're still in.'

'You'll be fine. We'll be fine – Rosie, your hands must be—'

'I think we will, Dina, because we'll be there for each other.'

I can't bear it any longer. I walk around the Saab and take Rosie's hands from the roof, and I can tell by her expression that she's only just noticed she was in pain.

'You see, Dina, we look after each other.' Rosie smiles up at me.

'But we can't stay in touch, remember? I've sold the house, Rosie. I'm moving away.' I let her hands fall from mine, but her smile doesn't falter and I can't be sure she's heard me. Understood me.

'So I was thinking, Dina,' she continues, 'to get through this final, delicate stage, we need to be strong for each other.'

'Rosie, I agree, but—'

'I knew you would, I mean, for either of us to turn to the bottle right now would be madness, you know, to throw it all away at the last hurdle.' She rubs my shoulder and walks by me to her car. 'And I'm sure it wouldn't be for long.'

'What are you talking about? What wouldn't be for long?'

'I've been rattling around in my little flat, and I didn't even give you a thought, Dina.' She opens the boot of her car and humps out a large suitcase. 'Especially when you're having to deal with what we're dealing with right now, in that empty chasm of a place, those memories... God, sometimes I can be so self-absorbed – can you grab one of these, please?'

Despite the heat, the suffocating heat of this moment, my blood chills. I walk over and grab the second little case Rosie has dragged from the boot and shove it back inside. 'You are not moving into my house, Rosie, so get that idea out of your head.'

'Oh no you don't, Mrs Dina Young.' Rosie wags a finger at me and I want to snap it off. 'You don't have to act tough with me. I know how close you are, because I feel the same way. The guilt of taking a life, I know now, doesn't wash off, just as I know alcoholism doesn't. It's a disease that can flare up at any moment, and this, Dina, is the moment of moments, and what kind of sponsor would I be if I let you face it alone.'

It feels like I've drifted out of my body and I'm looking down from above the wispy evergreens that box in this plot, as I watch Rosie Rey ferry her bags from her beat-up Beetle to my godforsaken house. And the out-of-body feeling rings true, because I am as useless as a ghost to stop her. Rosie isn't asking for my permission to move in, she's telling me. There was never a question in her mind. Her packed bags lay testament to that.

'Could you grab that last one for me, Dina?' she calls from my doorway, and as I oblige her, I have to fight the hysterical laughter that threatens to cackle out of my mouth.

What am I supposed to do? It isn't like I have the option of calling the police.

## 45

When Roy and I first moved into the house, we christened every room. Not in the crude way everybody else does – that's actually rather disgusting when you think about it – having sex in the bath where we would one day bathe our daughter, or on the kitchen table where she would no doubt eat an organic, low-sugar version of a cereal that doesn't have a cartoon animal on the box. No, that's not how Roy rolled.

The house in that first week was a shell, a dark and empty shell that still harboured the old-person musk left behind by Dotty Delevingne's mother, Mrs Lancaster. It wasn't necessarily a bad smell, it just wasn't ours, and Roy, lacking the designer's eye that I possessed, needed to erase as much of the lingering history of the place before he could even begin to imagine how we might live here.

We tore up the carpets and tore down the curtains, whitewashed over the trippy Graham & Brown woodchip that wrapped the house like a psychedelic Christmas gift, all to give Roy a clean canvas for his imagination. To give him the chance of seeing what I saw. But we couldn't quite get there, because he could still smell Mrs Lancaster, and while he could smell her, he could picture her living here, and so it would always be hers and not ours. So Roy decided we should christen every room in the house.

Our furniture was in storage, but we'd bought a cheap little patio set so we had somewhere to eat. And we did, in every room except the downstairs loo, and only then because we couldn't fit the table in there. We used scented candles and ate takeaways for two weeks, shifting the table and chairs every night and rewriting each room with new aromas and a history of our own making. It wasn't a deep cleanse, but it was enough for Roy to finally see the house it could be, the house I knew it could be.

While Roy was at the office during the day, I would trawl the interior design and housey magazines for ideas and colour schemes, block out squares in tester pots and tape wallpaper samples next to them. I didn't really understand what I was doing at first, I was merely mimicking the great designers, but Roy seemed to have a boundless confidence in me, which seeded my ambition to do more than just paint this house. I could be the designer I always wanted to be, and have magazines coming to photograph my work, to write about my concepts.

The last room we dined in was the little spare bedroom. I'd set out the table with the candles and the plates and cutlery, awaiting Roy and the Indian delivery I'd ordered. I was so buoyant with ambition, and couldn't wait to tell him of my plans for the future. But when he arrived home and I blurted out my new dream of becoming an interior designer, he didn't seem that impressed. In fact, he seemed irritated by the idea. The Indian arrived, and Roy dished us up the food, then we ate in silence. I assumed he'd had a problem at work, and when he told me that wasn't the issue, I went ahead and assumed it was the colours I'd chosen for this room, the wallpaper samples, but he told me that wasn't the issue either. I didn't believe him of course, and started to cry. Eventually he put his arms around me, whispered he was sorry for upsetting me, and a moment later we were kissing.

Becky was conceived on that night. In that little spare bedroom. Which is why I'm so upset that Rosie has unpacked all her stuff in here before I could stop her, and that I don't have the courage to tell her to move.

'Are you sure you wouldn't prefer the other spare bedroom?' I ask her. 'It's bigger. Looks over the back garden.'

'Absolutely not, Dina,' Rosie says. 'The last thing I want to do is put you out.'

46

I wanted to rise early the next morning, to be up before Rosie, to have her walk in and find me buttering toast in *my* kitchen, in *my* home, and so I could set out the rules of her staying here, and most importantly, when I was expecting her to leave. But it didn't work out like that.

When I walk into the kitchen, Rosie is already sitting at the table with a mug of coffee. She's wearing the white dungarees I first saw her in at the AA meeting, but this time paired with a lacy vest top beneath that shows off her shoulders – accentuated further by the messy bun she's fashioned her hair in, revealing her long and youthful neckline.

'Morning, Dina,' she says, and then, 'Take a pew. I'll make you a drink.'

As Rosie gets up, I sit down. On the table is my laptop, which is open, and next to that is my vodka bottle, frosted with condensation which has pooled around the base to form a dark ring on the tabletop. Next to the bottle is a little zipper pouch in hot pink. Rosie's make-up bag, I assume.

'Tea or coffee?'

I wait for the kettle to finish boiling. 'Tea.'

Rosie pulls open the cutlery drawer and takes out a spoon, knows which of the *Keep Calm* tins I use for the teabags. Which has the sugar. With her back to me, and her vest top cut so scant, I notice the cluster of red dots peppering her shoulder blades. At first I think it's a rash, but the deeper I look I can see the dots lack the red-rawness of fresh irritation, and they are not dark enough to be moles.

'I was thinking we should develop a kind of routine,' Rosie says, flicking the screwed-up teabag into the pedal bin as though she's done it a thousand times. 'You know, to help the recovery process along.' She places my tea down in front of me and retakes her chair. 'What do you think?'

'Well, I'm sure we'll naturally fall into some kind of routine, but really, I'll be spending much of my time sorting out the house. Packing and stuff.'

'Oh, that reminds me,' Rosie says, shoving my laptop towards me. 'You had an email from a Rachel Beatty? Apparently, the Delevingnes want to set the completion date for three weeks.'

'Umm, you checked my email?'

'God, no, Dina. I was gonna browse for a new pair of sneaks – I was thinking maybe a Union Jack pair this time – anyway, when I opened your laptop' – Rosie splays her fingers – 'boom, there was your email.'

'And boom, you read it.' I drag the laptop towards me and read the email for myself.

'Reflex. Won't happen again.'

Rosie is right. The Delevingnes want to rush the sale through, and Ms Beatty doesn't see a problem with the schedule. I sit back and cover my mouth, trying to hide the smile that wants to ripen there. Three weeks. In three weeks I will be gone from this house. Gone from Rosie Rey. I want to celebrate, and the glistening bottle of vodka in front of me is not doing me any favours.

'Can I put that back in the freezer drawer, please, Rosie?'

'Yeah, I wanted to talk to you about that.'

I close the laptop. 'Oh?'

'You see, Dina, the way I see our recovery playing out over the next few weeks is...'

*Three weeks.*

'...by having an alcohol-free zone – a safe environment to—'

'That's not how I do it, Rosie. I get strength from knowing it's there and choosing not to drink it.'

'I know, I know,' Rosie says, praying her hands together. 'But just look where you were only a few short weeks ago. Drunk on top of a scaffold tower? You could've killed yourself.'

'Look, that was a blip,' I say. 'I'd just found out about Grant Chapman. It won't happen again, I assure you.'

'It *can't* happen again, Dina. We both need to know that the other one is rock solid when we part ways. I can't have that shroud of doubt hanging over me that someday in the future you're gonna crack and I'm gonna get a knock on the door from Wallace and Co, questioning me about the murder of some fucking shyster solicitor.'

'Who said anything about murder?'

'You know what I mean, Dina. In the grip of alcohol, anything can spill out of your mouth. Our mouths. Do you have any other bottles hidden around the house?'

'What? No.'

'I had a quick look around this morning, but you know how slippery this disease can make a person. Toilet cisterns... Teddy bears... I even knew somebody who kept their gin in a hot-water bottle, if you can believe that – oh, by the way, what are these?' Rosie dives her hand into the pocket of her dungarees and pulls out a bottle of pills. 'I found them in your bathroom cabinet.'

I snatch the bottle from her. 'They're my husband's heart pills, and you have no right to be snooping around my house, do you understand?'

Again with the praying hands. 'If you're telling me you have no more booze hidden around the house, that's good enough for me, Dina. I trust you one hundred pesetas.'

I wish I felt the same way. I take a deep breath. 'Look, if you want to pour the bottle down the sink, that's fine by me, Rosie.'

'Hey, why don't we compromise? I'll hide the bottle!'

This is fucking insane and I want to scream. 'Whatever,' I say. Three weeks and it's over.

'Cool, I'm glad that's sorted,' Rosie says, and stands from her chair. 'But I do have one other thing I'd like to put in place, for both of us.' She unzips the hot-pink zipper pouch.

'What's that?' I ask.

'It's a breathalyser,' Rosie says, screwing a tube onto the device. 'I've got a mouthpiece for each of us, so I was thinking one in the morning and one in the evening before bed.' The device bleeps and Rosie blows long and even into the tube, then holds out the device. 'See, zero. Now you.'

'I don't think I will, thanks.'

'Oh, come on, Dina, it's easy,' she says, attaching the other mouthpiece.

'It's not about how easy it is, I just don't need to. I won't be drinking.'

Rosie offers me the breathalyser. 'It's not about that, as such. It's about structure and routine. It really does help, Dina.'

Good grief. Is this really how it's got to be? I take the breathalyser and blow, hand it back.

'Hey,' Rosie says, happy as a kid in a sweetshop. 'You're zero, too.' She offers her fist to bump.

I ponder her fist. Three weeks. I can do this. What choice do I have?

I bump.

An hour later, Rosie comes down with her make-up all done, and I notice she's hidden the red marks on her shoulder blades with concealer. That she's taken the trouble to hide these marks suggests to me that she's embarrassed of them. Which is why I won't mention them, even though I'm curious to know what they are.

'I've got to pop out this morning,' Rosie says while she's checking her phone.

I lean in the kitchen doorway with my tea. 'Of course, the meetings are on Thursdays. I forgot.'

'Oh, no. I pulled a sickie on Justin this morning. Need to swing by the flat for a couple of things – not sure what time I'll be back.' She drops her phone into her bag. 'Do you have a spare key I could have, Dina?'

'You can take the key for the lounge bifolds, if you don't mind coming in the back way?'

'Trade entrance is fine by me.'

We head to the lounge, ducking through the obstacle course that is the scaffold tower, and I pull the key from the bifold doors and hand it to Rosie.

'How come you left all the furniture covered up?' she asks, looking around the lounge and adjoining dining room, at the grandfather clock in the corner, the Welsh dresser and the dining table and chairs, all cloaked in the builders' dust sheets. 'Kinda ghostly, don't you think?'

I shrug. 'Never thought about it really.'

'Especially with the lack of pictures anywhere, it feels... unlived in – no, not unlived in, it feels like the house has lost its heartbeat.'

On that I would agree. The heartbeat of this house died along with Becky. Its spirit extinguished along with Roy.

'I'm sure the new owners will breathe life into it again,' I say.

'Maybe they shouldn't,' Rosie says, still looking around. 'Maybe it's a DNR.'

'DNR?'

'Yeah.' Rosie fixes me with a sombre expression. 'Do Not Resuscitate.'

*"The best rooms have something to say about the people who live in them."*

~ David Hicks

47

After I return the email to my solicitor confirming the three-week completion schedule, I find myself drifting upstairs, to Rosie's room. Call it snooping if you like, but I feel Rosie has a little payback coming for all the snooping she's done on me.

I grip the doorknob and gently turn it to step inside, but to my utter disbelief, the door is locked. The downright, bold-faced cheek of her! I throttle the knob back and forth and give the door a brief kick before pacing away. I have spare keys for all of the doors upstairs, but the bunch is in an old Harrods biscuit tin, and the tin is in the bloody loft, of which the hatch is in Rosie's bloody room!

What has she got to hide, I wonder? And as I pace up and down the landing, my mind conjures all sorts – none of it innocent, until I cool my thoughts and realise that, probably, most likely, Rosie has hidden my vodka in her room and is protecting me from temptation.

It still irks me, though, that this girl has wangled her way into my house, my life, and yet I know literally nothing about her. What kind of fool lets that happen, and how do I get free of her? She's like quicksand. The more I wriggle to escape, the deeper and tighter I become trapped.

I go downstairs to check the time. It's ten thirty. The AA meeting has been underway for half an hour, and Rosie said she wasn't going to be there. I know a man who will be, though, and he's the only person I can think of who might be able to give me some insight into who Rosie is, and perhaps then I'll have a better idea of how I can get her out of my life.

It takes me twenty minutes to walk into town, and a further ten minutes for the first of the AA group to leave the community centre. The old black guy and the plump but attractive woman with the good bag and great shoes. I watch them pour out from across the road, from where I sit baking in the Perspex bus shelter, my crappy sunglasses slipping down my sweat-soaked nose. When I think they've all left, I go over.

A cool breeze welcomes me as I step inside. All the doors in the entrance hall open, as are the windows beyond the doors, blinds drifting in the current of air. When I reach the meeting room, I find Justin stacking the chairs away, but also Ben, the denim-wearing guy, a folded newspaper sticking out of the rear pocket of his jeans. I tap on the open door with my sunglasses.

'We're just finishing up, I'm afraid,' Justin says, but then he recognises me. 'It's Dina, isn't it?'

'Well remembered,' I say, and go inside.

'I didn't think we'd see you again,' Ben snorts, and waddles with a stack of chairs to the far wall.

'Can I help you with something?' Justin asks, and comes over to me.

'I, umm, just wanted to speak to you about—'

'If you're concerned about coming back after missing a week or two—'

'It isn't that,' I say. 'The meetings aren't for me, I realise that now. No, I wanted to talk to you about someone.'

'One of the group members?'

'No.'

Justin judges me with a quizzical brow, then appears to fall in. 'Ben, could you give us a moment, please?'

'I can do better than that,' Ben says, and humps a final stack of chairs against the wall. 'I'll give you a week – as in, I'll see ya next week.'

'Thanks for your help, Ben,' Justin says, and Ben leaves us with a thumbs up. 'I have to get these away, so do you mind if we talk and work at the same time?'

'Sure,' I say, putting my bag and sunglasses down. 'I'll give you a hand.'

'So who's the someone?' he asks.

'Rosie. Rosie Rey?'

Justin lowers the stack of chairs he's carrying and leans on them. 'Is she okay?'

'Why do you ask that?'

'She quit this morning.'

'The programme?'

Justin squints his eyes a little. 'Rosie isn't in the programme,' he says. 'She volunteers. Volunteered.'

I insert a chair onto another. 'Volunteer?'

'Yes, she helped out. Teas, coffees, plates of biscuits for the end-of-meeting chit-chat. Stacks chairs for me. I'm sorry to lose her. She was a positive energy around here, people liked her.' Justin lifts his stack and humps it against the wall. I follow with my own stack of two.

'So she volunteered as a sponsor?'

'No.' He cuffs his forehead. 'You have to have been in the programme for quite some time before you can become a sponsor, and to be part of the programme you have to be...' He gestures at me with a shrug.

'An alcoholic.'

'That's how it generally works.'

'So you're telling me Rosie isn't an alcoholic' – Justin is shaking his head as I speak – 'and she isn't a sponsor?'

Justin's phone rings in his pocket. 'Rosie is sympathetic to the cause, that's what brought her to us, but – one second.' He answers his phone. 'Hello? Yes, this is he...'

I don't know what to make of this information. Why would Rosie lie?

Justin looks at his watch. 'I'll be here for the next... fifteen minutes if you can be here by then. Okay, I'll be here.' He pockets his phone. 'I'm sorry, Dina, but I'm going to have to wrap this up. Was there something in particular you wanted to ask me about Rosie?'

'Umm...' I want to unlearn what I've just learned, because Rosie Rey has become a deeper mystery to me now, more so than when I knew nothing about her. 'Umm... I suppose I wanted to pass on my thanks. She showed concern for me when I left here last time and I... umm...'

Justin goes back to stacking the chairs. 'Well, I'll certainly pass on your best wishes if I see Rosie again, Dina, and know that you're welcome to join us whenever you feel able. Our door is always open.'

I thank him and sleepwalk out into the lobby, where Ben appears to have been waiting for me by the noticeboard because he waves his newspaper to get my attention.

'You won't get anything juicy from Justin,' Ben tells me as he throws a shifty glance towards the meeting room. 'He's strictly by the book – and when I say *book*, I mean the Lord's book.'

'Right,' I say, and go to leave.

'You were asking about Rosie?'

I stop. He beckons me back with his newspaper. 'What about Rosie?' I ask him, my patience withering in the heat.

'She's a very troubled young lady, that one.'

'In what way?'

He cricks his stubbly mouth. 'Crown's just around the corner. Why don't we go for a quick drink and I'll tell you all about her.'

'You've just left an AA meeting and you're suggesting to another alcoholic that we should go for a drink?'

'Couple's all right, just don't go mad.'

I can't take another moment of this idiot's company, let alone join him for a drink. I go to leave again but he grabs my arm. 'Do you mind?' I say.

He lets go immediately and hands me his sweaty newspaper. 'My number's on the sports page if you change your mind,' he says, and walks out before I can tell him what he can do with his paper. But I am still holding it, fortunately.

Detective Wallace and Detective Anand are crossing the road from the car park behind the bus shelter I was sitting at a while ago, and are heading this way. I raise the newspaper to cover my face, because it's too late for me to exit the centre and escape. I do the obligatory dance left, dance right, then spot the ladies loos. As I lock myself into a cubicle, I realise that's who Justin had just spoken to on the phone, and I am damn sure they were calling him to discuss Rosie and me. *Shit, shit, shit!*

I use the time to pee – a frightened, semi-clenched pee, such as I haven't felt since I was a little girl. I dab. Flush. Use the cleansing wipes in my bag to clean my hands so I don't have to linger by the basins and risk discovery from a caught-short Detective Anand. And why am I frightened anyway? I have the right to be here. There is no reason I should have to stay locked away in this sweatbox, is there? No.

I step out of the cubicle and risk opening the door onto the corridor, can hear Justin speaking but not clear enough to make out his words. Same with Detective Wallace. I slip on my sunglasses and walk into the sunshine, not looking back, and as I head across the train track toward the river I realise why I was frightened. The only reason Detective Wallace is speaking to Justin is because he suspects Rosie and me are lying.

48

I didn't go directly home. I sat by the river for an hour or so, going over the many ways Detective Wallace was going to pick apart our alibis. *How long have Ms Rey and Ms Young been acquainted? Really? You didn't know they were? So when did Ms Rey become Ms Young's sponsor? Ms Rey isn't a sponsor, or in the programme? And you say Ms Young only attended the one meeting? That's interesting, Mr Campbell. Very interesting indeed...*

An old man takes the other end of the bench I'm sitting on, fills a little trough from his water bottle and sets it down for his equally old terrier, who is panting from the heat. It laps at the water too quickly and gives itself the hiccups.

'Too hot to walk him,' the old man says, taking in the river. 'But sometimes I've just got to get out of the house.'

I know how he feels.

'Are you finished with that, dear?' He gestures at the newspaper sitting between us.

'Please, I'm all done.' I shoulder my bag to head home. I'd already copied Ben's number into my phone anyway, but whether I call him or not is another matter. The way he described Rosie as a "very troubled young lady" was probably nothing more than word vomit to pad out a lazy chat-up attempt. Then again, it could be something else, something Rosie would prefer me not to know. After all, I have just found out that she's been telling me lies within our lies, so I'm not being unduly suspicious to wonder what else she might be hiding.

When I make it home, I'm surprised to find Rosie's car on the driveway. I don't know why, but I was under the impression she'd be out for some time, and I was going to try all the other upstairs keys in her bedroom door. Oh well, at least now she's home I can tell her I need to get up in the loft, and I can find the spare set of keys for when she goes out again. It's actually better if I don't make a fuss about her locking her door. Better if she thinks I can't get in there.

I call out to Rosie when I come through the front door, but she doesn't answer. I listen for the TV, the shower, the creaking of a floorboard to see if she's in my or Becky's room. I put nothing past her at this point.

The laptop is still on the kitchen table from this morning, but it's closed. I put my bag and sunglasses down next to it and walk into the larder and crack open the basement door, listen to the dark. Nothing.

'Rosie?' I call again from the entrance hall, and when I hear nothing in return I slip through the struts of the scaffold tower and go into the lounge, where I'm met by the smell of furniture polish.

The TV is off and the sofa is empty, but to my left I see Rosie in the adjoining dining room, sitting at the table, which has now been unveiled of its dust sheet and is instead covered in picture frames.

'What are you doing?' I ask, noticing the grandfather clock and the Welsh dresser have also had their dust sheets removed.

'Hello, Dina,' Rosie says, not looking up from one particular picture that is stood in front of her on the table. 'I thought I'd break open the furniture, give it a polish to see if we couldn't reboot the ole heartbeat, and found these in the dresser.'

'You had no right to take out all of my wedding photos, Rosie. No right.' I march over to her and start collapsing the pictures. I don't want to look at them, and certainly don't want her looking at them.

Rosie's eyes flick up to mine, though her face remains angled toward the picture she'd been staring at. 'They're not all wedding pictures,' she says. 'This one's of Becky. It's her birthday, Dina. Look.' Rosie brings the picture to me. 'See? Her cake has got ten candles on it, I counted.'

I step away from her, collect the pictures on the other side of the dining table.

'This must've been her last birthday,' Rosie says, lost in the picture again. 'How long after this did she...?'

I don't answer. I put the pictures back in the dresser, where they belong.

'I'm guessing she was a summer baby,' Rosie continues. 'I can see you in the background. You look quite flushed, Dina. Was it a hot day? Was Becky a summer baby?'

I snatch the picture from her. 'July,' I concede. 'And she died the following December. Now leave my things alone. They're mine and I don't want you touching them, do you understand?' I kneel to put Becky's birthday picture in the dresser, feel Rosie at my shoulder, standing over me.

'I'm starting to understand, Dina,' she says. 'It's painful to look at them, and so you hide their pictures away.'

And with that, Rosie leaves me, and a moment later I hear

her heavy feet on the stairs, followed by the slamming and the locking of her bedroom door.

I gather up the rest of the pictures, all of Roy and me on our wedding day, so happy. He'll now be on my mind for the rest of the day.

49

As I'd feared, Roy was in my dreams last night and I struggled to get any sleep. I can't blame Rosie entirely though. It was chokingly hot, and I'd made the mistake of keeping Roy's heart pills on the bedside cabinet with me. Nitrostat. Roy couldn't help saying the name without using his movie-trailer voice and adopting a wide-stanced superhero pose. *Nitrostat, the plant-based man of organically-sourced steel.* Becky thought it was funny, but I had seen Roy hunting for those pills while his chest tightened up from his angina. After three or four minutes of not being able to find them, I was on the phone dialling for an ambulance and Becky's cheeks would be flooded with tears as she sucked her bottom lip into her crying mouth, terrified her father was really going to die this time. Thankfully, she never had to endure that trauma, because Roy always kept a spare bottle of pills by the landline, for when I predictably went to call the ambulance.

I shower and dress, creep by Rosie's door, which is closed and undoubtedly locked. When I get downstairs she isn't in the kitchen or anywhere else, and her car is still on the driveway. I think briefly about calling up, to see if she wants a tea or something, but screw her. If she wants to lie in bed and sulk all day, that's fine by me. There are more important things I should be doing. Like finding somewhere to live.

I flip open the laptop and browse the local property market, but it's a hopeless task when I have literally no idea how to tackle the rest of my life. Do I buy small and live comfortably, or rent and invest the equity in a design studio? Go all out to realise my dream. God, my mind is so far away from work at this moment. Creatively, Rosie has left me barren, and the colour of that landscape is, I am ashamed to say, Magnolia. Flat, matt, Magnolia.

What I need is a break. A holiday, even. Somewhere I can decompress after leaving this house and somewhere I can reboot artistically before making any big decisions on where and how I should live. If only they did interior design retreats! No, that can't be a thing.

It is a thing! I search the internet and find many of them, but they're all too corporate. I need something more... bijoux. Something more... French. I think back to our last movie night, to *Revolutionary Road* and April Wheeler's dream of moving to Paris. I could do that for a month, rent a little Haussmannian apartment in the city centre and soak up the baroque and rococo architecture, the shabby chic cafés. Reboot. Recharge. Revitalise. Goodbye, Rosie. Goodbye, Magnolia. Hello, Apple Blossom.

I begin a search for holiday apartments in Paris when the laptop battery dies. A good omen, I think. I should walk into town and speak to a travel agent, re-engage with the world. I go upstairs to change into something a little more Parisian, but on my way back along the landing I pause at Rosie's bedroom door. It's gone eleven o'clock and I haven't heard her stir. I give a light knock.

'Rosie?'

Nothing.

'Rosie, are you okay?'

'I'm fine,' I hear her reply, but she's muffled and groggy.

'Can I get you a tea or something?'

'No.'

'Okay, well, I'm going into town for a while, do you need anything?'

'I'm *sleeping.*' Not groggy now, grumpy. At the very least, grumpy.

'Okay,' I say. I leave her to it and head out quietly.

I wanted to say more – apologise even, for snapping at her yesterday about the pictures, as I've clearly upset her. Perhaps Rosie's not as tough as I give her credit for. When I reach the coolness of the river, I realise her storming off into her room was really quite childish, and maybe her lying to me about being a sponsor was nothing more than that. A young girl trying to appear more grown up than she actually is, or feels. I am, after all, old enough to be her mother.

By the time I reach the town thoroughfare, my sandalled feet sore and my skin clammy in the heat, I wonder if I've misjudged Rosie completely. This could be her, the real her. Fragile and... troubled.

*A very troubled young lady.*

I grab my phone from my bag, and call Ben as I make my way to the travel agent.

# 50

I didn't make it to the travel agent. Ben answered straight away and said he was at The Crown, which was farther on. I can't remember the last time I'd been in a pub, and if Ben was already in there, drinking before noon, I don't know how I'll feel.

As it turns out, Ben isn't drinking, he's working behind the bar – well, as much as he can considering the place is mostly empty. When he sees me come in, he says something to a petite young barmaid who's browsing on her phone next to him, then nods me toward a little table by the window. From here I watch him pour himself a half of lager and sup the froth as he walks over to my table. In smart black shirt and trousers, he doesn't appear as rough and ready as he does in his denims, though the slight bounce he favours on his right foot as he approaches is a good reminder of the cocky chancer I peg him as.

'S'okay,' he says, taking the chair opposite me. 'I know you didn't bell me back because of my charm, so I'm guessing you're here to talk about Rosie?'

'You did offer,' I say, staring at his beer.

'Sorry, you want one?' He looks around to the young girl behind the bar.

'I'm fine, thank you. I'm just surprised that... you know.'

'That I'm drinking and go to AA?'

'Well, yeah.'

'Poxy stipulation from my ex-wife,' he says, taking another inch from his beer. 'I go to the meetings or I don't see my daughter.'

'How old is she?'

'Little Lacy? Six, and not so little anymore.'

Becky would have been twelve by now. She'll never grow up.

'So why were you asking Justin about Rosie?' Ben asks. 'She sniffing round your old man or something?'

'Why, has she got a thing for married men?'

'Nah, she's just got boundary issues.'

A group of people walk in and Ben gives his colleague a nod to see if she's all right dealing with them. She is.

'Boundary issues?' I press.

'Don't get me wrong, Rosie means well, but sometimes she can be a bit, you know.'

'No, I don't know.'

'A bit... overcaring.' Ben holds up his beer. 'Especially about the booze. She thinks everybody's gonna turn out like her mum, and I'm like, Jesus, Rosie, it's just a couple of drinks, and then off she goes.' He rolls his eyes before taking another inch from his beer.

'What happened to her mother?'

'How come you wanna know all this stuff about her? What is she to you?'

That's a good question. She's not my sponsor, I know that much.

'She showed concern for me,' I say, slightly warmed by that fact. 'On the day I left the meeting.'

Ben laughs. 'Forgot about that, you bolting out so soon, must be a record or something. Anyway, just don't let her make you a project.'

Too late for that. Her overcaring nature has left two men dead, but at least Rosie will only have me for a project for the next three weeks. I'm sure nobody else will die in that time. 'If you don't mind me saying, Ben, you seem to know Rosie quite well.'

He ducks his head and scrubs his ear. 'Yeah, we had a thing for a bit, but I ain't ready for all that again.'

'Settling down?'

'Nah, being told what to do.'

I suppose Rosie can be a little bossy, in a velveteen kind of way. 'You said something about her mother?'

'Did I? Oh, yeah.' He looks around as another couple walk in. 'I'm gonna have to—'

'The impression I get, is that Rosie is the way she is because of her mother.' I'm reaching now. Fishing without bait.

'You think?' He laughs, sees that his colleague has it under control and settles again. He sips his beer and eyes me, considering something, and says, 'Rosie told you about her mother dying, did she?'

'Yes,' I lie. 'But not how or when.'

Ben straightens in his chair. 'Okay – and this doesn't go beyond me and you.'

'You have my word.'

He studies me for a second. 'Rosie's mother died in a fire.'

'Oh, that's terrible...'

'It gets worse. Rosie saw it happen, from the roadside. Watched her house burn down with her mother inside.'

I cover my mouth.

'And it's even worse than that,' Ben says, glancing back towards the bar.

'How can it be any worse?'

He leans in. 'Rosie's mum used to abuse her – not sexually or anything – but she was a mean drunk, and used to hurt Rosie.'

'Hurt her?'

'Pulling Rosie's hair was her go-to for starters, but when she'd had a good drink, she'd start blaming Rosie for the old man leaving her – the mum's husband and Rosie's dad? Then she'd get really nasty.'

I wait for Ben to take a sip of his drink, don't like the way he's savouring this retelling, or for that matter, how I am.

'How nasty?' I prompt.

'She, umm... used to stub her cigarettes out on Rosie.' He gestures vaguely behind him with his thumb, but I know exactly where he means. 'But in the end, even that wasn't enough for her.'

Again, my hand raises to cover my mouth. How could a mother do such a thing to her child...

'In the end, Rosie's mum cracked.' Ben rings his ear with a crazy finger. 'She locked herself and Rosie in one of the bedrooms, I think, and poured petrol over them both, all over the room.' He nods at my gaping mouth. 'Yeah. She tried to set fire to herself and her daughter. Complete nutjob.'

'But Rosie escaped?'

'She jumped out of the bedroom window just as her mum lit the match. Broke both her ankles but managed to drag herself to the other side of the road. From there all she could do was watch helplessly while her family home and her mother went up in flames.'

'Dear God... How on earth did Rosie ever cope with such a thing?'

'Well, she didn't,' Ben says, finishing off his beer. 'She ended up doing stints in various head hospitals, if you know what I mean?'

'How long ago was this, do you know?' I ask.

'Rosie must've been about fourteen, fifteen at the time?' Ben questions himself. 'And what is she now, twenty-four, twenty-five? So about ten years ago, give or take.'

'And how long did she spend in hospital?'

'That I don't know, and didn't like to ask, but she's been helping out at the AA for a couple of years now, as part of some outpatient therapy programme. I got that much from Justin. Probably something to do with Rosie's mum being an alcoholic, and her getting something out of helping others with the "disease".'

Ben sees my reaction to his air quotes and his hands shrink back to the table.

'Sorry,' he says. 'I don't mean to trivialise what you're going through.'

'It's fine, I'm not a fan of the term, myself.' I shoulder my bag to leave, wishing my alcoholism *was* just a disease, and all I had to do was finish a course of antibiotics and be done with it.

51

I took a taxi home from town. Partly because of my sore feet, and partly because of the heavy shopping bags I had to carry. As hot as the afternoon was growing, I decided to cook a roast dinner for Rosie and me. Lamb has always been my favourite meat, but since Roy had taken the business down the plant-based path, I can't remember the last time I'd eaten it, so I thought I'd splash some of the soon-to-be-mine cash and treat us both to a slow-roasted shoulder with all the trimmings. I bought Rosie some flowers, too. Some white lilies called "Stargazers". The woman at the florist said they represented sympathy, and so I had to buy them. I don't expect Rosie will know what they represent, and I won't tell her, but after learning about her traumatic upbringing, I wanted to make some kind of gesture, especially as I've been thinking so poorly of her.

And I would love to say I was doing all this for purely selfless reasons. I realise now why Rosie reacted the way she did to the photograph of Becky and me on her tenth birthday. That picture represents the childhood Rosie never had. A relationship with a mother she never had. Having her father leave and having her mother blame her for it. Torture her for it.

So, yes, I feel awful for what she's been through, and I will try to make our last three weeks together as pleasant and homely as I can, but equally I'm doing it for me. If I can show Rosie how normal my life is – how sober – then maybe she'll see I'm nothing like her mother, that she doesn't have to worry about me slipping back into alcoholism and betraying us both for our crimes, and leave.

I unpack the bags and find a vase for the lilies, quickly check my emails before going upstairs.

'Rosie, are you in there?' I say, after I give a gentle knock.

No answer, and so I try the door. It's locked.

'Go away,' I hear Rosie's distant voice say.

'I've bought lamb for dinner, and—'

'Not hungry.'

'Well, it won't be ready for a few hours yet, so—'

'I won't be hungry later.'

I guess it's pointless telling her about the flowers I bought her. 'Well, I'm going to cook anyway, so if you change your mind.'

Rosie doesn't answer at all this time, and I don't push. She'll come out when she's ready. She's got to eat.

I get downstairs just in time to answer my phone.

'Hello, can I speak to Mrs Young, please?' an officious gentleman's voice asks, and I'm terrified Detective Wallace has handed his investigation over to some kind of serious crime squad.

'Speaking.'

'Hello, Mrs Young. My name is Vernon Penny, and I've been instructed by Mr and Mrs Delevingne to carry out a full structural survey upon your property and I was hoping to come along tomorrow morning. Ten o'clock, if that's convenient?'

My eyes wander up to the kitchen ceiling and I picture

Rosie lying in bed, curled beneath the duvet. 'Actually, Mr Penny, that might be awkward.'

'Fine, fine. I know it's short notice, but Mr Delevingne was keen to move things along as speedily as possible. My next available appointment won't be for another week, you see, which I understand will put the completion date back by as much.'

'Right.' Rosie will have come out by then, I'm sure. 'Okay, let's go for ten.'

'Are you sure that's convenient?'

'That should be fine, Mr Penny,' I say. 'I'll see you in the morning.'

'Good, good. Ten o'clock, Mrs Young,' Mr Penny says, and hangs up.

I just hope it will be good, good for Rosie by then, but all I can do for now is make a start on the lamb, and lure her grumbling stomach.

I know I was trying to fake the sense of normality by cooking a nice meal, by decorating the table with the lilies, but over the course of prepping the veg and making a batter for the Yorkshire puddings, studding the lamb with garlic and rosemary, I managed to trick myself instead. When I finally place the lamb in the oven and flop at the kitchen table with a glass of iced water, I feel wonderfully exhausted and calm in a way I haven't felt in such a long time. The lilies smell glorious, and soon the lamb will be filling the house with that gamey aroma and hopefully entice Rosie down from her bedroom. I used to enjoy cooking, but Roy gradually took over, and in the end I lost all confidence, both in how to cook and what to cook. I still wouldn't have the first clue what to do with quinoa, and according to Roy, I didn't know how to pronounce it, either – though I did joke that I knew how to pronounce *arsehole*, which is where I suggested he stuff his goji berry flapjacks.

In fact, I enjoyed the afternoon so much, I hunt through the kitchen cabinets for my cookbooks. I'm sure I have an old *Delia* of my mother's somewhere, and nobody does the basics better than Delia. I find the very one I'm looking for, jammed in amongst the many of Roy's vegetarian cookbooks, and I take it to the table and drop it down with a slap and open it up. Feel a new chapter in my life opening up too, and can't deny the rush—

What was that? I hear a loud bang from upstairs. I cock an ear for its repeat but it doesn't come. I go back to the book, a recipe for goulash—

There it is again, and this time I feel the faintest of tremors. I drift into the entrance hall, stalking toward the stairs while my ears tune into the next bang, though I can already guess where it's going to come from. I pad across the landing to Rosie's room, but I don't knock, I listen, and as I hold my breath, I hear nothing. Not the creaking of a mattress or the shuffling of her feet across the bare floorboards.

When I can't hold my breath any longer, I decide to head back to the kitchen. Perhaps it was a bird flying into a window, or just the growing pains of the house, even though I know it can't be either of these things. The house doesn't make sounds like that, and I've never heard of a bird flying twice into a window. And then there's the tremor. I'm about to check the arch window for smudges, to be sure it wasn't a bird, when I hear the hushing sound of a heavy object being dragged across wooden floorboards, but it doesn't come from behind Rosie's door. It comes from overhead. From the loft.

I go to Rosie's door and knock. 'Rosie, are you there?' I ask, knowing she isn't, but I've spoken loud enough for her to hear me, even from the loft.

And I'm right, silence falls, until I knock again, louder this time, and accompany it with a rattling of the doorknob. I hear footsteps above me, heading towards the loft hatch, and a moment later Rosie answers.

'What is it?' she asks.

'Can you open the door, please.'

'I'm tired, Dina. Trying to sleep.'

'Why were you in my loft?' She doesn't answer. God, I hope she didn't find her All Stars. I rattle the doorknob again. 'Rosie.'

'Rats,' she says.

'Rats? Is that what I could hear moving stuff around up there?'

'No, course not,' Rosie says. 'I was trying to sleep, and I could hear scratching and stuff. Thought it must be rats or something.'

'And so you went up in the loft?'

'Yeah.'

A pause. 'And?'

'Couldn't find any.'

'We've never had a problem with rats before,' I say.

'That's probably why I couldn't find any. I'm going back to bed now, Dina.'

'Rosie, wait—' The floorboards creak as she moves away from the door, and I'm worried the more I badger, the more she'll be reminded of her mother. I'll just have to be patient, and be supportive when she does emerge. Like any good mother would.

## 52

It's a shame Rosie didn't come down for dinner. The lamb, to my surprise, was melt-off-the-bone perfect. And as I sit here in the Saab, feeling slightly stuffed and savouring a cigarette as only can be savoured after eating a good meal, I try to remember the last thing I cooked for Becky, but I can't. When I think on it more deeply, I cannot remember a single meal I prepared for her – not an actual, from scratch, honest dinner. That is awful.

I do have my reasons, and I know they sound a lot like excuses, but with Roy keeping such a tight rein on us nutritionally, I felt it was okay to treat Becky with a trashy dinner here and there whenever Roy was away on business. I mean, it wasn't like either of us had heart issues to worry about, so the odd pizza or takeaway was fine as far as I was concerned. We even had a name for it, a code between us gals that was uttered with a nod and an exaggerated wink. A *don't-tell-your-dad* dinner. It was an innocent little secret we shared – something just for us, and not intended to exclude Roy in any spiteful way. Good-natured.

At least that's how it used to feel. Now it feels treacherous and deceitful and makes me bristle with shame to remember it.

And it's always when I'm sat in the Saab. For some reason the Saab is like a conduit to negative emotions about Roy, a naughty step for me to dwell upon my past misdeeds. I'm closer to him here than anywhere in the house, and I don't know how I'm going to cope with leaving the car behind. I should have sold it ages ago – God knows I needed the money – but where the house has subsidence, the Saab has an ugly dent in the rear bumper, and I couldn't bear to go through the same deflating routine of the car seeming great on paper, but hiding a price-reducing flaw, so I never bothered to try. The other reason I feel shame when I think about our little code, is that even on Becky's last day on this earth, I was still trying to bribe her with junk. What a shitty mother I was. A shitty wife.

I angle the wing mirror and hunch so I can see Rosie's room. The curtains are closed. I'm going to try to do better by that girl, to show her that there are still people in the world who care about her. What kind of a mother stubs a cigarette out on their own daughter? It's hideous to comprehend. I hold my cigarette to my palm, the embers close enough to the skin for me to feel the heat. I wonder what it must have felt like. To the giver and the receiver. I wonder what it felt like, for Rosie, to watch her mother burn.

I stub out the cigarette in the ashtray, look up at Rosie's window again. The curtains are still closed, but there's a sliver of darkness to the right, and in that darkness floats Rosie's face. I really hope she's going to be okay. When I go inside I'll take the photograph of Becky and me and hide it somewhere, because I don't want to chance Rosie seeing it once she's started to feel better, and slip back into this malaise. Thankfully, the rest of our photographs are boxed away in the loft. If seeing one photo can do this to her, what on earth could seeing dozens do?

That evening, I struggle to sleep, and every time I do manage to doze off, Grant Chapman is waiting for me. He's looking down on me from Rosie's room, and it's his blistered face that's peering out from between the curtains. I'm sure I didn't notice anything of the sort at the time, but when I think back to the moment I jetted acid into his face I now associate his burning skin with the smell of roasting lamb. It's ridiculous how your own memory can betray you. How it can rewrite reality. Change facts to fiction. I thought the subconscious was supposed to help you, to shield you from trauma, not to prod you with it.

And on the odd occasion Grant Chapman isn't there, Roy takes his place. He's so angry, his face buckled and flushing a deep crimson, his hands clawing at his chest, begging for his pills. His elusive bloody pills! I can't blame my subconscious for this one. I've got Roy's Nitrostat on my bedside cabinet for no good reason I can think of, his name neon-lit in the glow of the digital clock every time I wake. It's a sick kind of torture I'm putting myself through, when all I need to do is throw them in the bin. I deleted his voicemail greeting after only a week, without even getting too sentimental, so why I've kept his pills for so long, I have no idea.

I slip on my nightgown, quietly unlock my door so as not to wake Rosie. I'll throw the pills away now, while my resolve is strong, and try to salvage some sleep. I tiptoe along the darkened landing, past the bathroom. Past Rosie's room. Past the scaffold tower which still, disgustingly, has my vomit on the platform. When I reach the kitchen, I unceremoniously drop the pills into the pedal bin. Goodbye, Nitrostat. Goodbye, hopefully, grimacing Roy.

I return as silently as I came. Past the scaffold tower. Past Rosie's room. Past the bathroom—

'My God, Rosie, you scared the shit out of me!'

Rosie is standing in the bathroom doorway, in knickers and a T-shirt, unapologetic to my heaving chest, which I'm clutching to stop my heart erupting like an airbag. My mind flashes to Roy's pills. In case I need them.

'Why did you tell Detective Wallace I was your sponsor?' Rosie asks, with a tilt of her head. 'I thought we'd agreed to keep that between us, Dina?'

*Yeah,* I think, still catching my breath. *I can see now why she didn't want that mentioned. Her not being a sponsor or an alcoholic. But forget about that, Dina. Rosie Rey is a troubled young lady, as would you be if your mother tried to burn you alive.*

'Sorry. It just slipped out.'

'Yeah, this is exactly the kind of thing I'm worried about, Dina. The slips.'

'It's not a big deal, is it?' I say. 'You *are* my sponsor.'

'This time it might not be a big deal, Dina, but the next slip might be.'

'There won't be another slip, I promise.'

'Oops! Sorry, Detective Wallace,' Rosie says, fingers capping her mouth like Betty Boo. 'I didn't mean Rosie popped out for an hour or two on the night the solicitor was murdered.'

*Murdered?*

'Oops! Sorry, Detective Anand. I didn't mean Rosie was out on her bike the night Grant Chapman was murdered.'

'Murder? It wasn't murder, Rosie.'

'What I'm trying to say, Dina, is that you slipped up once, and that was sober.' Rosie steps a little closer. 'What happens if the drink calls you back, hmm? What happens if Wallace calls by when you're three sheets to the wind, jabbering like a loon and dropping truth bombs like confetti? How can I ever leave you, knowing that at any time in my life you're liable to send a prison stint my way, just because of a little slip?'

'I said I was sorry, Rosie, and I promise it won't happen

again. And as for the drink, I'm never going back to that place. Ever.'

Rosie studies me, as though she's reading my mind. 'Okay,' she says, and then, 'I forgot to test you.' She holds up the breathalyser. I take it.

'I plated you some food,' I say. 'It's in the microwave if you get hungry.'

'Thanks, Dina. I'll see how I feel tomorrow.'

I blow into the breathalyser and get a zero. Hand it back to her.

She grins at the readout. 'Great job, soldier.'

'Thanks,' I say. 'Nite, Rosie.'

I head off along the landing, toward my bedroom.

'Nite, Dina,' Rosie calls.

'Oh, I forget to mention, the Delevingnes' surveyor is coming in the morning. At ten. So he'll need access to your room. For the loft space.'

'Like I said,' Rosie says. 'I'll see how I feel.'

I watch her silhouette blend into the darkness and disappear into the bedroom. Hear the tumblers tumble as she locks the door.

53

I wake the following morning to a raking sound above me. Rosie is in the loft again.

I swing out of bed and look up at the ceiling, trace the path of what I can only assume is a tea chest being dragged across the dusty floorboards. If Rosie is on the hunt for rats, I don't know why she would need to haul a heavy chest from one end of the loft to the other. I have to unlock my bedroom door and step onto the landing to stay with her, though I have a good idea where she's headed.

I go to her bedroom door and rattle the knob. It's locked. I knock and the chest halts its journey across the loft. I knock again, and I'm about to call Rosie's name when I hear the doorbell ring. Shit, what time is it?

I dash back to my bedroom and see by the digital clock that it's five minutes to ten. Double shit! I drag on a pair of jeans and pull a top over my head, note in the tall mirror what a horror I look. The tea chest starts moving again.

Vernon Penny is a wiry-browed beanstalk of a man, and sweating profusely through a shoddily-tucked check shirt. Early to mid-sixties, married, and to an indifferent wife judging by his sagging corduroy trousers. 'Good morning, Mrs Young,' he says, eyeing the front of the house and ignoring me, thankfully.

'Sorry for keeping you waiting, Mr Penny.' I hold the door open for him. 'Where would you like to start?'

'I'm told you have a basement,' he says, looking at me for the first time and giving nothing away as to my ragged appearance. 'I'll work my way up from there, if you've no objections?'

'Perfect.' Gives me some time to deal with Rosie.

I lead him down to the basement. 'Excuse the mess, the builders left in something of a hurry.'

He steps down onto the basement floor and his greying hair brushes the boarded ceiling.

'The subsidence crack starts there in the corner.'

Mr Penny stoops a little as he walks over, fanning himself with the ledger he's carrying. He gives the crack the briefest of examinations, then turns his attention to the two holes in the concrete floor. 'I don't suppose you have the survey report on these, do you?'

'Not that I'm aware of,' I say, feeling my face breaking out in a sheen of sweat, as I notice from this distance that one of the holes looks decidedly more freshly dug than the other. 'The builders made them to see how far we could lower the floor. This was going to be my—'

'Can you remember how deep they went?' Mr Penny starts to write something in his ledger.

'I can't, I'm afraid.'

'Not to worry,' he says, snapping shut the ledger. 'At least they didn't put the concrete back. I'll just go and get my wand.'

'Wand?'

'Nothing magic about it,' he says, making his way to the stairs. 'It's a subsurface magnetic locator. Mr Delevingne was taken by your idea of lowering the floor – a studio, was it?'

'Yes, I'm an interior designer.'

'And I'm sure you would have created a beautiful space.' Mr Penny stalls on the first step of the stairs. 'Unfortunately, Mr *Delevingne* has hopes of creating a monstrosity out of it. A games room. Imagine, pool table, pinball machine, jukebox... *mini-bar*... Americans. They really are vulgar. Won't be a second.'

I glance at the freshly dug hole, can picture Mr Penny digging up the acid bottles. The bloodstained Elvis top. I catch him crossing the kitchen. 'Mr Penny, out of curiosity, what does it involve? With your wand, I mean, do you have to dig or anything?'

'No, no,' he says. 'It's basically a metal detector. It'll show up any utility lines or mains beneath the concrete – merely a heads-up to our American paymaster, and not part of the survey, don't worry. I will bring my trowel, though. You'll be surprised how many Roman coins I've unearthed for homeowners – and did you hear me say "heads-up"? I swear the Americans are using satellites to beam their lazy lexicon into the minds of the distracted. I think it must have been when I uttered that horrific word "jukebox" that my guard was temporarily lowered.' He taps his nose. 'Don't let the buggers in, Mrs Young.'

This is turning into a living nightmare. There is no way I can let Mr Penny dig around in that hole. Not while our incriminating evidence is buried there. He'll have to start upstairs.

I dart out into the entrance hall and see Mr Penny opening his car boot. I close the front door quietly and lock it, run upstairs and knock on Rosie's door.

'Rosie? Are you in there?' She doesn't answer, but I think I hear her clambering around at the back of the room. In the wardrobe, perhaps. Climbing down from the loft, perhaps. 'Rosie, the surveyor really needs to get in the loft. I'm sorry but you'll have to come out, just for a little while.'

Still no answer, but her room has fallen silent.

'Rosie!' I bang on the door.

'What is it, Dina?' Rosie finally answers.

'You have to open the door, the surveyor's here and—'

'I'm tired.'

The doorbell rings.

I take a deep breath, resist the urge to kick the door and scream at her. *One, two...* Breathe. 'Rosie, it is really important that the surveyor gets access to the loft. Can you please open the door. He won't be long, and then you can—'

'I'm going back to bed, Dina,' she says. 'I'm not feeling great.'

The doorbell rings again, and my clenched fist becomes the stopper of a scream. *One, two...* 'Okay,' I say. 'I hope you feel better soon, Rosie.' *Aahhh!!!*

'Mr Penny, I'm so sorry, the wind must have blown the door shut.'

'Not a problem,' he says, now holding a little garden trowel and with a long pole thingy slung over his shoulder and sheathed in a canvas carry case, which he pats. 'The wand.'

'I am so sorry to do this to you, Mr Penny, but I've suddenly been struck with one of my horrendous migraines.' I cup my forehead and dim my eyes.

'I will be as quiet as humanly possible, Mrs Young, I assure you.'

'I'm sure you would be,' I say, 'but the only thing for me now is to close the blinds and go to bed. Could we reschedule, I'm so sorry...'

'Please don't apologise, Mrs Young. My mother suffered from the same. Next week, then.'

Mr Penny backs away as though from a sleeping baby, and as I close the door, all I want to do is scream, but I can't. I don't want to disturb Rosie.

54

The plan isn't great, I know that, but what else can I do? Rosie is locked in her room, and I can't risk her finding out that I haven't disposed of the evidence yet – just look how she reacted to me telling Detective Wallace about her being my sponsor. This would be a second, more serious slip, in her mind, and she'll never leave. So I can't burn it all in Roy's metal bin in the garden, in case she comes down for some reason, and I certainly can't leave it where it is for Mr Penny to find. Or the Delevingnes, for that matter, when they start excavating the floor for old Joe's games room. Complete destruction of the evidence is the right way to do it. The safest way. But burning it is no longer an option. That only leaves disposal, and with Rosie sleeping in her room, it's now or never.

After listening at Rosie's door for a good five minutes and hearing not a sound, I take a clean carrier bag down into the basement and dig up, with my bare hands, the old carrier containing all the incriminating evidence, including Rosie's bloody Elvis top. Then, with my hands washed and the dirty bag inside the clean one, I wait by the front door, listening for any noise coming from Rosie's room, and after hearing nothing again, and knowing I still look like a homeless person, I leave the house and head towards the river.

It's cooler down by the river, and even more so at this time of the morning, which is why the number of dog walkers and joggers is greater now than at any other time of day. Ideally, I would've liked to have done this at night, distribute each item in the carrier bag between each of the many rubbish bins that line this river pathway – nobody around and with it too dark to see my face if there were. But no. It's a circus.

I arrive at the first rubbish bin, which is handily adjacent to a bench so I can sit and enjoy the light reflecting on the water and wait for the traffic of people to thin out. First, an older couple passes with a ratty little dog, then a skinny young woman jogs by in Lycra and a bum bag. Next, only thirty seconds behind her, is a man with a ginger lab, and behind him, no one for at least two minutes. I reach into the carrier bag and grope for the lighter fluid. The man with the lab goes by. I drop the lighter fluid into the bin and continue my walk along the river.

The next bin I come to has no bench to sit on, and is full to the brim with burger cartons and coffee cups from the caravan café at the quay, which I can see from here, about a quarter of a mile away, is fairly busy with customers. I walk on a hundred yards or so to the next bin, but it's for dog waste only.

I come across one last bin before I would have reached the small crowd queuing for breakfast rolls at the café, but there's a hippyish, middle-aged woman sitting directly opposite on a makeshift jetty of planks next to where her grimy little houseboat is moored. She's selling artsy pieces of driftwood with saccharine messages of love hand-painted on them, such as *Heart & Harmony*, and *Passion & Promises*. I make the mistake of lingering, which she mistakes for interest, when I'm only considering whether or not to dump the whole carrier bag of evidence into this bin and be done with it.

'All the pieces here were found along this stretch of the Deben,' she tells me, 'and I hand-paint them myself.'

'They're beautiful,' I lie, and we both turn toward the sharp outburst of, 'Jackson, no!' as a little girl has her polystyrene tray of chips knocked from her hand by the family terrier. The girl starts to cry while her mother yanks the terrier's lead to prevent the dog from snaffling up the fallen chips.

'These are on offer today,' the woman continues. 'Only ten pounds for the larger pieces and eight for these ones.' She casts a hand over the smaller pieces of driftwood laid out on the grass verge beside her. *Flowers & Friendship. Comfort & Caring.*

I glance toward the mother and daughter. The mother has given her chips to her daughter and is fending off the terrier with one hand and clearing up the fallen chips with the other.

'I'm happy to do two for fifteen?' the hippyish woman offers. 'For one small and one large?'

The mother has now cleaned up the chips and is heading this way with the hopping terrier. For the bin I have to assume. 'I'll take one of the smaller ones,' I say to the woman, and unzip my purse.

'Which one?'

'Any one,' I say, handing over a ten-pound note. 'They're all so lovely.'

The woman takes the note and begins the hunt for my two pounds in change. The mother with the chips and the dog is only a few steps away now, and so I stuff the carrier bag of evidence into the rubbish bin and push it down deep. The mother smiles at me and the terrier has one final lunge for the chips, but with no luck. The mother dumps the chips and the polystyrene tray on top of the carrier bag and walks away. The hippy woman hands me my change and a piece of driftwood of her own selection – a silvered shard from what looks like an old rowing boat.

I decide to head home via the town route, so I can walk through Dreydon Park. As I approach the spot on the path where Grant Chapman drew his last breath, I surprise myself by sitting on the bench to consider my feelings, and am surprised again to find that my hatred of the man has evaporated. I wish I could take it back, and not just for purely selfish reasons. I think deep down I could have, over time, forgiven him.

Before I leave, I prop the little driftwood shard on the bench. A sort of memorial for us both.

*Hearts Remember What Minds Forget.*

## 55

It's a full hour and a half later when I get back home. I stopped at the travel agent to pick up some brochures, but all they had were city break leaflets for Paris. Something to stick on the fridge, though. Something physical to daydream about over tea. I close the front door and head into the kitchen, where all thoughts of Paris are abruptly scratched from my mind. Rosie is sitting at the kitchen table in joggers and vest. Her hair raked back in a ponytail, with errant strands sticking to her sweaty neck and shoulders. Feverish-looking.

'Oh, hi, Dina,' she says, gesturing at the roast lamb dinner before her. 'Hope you don't mind, but you did say you'd left me something to eat in the microwave if I got hungry, and boy am I hungry.'

I'm frozen in the doorway for a second, the Paris leaflet burning guiltily in my fingers. 'Umm, no. You tuck in, Rosie,' I say. 'And there's more lamb in the fridge if you want it.'

Rosie spears a soggy roast potato and aims it at the leaflet. 'What happened to your bag?' She stuffs the potato into her mouth.

'My bag?'

Rosie nods as she chews and swallows. I feel the potato catch in my own throat.

'You had a carrier bag with you when you went out this morning.' She spears some lamb this time.

'Did I?'

'Yup. Saw it from my bedroom window.' Rosie pokes the lamb into her mouth and bites the fork clean with a chime of teeth on tines.

'Oh, yeah,' I say, folding the Paris leaflet into the back pocket of my jeans. 'Just some old clothes I took to the charity shop.'

'Right.'

'You look better,' I lie. 'Are you feeling better?'

Rosie smiles up at me. 'Much better, actually. Thank you for asking, Dina.'

'That's good to hear,' I say, fanning my top against my sweaty skin. 'I should get showered.' I go to leave.

'Beautiful flowers,' Rosie says, stopping me in the doorway.

'Yes. Lilies. I bought them yesterday.'

Rosie's face lights up. 'For me?'

'Well, you seemed upset and so... I thought they would cheer the place up a bit.'

'White is such a peaceful colour,' she says, and lays down her fork. 'In fact, I was thinking of cheering up my room a bit, too.'

'Please, take them.'

Rosie turns in her chair to face me. 'What I mean is, Dina, you've got all that leftover white emulsion, and bare plaster walls are so, well, bare. And with me staying on here for a while longer, I was hoping you could let me have some of that paint so I could brighten up my room?'

I squirm inside. 'Is it really worth it? For three weeks?'

'Four,' Rosie corrects me. 'If you count the extra week for rescheduling the surveyor.'

*Eavesdropping little...*

'Please, Dina? It really would make me feel better.'

I suppose it can do no harm, and if it keeps Rosie happy, that can only be a good thing.

'Take all the paint you need,' I say. 'I'll sort out some brushes and stuff for you.'

Rosie silently screams with joy and claps her hands together, the way Becky used to do when I told her she could sleep over at one of her friends' houses. And just like with Becky, it makes me feel a little sad.

## 56

Two days crawl by, and although Rosie has been released from her self-imposed quarantine, I only see her twice during this time, when she came to find me, all paint-spattered and sweaty in her dungarees, to give me my breathalyser test. Apart from that, we became the proverbial ships passing in the hot and sticky night, and the only evidence of there being somebody else living with me in the house is the clatter of stepladders coming from her bedroom, and the occasional scuffing sounds coming from the loft. That and the locking of her door, of course, as I'm still not allowed inside. Not until the decorating is finished, Rosie tells me whenever I knock to see if she's okay or needs some help. *The big reveal is coming soon*, she always replies. *Be patient, Dina, jeez.*

And I don't know how Rosie is even functioning. She seems to subsist on toast and paint fumes, as I sometimes catch a burnt charcoal scent lingering in the kitchen, or the chemical waft of gloss as I pass her bedroom door – the only other evidence I have of Rosie leaving her room. Not that I am one to talk. I'm getting by on cigarettes and fingernails, waiting for Detective Wallace to ring my doorbell and present me with a carrier bag full of evidence, evidence I've been seen disposing of in a public rubbish bin. No, I mustn't give in to those thoughts. There's no way in hell—

My phone buzzes on the passenger seat of the Saab and I almost burn my lip on the cigarette. Thankfully it isn't Detective Wallace. It's Darryl.

'Mrs Young, it's—'

'Hi, Darryl.'

'I've just got off the phone with Mr Delevingne. He's asking why he's had to reschedule the surveyor?'

'Right,' I say, leaning out of the Saab to look up at Rosie's room. 'That was completely my fault. Just epically bad timing of a migraine. If the Delevingnes have incurred any financial penalty over that, please tell them to knock it off the asking price.' Rosie appears at the window and pulls the curtains closed. Not that I could see anything.

'It isn't the financial aspect, Mrs Young,' Darryl says. 'It's a timing issue. The Delevingnes are flying back to the States within the next few weeks and won't be able to return for a couple of months after that. Mr Delevingne has a contractor lined up for the initial renovation works, and he wants to be around for the first two weeks to oversee—'

'I promise you, Darryl, there'll be no more hold-ups at my end.'

'That's good to hear, Mrs Young,' Darryl says, and I can sense his relief. 'I'll let Mr Delevingne know.'

'Bye, Darryl,' I sign off, and my attention is drawn to my opening front door, where Rosie is stepping outside. I toss my phone back onto the passenger seat and toot the Saab's horn. Rosie looks my way.

'Oh, hi, Dina,' she says, swirling her car keys around her finger. 'Just nipping into town to get some Blu Tack. You want anything?'

'I think I've got Blu Tack somewhere,' I say, climbing out of the Saab.

'S'okay, I need a lot.' She pops the boot and wrestles free her silver racer, pushes off without another word.

I step on my cigarette and watch until Rosie is out of sight before I go inside and hurry up to her room. Find it locked. Damn it!

What can Rosie possibly want with *a lot* of Blu Tack?

I go back to the Saab to retrieve my phone and to get another much-needed cigarette, but when I grab my phone I notice I've just missed a call. I listen to the message that's been left, my breath held and my heart skipping beats. It's from Detective Wallace. He wants to talk to me about something but doesn't say what. I swallow. The evergreens that surround this plot constrict. I dial.

'Mrs Young,' Detective Wallace answers. 'Thank you for returning my call.'

'You wanted to speak to me?' I say. 'Is everything okay?'

'There's been a development in the Rolland Childress case that I'd like to discuss with you.'

'But I had nothing to do with that.' I sit back inside the Saab and snick the door closed. I want to hide.

'Are you currently at your house?'

'Yes, why?'

'Could I come over?' he asks. 'It would be better to talk in person.'

'Well...'

'I understand that Ms Rey has been staying with you. Is she with you presently?'

'No, but...' But she won't be long. What if Detective Wallace is here when she gets back? What if he sees Rosie's silver racer? He mentioned a person of interest with a silver bike. 'I can come to the station if you like?'

'If you'd prefer. I can send a car over to collect you?'

'That's okay,' I say. 'The station's not far, I'll walk.'

'If you're sure. Have them buzz me at the front desk when you arrive and I'll come down.'

I nod as if he can see me, which is silly. If Detective Wallace *could* see me, I'm sure he'd ask why my hands were shaking.

## 57

It was Detective Anand that collected me from the police station's front desk, and led me through a warren of corridors and into what I could only guess was an interview room, as there was nothing inside but a school-type table and four chairs tucked smartly beneath. A narrow floor-to-ceiling window to my right was the only natural light source in the room, and I could barely make out the station's car park beyond the obscured safety glass, through which I also glimpsed my future should I end up being detained here for my crimes – a double sentence of sorts, both in the confinement and the torturous institutional décor I would endure. I sat in the chair Detective Anand offered me and she told me Detective Wallace wouldn't be long. That was twenty minutes ago, and when Detective Wallace finally did walk in, I still didn't have a name for whatever colour these walls had been painted, though I was torn between Urine and Bile.

'Mrs Young,' he says, standing the tall electric fan he's carrying in the corner by the window. 'Sorry about the room. It was the only one free.'

'It's fine,' I say. 'I prefer rooms not to have oxygen in them.'

'Is that a feng shui thing?' he asks, plugging the fan in and switching it on.

No, I want to answer. It's a nerves thing.

He switches on the fan and it slowly shakes its head at me, basting the room in a warm current of air. 'It isn't great, but it'll have to do,' he grumbles as he takes his notebook from his back pocket and places it on the table, takes the seat opposite me. It's the first time I've seen him without his jacket on, though his tie, despite the oppressive heat, remains nipped tightly to his throat. He must really have loved his wife.

'You said there'd been a development?' I ask. 'With Rolland Childers, is it?'

'Child*ress*, yes.'

'Sorry, Childress. I take it you've caught the person who started the fire?'

'Not yet, no.' Detective Wallace crabs his fingers on the table as though he's about to play the piano, but removes them again and looks up at me. 'You said Rosie Rey is living with you currently?'

'No, you said that.'

'So she's not staying with you?'

'Staying, yes, but she's not living with me.'

He nods but doesn't reply. The fan whirrs on.

'It's just for a few days,' I say, filling the silence. 'Is that a problem? Am I harbouring a fugitive of the law or something?'

'What makes you say that?' he asks.

I dim my eyes and gesture at his notebook. 'Shouldn't you be writing this down?'

'I'm not taking a statement, Mrs Young. It's just an informal chat.'

'Informal? About a man who died in an arson attack, that had absolutely nothing to do with me?'

'Well, that's not entirely true.'

'So you *do* think I had something to do with it.' I let my jaw drop open as I look away in disbelief. And fear.

'What I mean is,' he continues, 'Rolland Childress didn't die of an arson attack.'

I snap back to attention. 'What do you mean he—'

'If we could just focus on your relationship with Rosie Rey for a moment.'

I sit forward. 'I do not have a relationship with Rosie Rey.'

'But she is staying at your home.'

I take a deep breath and try to let the fan cool me. 'It's just a support thing,' I say. 'I had a little wobble and Rosie offered to stay for a bit until I felt stronger.'

'As your sponsor?'

'Yes, as my sponsor.'

Detective Wallace wipes his mouth.

'Is there a problem with that?' I ask, but I know there is.

'How well do you know Rosie?'

If he knows that Rosie isn't a sponsor (which he does), and knows she's never been in the programme (which he does), then he knows I've only been to one AA meeting and why the hell have I invited this woman into my home, let alone shared two movie nights with her? But then again, what business is it of the police to question who I invite into my home and how well I need to know them if I do.

'Well enough,' I say. 'Now what's this about Rolland Childress not dying—'

'Has Rosie talked to you about her mother?'

I retreat into my chair. 'Bits and pieces, why?'

He nods faintly. 'Any of those bits and pieces cover their relationship or... how Rosie's mother died?'

It isn't obvious on his face, but Detective Wallace has the smug air of someone who already knows the answers to the questions he's asking. At least if I tell him what I know about

Rosie's past it shows we're not complete strangers, which I get the distinct impression he thinks we are.

'Her mother was an abusive alcoholic,' I say. 'She used to hurt Rosie, burn her with cigarettes. Then one day she tried to kill her.'

'Tried to kill Rosie?'

'And herself. She poured petrol over herself and Rosie and tried to, you know, but Rosie escaped from her bedroom window and watched her mother burn from the roadside. I think Rosie spent some time in various hospitals after that. As would anyone.'

Detective Wallace reaches for his notebook. Flips it open. 'After Rosie's detention at Hollesley Bay Colony, she spent time in three different medical facilities over a seven-year period, starting off on the juvenile ward at the Willow Peak secure psychiatric unit and finishing out her treatment as an inpatient at Highbridge Mental Health unit.'

'Wait, Hollesley Bay's a prison, not a mental hospital.'

'The colony is a young offenders institution, yes.'

'But why...?'

'You mean why was Rosie in prison for escaping her abusive mother and watching her set herself on fire?'

I don't want to know the answer, but this is why I'm here. 'What did Rosie do?' I ask.

'Rosie killed her mother, and then set fire to the house.'

The Urine or Bile walls close in and I cave into my chair. Detective Wallace goes on.

'Rosie's mother – Jane Rey – had intended to burn down the family home, and while Rosie slept, she doused Rosie's bed in petrol. Rosie woke, thinking she'd wet the bed again, as she sometimes did, and crept into the hall to go clean herself up before her mother found out. But on her way to the bathroom, Rosie saw her mother in the kitchen, pouring the last of the petrol over her head, and when she turned and saw Rosie she started trying to spark the lighter she was holding...'

'Dear God...'

Detective Wallace nods sombrely. 'But the lighter wouldn't spark, and it gave Rosie enough time to rush into the kitchen and pull a carving knife from the block and—'

'That's enough,' I say, covering my eyes as though that could stop the scene unravelling in my mind. Instead, I hug my arms to stop myself from unravelling. 'Why are you telling me this. *Should* you be telling me this?'

He closes his notebook. 'Rosie's arrest is a matter of public record, but the details I thought you should know.'

'Why on earth would I want to know that?' I snap.

'If someone was staying in your home, someone with this kind of history, wouldn't you want to know? Especially if that someone has lied about that history.'

'She never lied,' I say, almost to myself.

'But the story she gave you isn't true.'

She didn't give me the story. Ben did. 'Rosie was abused, wasn't she?'

'Yes, that part's true.'

'And if her mother was going to kill her, that's self-defence, surely?'

'That's how the jury saw it, yes.'

'What, somebody saw it differently?'

'According to the reports, the prosecution wasn't entirely happy with Rosie's version of events, but what with her mother's clear case of abuse, it wasn't pursued as vigorously as it could have been.'

I swallow. 'What wasn't the prosecution happy with?'

'Rosie was found to be right-handed, but her mother's knife wound was located on the right side of her neck.' He demonstrates with two fingers on his own neck, as though he's checking for a pulse.

'And?'

Detective Wallace leans towards me and beckons for me to do the same, which I do, hesitantly. 'And that would mean Rosie stabbed her mother like this.' He raises his right hand in a fist and crosses my face to mock-stab me in my neck – my right side – his curled pinkie finger brushing my skin. 'You see, naturally, if somebody was standing in front of you, you would attack them like this...' He strikes again, this time brushing the skin of my sweaty neck on the other side. My left side. 'See?' He sits back as though he's proved his point.

I rub away his touch from my skin, though I can still feel the lingering presence of his first fake blow. 'It's awkward,' I concede. 'Or maybe Rosie just used her left hand in the heat of panic.'

'Or as the prosecution suggested at the time, Rosie struck her mother from behind.' Detective Wallace goes to stand, presumably to stab me again.

'I get it,' I say, and he sits back down.

'This theory obviously raised other questions, such as, did Rosie then go on to set fire to the house to erase evidence rather than to obliterate a lifetime of horrific memories – as her psychological evaluation concluded – and did Rosie's mother even douse the place in petrol or did Rosie do it after the fact – which then brings into play an element of premeditation.'

The fan rakes another wave of warm air across me, and the Urine or Bile-coloured walls close in further. 'Look, as you said, these are just theories the prosecution had, but the facts are, the jury returned a vote of self-defence, correct?'

He blinks in affirmation.

'Then you'll have to explain to me, Detective Wallace, how two completely unrelated accounts of arson – ten years apart, I might add – have anything to do with me, or for that matter, Rosie Rey?' A tall glass of vodka, bobbing with ice, beams into my mind, and I'm thankful that Rosie has hidden the bottle I kept in the freezer.

Detective Wallace reaches for his notebook and peels back a few pages. 'If it were the arson attacks alone, I wouldn't have asked to speak with you—'

'Then why have you?' I ask. 'We've established that I had absolutely nothing to do with Rolland whatever-his-name-is—'

'Childress.'

'Yes, him – hang on...' The glass of vodka I'm holding in my mind suddenly slips from my grip. 'You said he didn't even die in an arson attack, didn't you?'

Detective Wallace reaches for the knot of his tie. At last, the heat has gotten to him. But no. He cinches it tighter and adjusts his cuffs. 'The coroner didn't spot it at first—'

'Spot what?'

'—because the body was so badly burned. But when she opened up Childress's lungs, they were clean.'

'So he didn't smoke, good for him.' I roll my eyes away to the whirring fan, as though to get a second opinion on this trivial point.

'It means that Rolland Childress was dead before the fire was lit.'

I slowly return my attention to Detective Wallace. The fallen glass of vodka so many vicious shards in my mind. 'Then how did he die?'

He places two fingers again on his neck, but I know this time for sure there'll be no pulse. 'Single stab wound,' he says.

58

Roy always used to say I made terrible jokes when I was nervous. He also used to say I got terribly nervous when I was lying, and that if I was more truthful with him my jokes might improve. I would obviously make a joke about that, and obviously he wouldn't laugh. I don't see this evasive ploy working on Detective Wallace, though.

Detective Anand had ducked into the room and called him away about five minutes ago, leaving me to sweat in the knowledge that I might have a murderer staying at my house. The problem is, I'm having real trouble believing any of it – that Rosie could be capable of such a cold-blooded act, or that the timing of Detective Anand stepping in when she did was anything but calculated. The visual cue of Detective Wallace tapping his neck, followed so quickly by Anand's knock at the door... It was just too perfect. *Let her percolate for a bit*, I can hear them say. *Let her stew until her lies fall off the bone like a slow-cooked shoulder of lamb...*

I go and stand in front of the fan, but not to cool down. I'm looking for the camera that must be in here somewhere – the spying eye that Detective Anand used to spot her cue, as there is no two-way mirror like they use on TV. I glance up at the four corners of the room, but they're bare, as is the ceiling, apart from a rust-tinged striplight. The rest is just clean walls and carpet tile, so I suspect they must have done it the old-fashioned way, and Anand had watched through the window in the door.

I meander around the table. I'm becoming paranoid – and yet, when I notice Detective Wallace's notebook lying open in front of me, I don't think it's unjustly so. It's mostly indecipherable chicken scrawl from this distance, apart from the bottom line, which he's kindly written out in all caps and bookended with two question marks.

*? SEX ON A HICKORY STICK ?*

I make it back to my seat just before Detective Wallace returns.

'Sorry about that,' he says, retaking his seat. 'Where were we?'

'I think you were just about to say: "Apologies for wasting your time, Mrs Young. Thanks for stopping by and enjoy the rest of your day"?' Roy would call this nervous humour again, but it isn't. It's cold, hard confidence. They've got nothing but suspicions, and this whole "Rosie may have stabbed her mother from behind" crap, is just, well, crap. Rosie's scars don't lie.

Detective Wallace closes his notebook. 'I think you're caught up in something here, Mrs Young' – he raises his hands before I can protest – 'just hear me out. I think for some reason Rosie has become protective of you, perhaps you losing your daughter the way you did—'

'Becky,' I say. 'Her name is Becky.'

He nods. 'The way you lost Becky, and that perhaps Rosie has taken this too far and sought to—'

'You have literally no grounds – or evidence – for thinking such a thing.'

'But I do have grounds. Grounds for questioning your stories.'

*Alibis.* 'I can't help you with that, I'm afraid,' I say. 'What is it they call it, the "inconvenient truth"?'

'For instance,' he continues, as though I haven't said a word, 'I spoke to Justin Campbell, at the AA centre, and he told us you barely attended one meeting?'

Here we go. 'It wasn't for me.'

'He said you became quite upset when you started talking about Becky, and that Rosie went after you to see if you were okay. Is that correct?'

I shrug. 'More or less.'

'And is that when she offered to be your sponsor?'

Okay. Let's get this over with. I don't care if Detective Wallace thinks I befriend beggars off the street and invite them round for barbecues and Jägerbombs. It's my house and my life, and I'll fill each with whoever the fuck I please. 'I was upset, and so I went across the road and bought a bottle of vodka. Rosie saw the bottle as I was climbing into the taxi, was worried I was going to do something I'd regret, and so followed me home. She knocked on my door, knew what I was about to do, and talked me down.'

'And that's when she offered to be your sponsor?'

'You spoke to Justin, you know Rosie isn't a sponsor. I don't know why you're making such an issue of it. You don't have to be a sponsor to offer support to someone like me. Just like you don't need to be a therapist to be able to listen to someone's problems.'

'That's true,' Detective Wallace says, 'but Rosie made a point of telling us that she was in recovery, and that most definitely is not the case.'

'Did you get that from Justin, too?'

'Does it bother you that Rosie lied to you about being a sponsor, about being an alcoholic?'

'Like I said, the sponsor thing is your issue, not mine. And she's young! Maybe she let me believe she was in recovery in case I didn't think she was credible. Maybe she thought if she hadn't woken up on a toilet floor with puke in her hair I couldn't possibly accept her platitudes about the virtues of quitting the demon drink, and she'd be right. I wouldn't have.'

He looks away. To pacify me, I think, because if I can feel my anger rising, Detective Wallace can certainly see it. I notice my hands on the table, let the fists they've become loosen and withdraw them into my lap.

'So, Rosie took on the supportive role as your sponsor?'

'If you like.' I tug my earlobe. 'A few days later I wobbled again. I called Rosie, she came round, sobered me up. I think we both realised then that I couldn't be on my own and so we agreed that she would come over sometimes to check on me.'

'A movie night, for instance.'

I glance toward the door, return with what I hope is a resigned look on my face, as though the great detective has begrudgingly pried the truth from me. It's over now. The only thing I was ever trying to conceal was my own pathetic helplessness.

He crooks his mouth. 'There's one thing that bothers me, Mrs Young...' He reaches for his notebook, but I know already what's bothering him. *SEX ON A HICKORY STICK* is bothering him. The fact that me and Rosie both used the same odd way of describing Leonardo DiCaprio, like we'd polished our stories a touch too much. But it was nothing of the sort! The silly phrase just stuck in my head because Rosie says stupid things like that. It was a Rosie-ism! I'll just tell him I parroted a Rosie-ism—

He opens his notebook again. 'It's the taxi that bothers me.'

'What? What taxi?'

'The taxi Rosie took to your house, for your first movie night.'

'That bothers you?'

'You both in interview stated that neither of you drank that evening. Is that still what you maintain?'

I stare at him for a moment before answering. 'Yes.'

'That's what bothers me. You are clearly in recovery, and Rosie, at the time, was posing as your sponsor and therefore could not drink in your presence for obvious reasons – in fact, if I remember correctly, she mocked me for asking the question. So why would she need to arrive in a taxi when she has a car, and given the fact that she knew she wouldn't be consuming alcohol?'

'I really have no idea,' I say. 'Flat battery?'

'No. I checked with all the local garages and Rosie's Beetle hasn't been in with any of them, and Rosie herself confirmed with me that her car was running fine.' Detective Wallace sits back in his chair and looks at me, as though I'm supposed to solve this mystery for him. But I'm happy to wait him out, I tell myself, and immediately cave to the silence.

'You'll have to ask Ros—'

'We call it a time stamp.' He sits forward again and laces his fingers together on the table. 'Where an innocent third party inadvertently corroborates the whereabouts of the... guilty party, at a specific time. In this instance we have the taxi driver, who confirms the drop-off and pick-up of a very chatty young lady in animal-print PJs. Seven o'clock, and ten thirty. It's the duration between that—'

'Let me see if I understand what you're getting at,' I say, my wide eyes blinking to illustrate the incredulity of his fantastical notion, when really my eyes are wide and blinking because I cannot see how this man has come to the correct assumption based on so little evidence. 'You think that Rosie arrived in the taxi and then left to go and murder Grant Chapman—'

'Not murder,' he says. 'I think it was a viscous attack gone wrong.'

'Whatever...'

'And the funny thing is, at first, I thought it was you, not Rosie. But after Rolland Childress, the stabbing, the fire... Rosie's history...'

'This is utterly ridiculous,' I blurt, and stand from my seat. 'I was – I mean, Rosie was...' I take a breath. 'We were together all night, and neither of us left my house. We ate a takeaway and we watched a film together. That's it. All this shit about Rosie plotting to kill her mother and Rolland whatever-his-bloody-name-is being stabbed in the neck before his house burned down...'

'Is entirely true, Mrs Young.' He stands to join me.

'Well, then show me the reports. Show me the prosecution's concerns about Rosie in black and white. Show me the autopsy report that says the solicitor didn't die in a fire!'

'I can't do that.'

Of course he can't. 'Am I free to go?'

'Mrs Young, don't let Rosie drag you so deep that you feel you can't escape. Talk to me, before it's too late.'

'Am I free to go?'

He sighs through flared nostrils. 'I'll see you out.'

59

I walk back along the river to clear my head, though I don't live nearly far enough away for that to happen before I get home. Detective Wallace has somehow divined a version of the truth, but knowing the truth and proving it are two very different things, and unless Rosie or me confess, his suspicions alone are not enough to undo us.

That must be the reason he tried to bluff a confession out of me. Plant the idea that Rosie might have murdered her mother in a cold-blooded, premeditated act of revenge, and then years later mirror the very same horrific crime upon Grant Chapman's solicitor. And for what? For me? Complete and utter nonsense, and proven by the fact he wouldn't show me the reports, and why our little chat was "informal" and off the record. An on-the-record chat would have recorded his lies, but I'm sure it would have quickly become on the record had I folded to the pressure and started singing to save myself. Unfortunately for Detective Wallace, he has no idea how truly deep I am muddied (*bloodied?*) in this mess, and he can never know. The shame would kill me.

No. Detective Wallace is clutching at straws, or rather,

hickory sticks, and the sooner I can get Rosie out of my house, out of my life, the sooner I can move far away and forget this ever happened. Create a new colour for myself. Yes, I can see it, in the sun's blazing reflection as it scorches the surface of the river. I think I'll call it... Phoenix Gold. That's it. That's the colour of my future without Rosie Rey.

*"Remember, colour is not just colour, but mood, temperature and structure."*

~ Van Day Truex

## 60

Rosie's car is still on the driveway when I get home, her silver racer leaning against the boot. She must have been in a hurry to get inside and use the Blu Tack she'd dashed out for if she couldn't be bothered to put the bike away. Or maybe she's planning on going out again.

Either way I can't face her yet, so I go and sit in the Saab and smoke a cigarette, my body frying against the leather seat. The spider I squished under the wiper blade is nothing more than a crusty arc now. Its brief dance with agony long over. I have to believe that one day this episode of my life will be nothing more than a crusted streak in my memory. Painlessly observed from a distance and lacking the sting of the present. There was a time when I couldn't think about Becky without breaking down, or sit in the Saab without sobbing for Roy to forgive me. By comparison, Rosie should disappear from my mind like the details of a Friday night pub crawl on an empty stomach.

I lean out of the Saab and squint up at her window. Rosie has pulled the curtains wide open, but all I can see is the glare of the sun against the glass. I take a final drag of my cigarette and bury the butt in the overstuffed ashtray, stoking the aromas of soot that Roy hated so much. 'I'm sorry, Roy, but I think it's time I sell the Saab, for whatever I can get.' It has become a morbid place to be, and not just because of the dead spider.

The house is quiet as I linger at the front door, the scaffold tower seemingly holding its breath, from the smell of the vomit, perhaps. I shudder at the thought of it still up there on the platform, at what I must have been thinking to make such a dangerous climb. I step into the kitchen and place my bag and phone on the table. The vase of lilies has gone. Wishful thinking that Rosie has gone, too. I step back into the entrance hall and close the door, loudly enough to be heard.

A flurry of footsteps on the landing, and for the briefest moment, as I turn, I expect to see Becky. My beautiful daughter.

'Hey, Dina,' Rosie calls from the gallery rail, her head and shoulders framed within the struts of the scaffold tower and the arch window behind her, casting her face in semi-shadow. 'I've finally finished the bedroom, come see!'

'Just let me get a glass of water and I'll be up.'

'No, no,' Rosie says, flitting down the staircase and putting me in mind of Becky again. 'You have to see it now, come on!' She takes my hand and guides me to the stairs.

'Actually, Rosie, we need to talk.'

'Sure, whatever,' she says, drawing me up the stairs. 'You're gonna love this room, it's so peaceful, Dina.'

'I'm sure it will be,' I say, cringing inside at how I'm going to broach the subject of Rosie leaving. At how she's going to react.

'And I hope you don't mind, but I totally stole the flowers from the kitchen table.' We turn onto the landing and Rosie lets my hand fall, walking backwards and encouraging me to follow. 'When I was staying at the institute, they always made sure I had fresh flowers in my room, something for me to look after, to water, you know?'

Did Rosie just mention the institute? I'm not sure she's ever mentioned it before to me.

She reaches the bedroom door and steps aside, nibbling her knuckles. 'I'm so nervous, Dina, I hope you like it!'

The door is open and daylight is reaching into the landing. It feels strange, as the door has been locked for so long. Rosie takes my arm and stands me just outside, the smell of fresh paint cloying in the heat of the afternoon.

'Well?' she says.

The floorboards are silvered bare pine, but everything else is stark white. The ceiling, walls, the skirting and architrave.

'Go in, Dina. See how it feels.'

As Rosie moves around behind me, I notice the paint pots and dust sheets piled against the landing wall. The stepladders and the roller sleeve drying in its tray, the tin of Jewel Teal I'd used in the snug.

'Don't worry about all that,' Rosie says, her hand on my lower back, gently coaxing. 'I'll clear it up later. Go on, see how it feels.'

I take a couple of steps and I can see the corner of the bed, crisply cornered in the white linen I gave her. Then the chest of drawers against the back wall, which displays the vase of lilies. I still can't see the window to the left as the door is obstructing that side of the room, but the sun is almost blinding with the golden ribbons of light blazing along the floorboards, and I wonder if I can even tolerate the purity.

'There's something about white, the absence of colour, Dina, that just clears the mind, you know, like a mental spring clean. It really helped me at the institute, and I think it'll help you.' Again, Rosie's hand on my back. Gentle, but undeniable.

I take another couple of steps and I can now see beyond the open door. The window, the en suite, the chair in the corner that is usually in my bedroom. I don't dwell on the fact Rosie has been in my bedroom and taken the chair, because my mind is catching on the tin of Jewel Teal, when everything in here is so brutally white.

'You see, Dina,' Rosie's voice soft in my ear, 'I think taking a little time for yourself, without all the clutter that life bombards us with, I think you'll be able to find what it is that's stopping you from healing, you know?'

'Healing? But I've been dry—'

The slamming of the door startles me, but the key turning in the lock sends my stomach lurching. 'Rosie!' I whirl. The flash of colour, the flash of Jewel Teal scarring my eyes.

'I just want you to know, Dina, that I'm going to be here for you, okay? We'll work through this together.'

'What the fuck, Rosie!' I pound on the door, rattle the knob. 'Let me out!'

'Only you can open the door, Dina, but you've got to start telling the truth.'

'What the fuck are you talking about? I've never lied to you, Rosie! Open the door!'

'Get some rest, Dina. I'll bring you some tea in a few hours.'

And with that, I hear Rosie's footsteps recede, leaving me to stare at the wall behind the bed, which is filled with photographs, every inch. Photographs that I'd buried in the loft and hoped I would never have to look at again. And there, written on the back of the door in bold strokes of Jewel Teal, a bleak beacon in this sea of white. A message from my captor, my sponsor: ***DINA IS A LIAR.***

61

I'm dreaming, at least in part. I can feel the pillow wet from my tears, my cheeks becoming sore, but I'm also sobbing in the dream.

Roy is clutching his chest, by the Saab where I left him, and I'm thrashing around the house in search of his pills. At last, when I find them, I race outside where he has collapsed on the driveway. I somehow haul him onto the driver seat, his arms in paralysis around him, and sit him up. I fumble the cap from the pill bottle and toss a few into my palm, but when I see the look on his face I know I'm too late. His eyes have rolled back into his head, and his lips have turned an awful shade – Grape, no, Byzantium. I force the pills onto his lolling tongue, but he won't take them into his mouth. Then his arms slacken and he starts to topple. I rush around to the other side of the Saab and climb in, cradle his head as my tears rain down on his face...

When I wake, the room is bathed in the honeyed light of the sun, which has almost sailed beyond the wispy evergreens that cage this house. I go to the door and try the knob, half believing I've dreamed this part too. But no. The door is locked. I take the chair in the corner and face the window, so I can't see the photographs on the wall. It's no mystery why I dreamt of Roy, with so many pictures of him watching me. So many pictures of us as a family. There's a reason I kept them hidden in the loft – sure, I glance at the odd photo now and then, but as a whole, as an album of our lives, for some reason I could never bear to look at them.

'Dina?'

I turn towards the door.

'I've made you some tea and a sandwich,' Rosie says. 'You want?'

'I want you to let me out of here.'

'That's up to you, Dina. Leftover lamb with mint sauce, if you're interested. It's a pretty epic sandwich—'

'It's up to you if you let me out, it has nothing to do with me.' I creep to the door and listen. I imagine I can hear Rosie breathing, but it's me, and every breath I take I inhale the chemical tang of the freshly-painted Jewel Teal message.

*Dina is a liar...*

But it's not me who is the liar. 'Did you kill your mother, Rosie?' I whisper through the door, half-hoping she doesn't hear the question.

'Now wherever did you get such a notion, Dina?'

Which source do I name? Ben or Detective Wallace? Which version of events do I use? Self-defence or premeditated murder?

'I noticed on your phone you've been chatting to Ben,' Rosie says. 'What did *he* tell you?'

'I don't know, what did you tell him?'

'The truth, Dina, though he didn't deserve it. He talks like he wants to get sober, but really he's a lost cause. Not like you.'

'Is that why I'm locked in here? You think you can save me?'

'Did Ben tell you he has a daughter? Six years old. He only gets to see her every other weekend, and do you think he can stay sober for five fucking minutes for her? Some people don't deserve kids, Dina. Just look at Grant Chapman, his daughter is better off without him.'

'You didn't answer my question, Rosie.'

'Which one? Did I kill my mother or am I trying to save you?'

'Both, if you like.'

'Well, only you can save you, Dina, but I am here to help. As for my mother, one of us was going to die. I didn't want it to be me. Do you want this sandwich or not?'

*Did you kill Rolland Childress!* I want to scream. *Did you stab him in the neck and then burn down his house!* I think back to that night, when Rosie came home and there was blood all over her Elvis top. She'd said it was a nosebleed and I had no reason at the time to disbelieve her, but now... What if Detective Wallace was telling the truth?

'Dina?'

'I'll take the sandwich.'

'Ace! If you could go into the en suite and close the door loudly behind you—'

'Wait, how will you know if I'm on the other side of the door or not?'

'Because, der-brain, you're gonna flush the toilet for me. Then I'll unlock the door and put the tea and sandwich inside.'

I do as Rosie says. I close the en-suite door and flush the loo, hear her unlock the bedroom door and enter, but she doesn't rush to get out again. Is she so sure I won't try to escape? As young as she is, does she believe I couldn't overpower her? I couldn't, I know that, but how does Rosie?

Seconds tick by and she still hasn't left. I crouch and place my eye to the keyhole. The bedroom door is open, but I can't see her from this narrow viewpoint.

'I'm coming out now,' I say, not moving, and then I see Rosie cross the room and leave, locking the door behind her.

'Okay, Dina,' she calls.

I come out of the en suite to find the cup of tea and the sandwich on the chest of drawers. My stomach gurgles, but not from hunger.

'Don't take the photographs down, okay?' Rosie says. 'If you do I'll make you put them up again and this process will just take longer.'

'What process?'

'The healing process, Dina, and that can't begin until you admit there's some healing to be done – what do they say: the first step in beating alcoholism is to admit you're an alcoholic.'

'But I am an alcoholic.'

'Yeah, Dina, it's just the details of your alcoholism you're fuzzy about. But we'll get to that in the morning. Nite.'

I listen as Rosie's footsteps disappear along the landing, and I take the chair and watch the sun disappear beyond the trees. At least I know now why she wasn't in a hurry to leave the bedroom. Why she was so confident that I wouldn't overpower her and escape.

She'd been holding a carving knife.

## 62

I wake the following morning to the sound of the bedroom door closing and locking, and to the aroma of tea and buttery toast. I sit up in bed and see the fresh mug and plate on the chest of drawers, the Turmeric sun burning through the open window. I don't want to start thinking in these terms, to start marking my time in capture with notches on the bedpost, but the words flash in my mind before I can stop them: *Day two*.

After a cooling shower I put on yesterday's clothes, decide I should eat something. I'd drank the tea already, but couldn't face the toast. Now though, with Rosie Rey my jailor, who knew when my next meal would come.

I take the toast and go to sit in the chair by the window, notice the folded sheet of paper that had been tucked beneath the plate. I pick it up and open it out. Inside is a message that reads: *Dear Dina, today I'd like you to study the photographs and tell me what you see. On this occasion, I'd like you to pay close attention to your husband, Roy (who's a dish BTW!). Regards! Your sponsor, Lois Lane* ☹

If Rosie has gone through my phone and noticed her own number under a different name, I can assume she knows

Detective Wallace called me yesterday and I called him back. I wonder why she hasn't mentioned it? Perhaps that's why Rosie has signed off with a sad face. I suddenly lose my appetite and tip the toast out of the window, march over to the bedroom door and start pounding.

'You may as well let me out of here, Rosie!' I shout. 'I'm not going to spend all day looking at old photographs!'

'Shouldn't take you all day, Dina.'

I jump back, startled at the closeness of Rosie's voice on the other side of the door.

'I told you what you need to do,' she continues. 'Bang on the door when you're done and we can discuss.'

I charge the door and pound again. 'Discuss what? I don't know what you want from me, Rosie!'

'Jeez, Dina, I gave you a clue.'

'What? What fucking clue?' But Rosie doesn't answer, and I hear her footsteps retreat to the stairs.

I go to the window and look down at the Saab, which brings on a painful thirst for a cigarette. I gauge the drop to the paving-stone path below and know it would certainly result in a broken leg or worse, and crying out for help would be equally hopeless. Even if someone heard me (and they never seem to, as I've blasted the Saab's horn so many times in frustration), what could they do? Call the police? If I had my phone, the last person I'd call is Detective Wallace. No. I'm trapped within this room as I've been trapped within this house, within these grounds, but I'm so close to being free. I just need to hang on a little longer. Play Rosie's twisted game if I must.

I pick up the note and read the last part again:

*...I'd like you to study the photographs and tell me what you see. On this occasion, I'd like you to pay close attention to your husband, Roy...*

Whatever. I drag the chair to the foot of the bed and take a seat. What does Rosie see? What does she want me to tell her?

There are dozens upon dozens of photographs, all family get-togethers of some description – whether they be birthday parties, barbecues, or the semi-work functions Roy would host at the house for his colleagues – dinners that he would have catered with all the finest vegan food available. He was always trying to convert people to his new "religion".

I stare at the pictures, but nothing jumps out. They all feature Roy, Becky, or me – either all together (as in Becky's birthdays and the occasional family barbecue) or of only Roy and me at one of his work dos. I try to look through Rosie's eyes, at what she might be seeing that I can't, and my head starts to hurt.

'I give up,' I shout, as though Rosie can hear me through the floorboards, but then I read her note again, trying to find the clue she's supposedly left me.

*...On this occasion, I'd like you to pay close attention to your husband, Roy...*

I toss the note onto the bed. 'There's no clue here,' I shout again, and go to the window to second guess the drop to the paving stones, only to picture myself crumpled on the ground with a shinbone poking through my skin. I go back to the note.

*...I'd like you to pay close attention to your husband, Roy (who's a dish BTW!). Regards! Your sponsor, Lois Lane* 😞

So Rosie thinks Roy was attractive, what has that got to do with anything? And what has her being my "sponsor" got to do with the photos, or that she wasn't happy about me putting her number in my phone under the contact "Lois Lane"?

I fan my face with the note, but it doesn't have any cooling effect against the climbing heat of the morning. If Rosie had been upset that I'd listed her as Lois Lane in my contacts, I'm surprised she didn't mention it. She has no qualms about speaking her mind – has no inner dial for social sensibilities. Tagging a sad face on the end of the note seems so passive and out of character—

Unless she doesn't mean *her* sad face.

I go through the photos again, this time studying Roy's expression, seeing for the first time what Rosie sees. In each picture, to some degree, Roy does look sad.

I've never noticed this before, because, well, that's just how Roy looked. But did he always look this way? He was intense when we first met at college. He was studying business and I was flunking an Art and Design degree. He had a three-year plan, for his personal and professional life, which he would tell me as if he were reading the evening news, that I should adopt. He even printed out a template for me to fill in (twice, actually, as the first one I plotted my dream career as a pole dancer, which Roy crushed by saying that my personal life plan of having eleven children would effectively hobble my growth potential in the adult entertainment industry). The second template I filled in was a shameless rip from his own three-year plan, inserting an interior design company in place of his, and dropping the child-count down to one, where Roy had put two. A boy and a girl. I meant for it to be a gentle push-back to his regimented approach to life, that artistic temperament is fluid and cannot be constrained. But Roy completely missed the point, and told me with not a hint of humour that I'd go far implementing his business models.

So Roy didn't walk around with a big goofy grin, but he wasn't sad, or even uptight. Occasionally he used to smoke marijuana, and the real Roy would come out – chilled and easy and sexy as hell – but as his business plans started to blossom, those occasions grew fewer and farther between, and then when he got arrested for possession at a college mate's house party, he stopped smoking it altogether. I think that's when he lost his spark, and that chilled and easy Roy disappeared forever, and without me even noticing, this joyless professional version of Roy took over. Either that or when he caught me with... God, what was his name?

I bang on the bedroom door and wait, and a minute later Rosie arrives.

'Got something for me, Dina?' she asks.

'Roy, he looks a little sad, whatever that signifies.'

'Doesn't he, though?'

'I suppose.'

'But not just sad, Dina, he looks...'

I move closer to the door, as though I can hear Rosie's mind turning over.

'He looks disappointed, resigned, hollowed the fuck out.'

'I don't get that from the pictures,' I say, 'and I don't agree with that, because I was married to the man. He was just serious, always preoccupied with the next big idea.'

'Oh well, at least you gave it some thought,' Rosie says. 'That's all I asked, Dina.'

I wait, listening, but Rosie stays silent. 'Does that mean I can come out now?'

'Not yet, silly. Tomorrow we'll work on the next part of the process. I'll bring you up some dinner later.'

'Wait, Rosie!'

'I'm still here, Dina.'

'What's the next part?'

'I'll let you know in the morning, give you more time to think about Roy.'

'Tell me now, please.' I don't want to think about Roy anymore.

'I'll bring you some fresh clothes, too,' Rosie says, and starts to walk away.

'Rosie, wait!' I hear her stop. 'Cigarettes. They're in the Saab. Can I have them, please?'

She moves on again. I hope that means yes.

63

Day *three.*
Rosie had picked out for me some black leggings and a tie-dye ruched top in shocks of Vermillion and New York Taxi Yellow. She must have dived deep for this one as I haven't seen it in years, and can only vaguely remember wearing it once or twice. Doesn't suit my mood now and jars with my psyche to put it on this morning, though it's nice to be wearing something fresh, along with the clean undies.

She hasn't brought me breakfast yet, which is fine because I now have cigarettes, but neither has she come to give me the next part of the "process". I don't know what I'm supposed to achieve being locked in here, staring at these photographs, and I'm not entirely sure of what I'm supposed to have lied about, though the proclamation painted on the back of the door jars me as much as the top I'm wearing.

When Rosie does finally knock, I step into the en suite and close the door, flush the loo and wait for her call. When I come out there is a mug of tea and a plate of toast on the chest of drawers, and last night's half-eaten bowl of cheesy pasta is gone.

I check under the plate but there is no note this morning. I take the mug of tea to the door.

'Rosie?'

'You didn't like the pasta?'

'Wasn't really hungry.'

'Gotta keep your strength up, Dina,' she says. 'It'll keep your focus on the process and not the rumbling of your tummy. Make sure you eat the toast.'

'What's the next part of the process, Rosie?'

'Was gonna let you have your breakfast first, but okay. Do you remember when I found that photograph downstairs of you and Becky on her tenth birthday?'

Yes. That was when Rosie's whole mood changed towards me. 'Yeah, I do. Why?'

'Well, do you remember me asking if Becky was a summer baby?'

'Yes...'

'Well, that was a lucky guess, Dina.'

'What's that supposed to mean?'

'It means I wrongly assumed it was summer until I saw all the photographs. When I bring you your lunch we can discuss.' Rosie starts to walk away.

'Wait, Rosie, what am I supposed to do?'

'Look at the pictures, Dina,' Rosie calls back. 'Can't all have been taken in the summer.'

'That doesn't make any sense! Can't you give me another clue? Rosie?' I hear her footsteps return.

'You really need a clue?' she asks, so close to the door.

'Of course, I've never been any good at that cryptic stuff.'

Silence, and then: 'Okay, here's the clue: it's the reason you're a fucking liar, Dina.'

'What? But I'm—'

'Do you have a hose, Dina?'

'What?'

'A garden hose. D'you have one?'

'Umm, yeah, in the back garden, why?'

But Rosie doesn't answer, and I hear her footsteps once again retreating to the stairs.

64

I refuse to look at the photographs. I refuse to play her ridiculous game. Who cares if the pictures were taken in the summer, winter, or in the middle of the bloody Sahara Desert. What's clear is that I have to escape this room, this wretched house, and get as far away from Rosie as I can. Darryl has keys and can oversee the sale even if I'm not living here, and I can find a cheap room to rent in the meantime and coordinate things from there and Rosie won't be able to do a thing about it. But first I need to escape this room.

I open the walk-in wardrobe door and, as quietly as I can, lower the loft hatch ladder. I know the keys to all the doors are up here somewhere, in the little Harrods biscuit tin. I only hope the tin isn't buried in one of the tea chests, as digging everything out will inevitably make noise. Rosie mustn't know I've been up here.

Mid-morning and the temperature inside the loft space is brutal, and I wonder how Rosie managed to stay up here for so long, especially since she's dragged every tea chest and box over near the rose window. I would surely have passed out.

I pad towards the rose window, ducking the beams, and as if

by a miracle I see the biscuit tin sitting on top of one of the boxes, illuminated in a shaft of dusty sunlight. But before I even reach it my stomach knows ahead of me that I'll find it empty, and when I pick it up and pop the lid, it's confirmed. Of course it's empty. Rosie's been through everything.

As I go to leave, I have a horrible thought. If Rosie *has* been through everything, she would have certainly found her... Bugger.

I climb down out of the loft and quietly raise the ladder again. That's why Rosie wrote the message on the back of the door, because I kept her All Stars. She probably thinks I've still got all the other evidence, too. The acid bottles and her bloodstained Elvis top. As far as Rosie Rey is concerned, Dina Young *is* a liar.

I don't need to wait until lunchtime to put this to bed. I'll get Rosie up here right now and apologise, reassure her that although I didn't burn the evidence, it *is* gone and we are in the clear. Keeping her All Stars was just a silly, stupid mistake and we can burn them together!

I pound on the bedroom door and call her name, and a couple of minutes later she arrives.

'You okay, Dina?'

'I know why you think I'm a liar.'

'You do?'

'You found your shoes in the loft, the ones I was supposed to burn.'

'I did.'

'And you think I didn't dispose of the other evidence or I've kept it for some reason—'

'Oh, no, Dina,' Rosie says. 'I took my bike out for a spin when you left the other day and I watched you dump it all in those bins, you know, down by the river?'

'You saw me do that?'

'Let me ask you something, Dina: do you think the extent of your lies runs to keeping a pair of my fucking sneaks?'

'I don't—'

'Have you even looked at those photographs?'

'Yes, but—'

'And?'

'And what? Were they taken in the summer, the winter? I don't know what you're getting at, Rosie, this is ridiculous!' I bang the door. 'Let me out!'

'Dear God,' Rosie says. 'Your delusion runs deeper than I thought.'

'What delusion? I'm an alcoholic, for goodness' sake. How many times have I got to bloody say it!'

'Wow. Looks like we're gonna have to try this a different way.'

And with that, Rosie walks off and I can barely contain a scream. Instead, I channel my anger and frustration onto the wall of photographs, ripping them from their Blu Tack buds and tossing them up into the air in a frenzy until I'm exhausted and crying on the bed. I lay here panting and sobbing for how long I don't know, until a noise at the window stirs me.

When I look down I see Rosie by the Saab. She's holding a petrol can in one hand and a length of what looks like my garden hose in the other. I then notice the Saab's petrol cap is open.

65

*Day four.*
Rosie served me my tea and toast this morning and then left the house without a word. I drank the tea and saved the toast, counted out my remaining eight cigarettes and decided I would allow myself two per day from this point on. I shouldn't be thinking in these terms – rationing – but my captor may have murdered two people in cold blood and set fire to their homes with them inside, and if I marry this to the fact that Rosie now carries a carving knife and has a can full of petrol, I'm going to do everything she says to the letter and pray I get out of this house alive.

By noon I've tacked all of the photographs back onto the wall, and even tried to break Rosie's cryptic clue about her lucky guess at Becky being a summer baby. If these photos point to me being a liar, based on the time of year they were taken, I can't see how. I eventually eat one of the two slices of toast, then fall asleep on the bed.

When I wake, the glare of the sun has slipped behind the evergreens, and I hear the frenzied chatter of birds as they prepare to settle in for the evening. I go to the window and smoke my last cigarette of the day, my stomach lurching at the thought of the last slice of toast.

Beyond the Saab the base of the trees is shrouded in darkness, and I'm thrown back into the dream I was having before I woke. Rosie is sitting there, looking up at me, the house ablaze in every room and thick smoke rolling by me into the gathering night. I turn towards the flames and know there's no escape, but – and this is why I call it a dream and not a nightmare – I'm unafraid, and relieved almost. When I glance down at Rosie again, Roy is sitting with her, as I knew he would be, and Becky is staring up from the driver seat of the Saab, her arms folded out of the window, her little chin resting on them. Who was I in that dream, I wonder? A wife? Becky's mother? Rosie's? Why didn't I care that I was just about to die? I take one more lug on the cigarette and drop the butt to the paving below, duck back inside just as Rosie's Beetle splashes onto the drive.

I take a seat in the chair and listen, hear the car door open and Rosie's feet crunch the gravel, followed by the rummaging of what I imagine is Rosie searching her bag for my keys. But then I hear another car door open and a second pair of feet hit the gravel.

'Hold up,' a man's voice says, and I peer over the windowsill.

The man's face is hard to make out in the semi-dark, but the denim jacket is a giveaway. It's Ben, from the AA meeting. He walks around the car and joins Rosie.

'You sure she's up for this?' he asks her, leaning into her ear as she unlocks the front door.

'I told you,' Rosie says. 'It was her idea.'

They enter the house and I hear the door being locked, the silence that follows, on and on. I go to the bedroom door, but again I can hear nothing. Why on earth has she brought him here? What was supposedly "my idea"?

Twenty minutes or more go by, and a third cigarette, when finally there's a knock at my door.

'Dina?' Rosie calls, but I don't answer. 'I'm coming in.'

I back away as Rosie unlocks the door and enters. She's holding the carving knife.

'Is that really necessary?' I ask?

'That depends on you, Dina. Gonna play nice? I've brought a friend.'

'Yeah, I saw. What's he doing here?'

'He just wants to hang,' she says, and without lowering the knife, she backs out onto the landing. 'You can lead the way.'

I'm frozen for a moment, but then I manage to move my feet. 'Where are we going?' I say once I'm out of the room.

'Basement,' Rosie says.

66

It's dark when I step into the basement, until Rosie switches the light on behind me.

'About time,' Ben says from somewhere down below. 'Starting to think you were pranking me.'

'No, no, honey,' Rosie says. 'Not a prank.'

When Ben comes into view, over in the corner, I first think he's on his knees, but when Rosie nudges me closer I can see he is in one of the excavation holes, sitting on a kitchen chair.

'I don't see why we can't do this upstairs,' he says, straining to look around at us, and then I see why he's straining.

There's a slim rope tied around his neck, which in turn trails down the back of the chair to his bound wrists. From there the rope trails under the chair to his ankles, where every time Ben shifts, he pulls the rope tighter at his throat.

'What's going on?' I ask Rosie, who skips over to Ben and straddles his lap, gnawing playfully at his neck with the childish sound effects to go with.

'Ben, here, thought he was onto a three-way, dintcha, dirty boy.' Rosie touches the tip of the carving knife to the underside of Ben's chin.

'What the fuck, Rose!' he shrieks, bucking under her weight, though still in semi-good humour.

Rosie kisses his cheek and climbs off  him.

'What the fuck's up with the knife, Rose?'

'Ssshhh, just a prop, to heighten your pleasure.' Ben goes to speak again. 'Uh-uh,' Rosie cuts in. 'You be quiet now, and let the grown-ups talk.'

'Why are we down here?' I ask.

'Did you give those photos another look-see today, Dina?' Rosie jumps into the hole with Ben and takes a seat on the concrete edge, gestures with the carving knife for me to do likewise in the adjacent hole. I do as she suggests.

'I did, yes.'

'Any more thoughts as to why Roy looks so... undone?'

'Rosie, that's just how he looks. Looked.'

'Wait,' Ben pipes up. 'There's not another guy turning up tonight, is there? That's not my scene.'

Rosie glares at him and he quiets again. 'Let's forget about Roy for a second. What did you make of *your* pictures, Dina?'

'Umm, I looked at them, I did, but even with your clue I couldn't—'

'Which clue? The one about the summer baby or the one about you being a liar?'

'Well—'

'Wanna know why I wrongly guessed Becky was a summer baby?'

'Okay.'

'You looked so flushed in the photo, and I thought, okay, it must be summer, coz you looked so hot and you were wearing a nice dress and shoes and not a jog suit and trainers, you know, you hadn't just come back from the gym or something. But then I thought, I've seen a face like that before, all flushed like that, and so I had to hunt through all your other photos to check, and that's how I knew you were a liar.'

'I don't see how.'

Rosie slants her head to look at Ben. 'She doesn't see how.'

'Look, Rose, I can see you two are getting into something here, so why don't you untie me? I can't feel my fucking feet anymore.'

'Soon, honey,' Rosie says, patting his thigh. 'But Dina doesn't see how, and as her sponsor, it's my responsibility to help her see.' Rosie climbs out of the hole and starts to pace around.

'Sponsor?' Ben asks, more to himself.

'You see, Dina, you're flushed in *all* of the pictures, but not *all* of the pictures were taken in the summertime. Agreed?'

I shrug.

Rosie looks back at me, from over where the cement mixer is standing. 'They're not.' She takes a seat on a stack of sandbags. 'Yeah, you've got the barbecues and the dinner party pics where everyone is dressed in their summer duds, but there are also pictures that are defo not taken in the summer.'

'Can't say I'd given it much thought.'

'I get that,' Rosie says. 'Why would you? Anyway, in a few of the pictures you can see your lovely coat stand in the background, and it's loaded with winter coats and scarves – winter, yeah?'

'I guess.'

'And in one there's a Christmas tree, so winter there for sure.'

'Okay.'

'Ladies, can I just—'

'Shut the fuck up, Ben,' Rosie shouts, and stabs the carving knife into the stack of cement bags next to her. 'Jeez, can't you fucking see we're talking?'

Ben actually looks like he is about to speak again and so I distract him, shake my head for him to be quiet. For God's sake be quiet.

'So, my issue is, *Dina*, why were you flushed in wintertime? Did you really have the heating jacked up that fucking high?'

'Not that I'd recall.'

'And nobody else is flushed – and I'm looking at you now, in this air-sucking heat, and well, you ain't flushed, Dina.' Rosie shrugs. 'A true fucking mystery, wouldn't you say?'

'It is strange, yes.'

'Oh, wait!' Rosie jumps down from the stack of sandbags, pulling the knife from the cement. 'Would you mind if I speculate, Dina?'

'Sounds like you're going to whatever she says, Rose,' Ben says.

I cringe, waiting for some form of retaliation, but thankfully Rosie doesn't bite, and comes closer.

'I speculate, Dina, that you are drunk in every single picture, and I can tell because I woke up to that face every day of my life – the flaming cheeks, the eyes like marbles...'

I swallow. 'Maybe. I never said I was teetotal before Becky.'

'No,' Rosie says, 'but you did imply at the AA meeting that it was Becky's death that drove you to alcoholism.'

'Actually,' Ben says to me, 'you did imply that.'

Rosie starts pacing again, waving the knife around as though she's regaling an invisible audience. A jury. 'Now I'm wondering if you weren't a drunk waaay before Becky's death, and waaay before Roy's ticker ticked its last tock. Just look at the poor man's face, Dina. He's not sad, he's destroyed, disgusted – he's seen it all before and he's sick of it.' Rosie stops and turns to me. 'Sick of you, Dina.'

'Roy loved me,' I say, 'and you have no right—'

'Loved!' Rosie's mouth drops open. 'He looks like he could crash a wine bottle over your head at any moment!'

'That's not true, we were very happy.'

'Girls, please, I can't feel my feet.'

'I don't get why he didn't leave you, though,' Rosie continues, tapping the knife blade against her chin in curiosity. 'My dad left my mother, eventually – she totally blamed me for it, as if being a lifelong gin sponge had nothing to do with it – but Roy supposedly stuck it out with you... hmm...'

'I was not a drunk!' I shout.

'Doesn't matter,' Rosie says. 'Getting off topic anyway. This process was never about whether or not you were a drunk – are a drunk, whatever, who gives a flying fuckeroo – it's all about when and why you decided to get sober. That's the crux of it, right there. And the important thing to remember, Dina, is that if I didn't think I could help you or couldn't save you from losing yourself to the oblivion, I would never have offered to be your sponsor.'

'You are not a sponsor, Rose,' Ben says. 'Now un-fucking-tie me!'

With her eyes still focused on mine, Rosie says, 'Which brings me to this weak excuse of a man.'

Ben bucks in his chair. 'Untie me, now, Rose. Dina, untie me, please.' But I can't. I am frozen in place.

Rosie puts her hands on Ben's shoulders and calms him. 'You see, Dina, Ben here is not like you. He's a lost cause, aren't you, Ben?'

'Rose, please, this isn't funny.'

'Did he tell you he has a daughter?' Rosie asks me, and I nod. 'Yeah, Lacy. Six years old and he only gets to see her once a fortnight, and you'd think that only being able to see her once every two weeks it would be easy to stay sober for long enough to give her the quality time she deserves, and not palm her off on a neighbour so he can go to the pub and get pissed with his waster mates. That to me, Dina, is not what I would call a "good" father.' Rosie tilts Ben's head back so she can see his upturned face. 'No, Ben, in fact I'd go as far to say that Lacy is better off without you.'

Three violent stabs to the neck and Ben doesn't even make a sound. He convulses, as an arc of blood paints the brick wall over two metres away and weakens to a wellspring erupting from his throat and mouth as he winds down like a child's toy.

I hadn't realised I'd been screaming until I ran out of oxygen, and then I scramble to my feet and stagger backwards to the nearest corner of the basement.

'You don't have to worry, Dina,' Rosie says, seemingly unaware of the blood she's covered in. 'I'm not going to hurt you.'

'You, you, you killed him, he's dead.'

'Think of Ben here as another Grant Chapman, or a Rolland Childress – the world's a better place without them.'

Rosie walks towards me, her hand out like I'm a child, and I can't crawl deep enough into the corner to get away from her.

'Come on, Dina,' she says, gently prising my trembling hand away from me. 'I'm going to get some soapy water and a scrubbing brush for the mess on the wall, and you're in charge of burying the body. We're both in this together, remember?'

'I can't,' I say. 'Don't make me.'

'Sure you can. I'll cut him from the chair and you can pour the concrete over him.'

'I don't, I can't...'

'Plug the mixer in,' Rosie says. 'Five parts sand to one part cement and add water to make a thick slurry. I googled it.'

Rosie lets me go and cuts Ben free from the chair. I stare at the blood she's left on my hand.

'Wakey, wakey, Dina. Here, take the chair. I'll run the hose down the stairs in a second.'

I shuffle over and take the chair from Rosie, stand it against the far wall. When I get back, Rosie has arranged Ben's body in the excavation hole. He looks like an unborn baby. A pending stillbirth.

*"There seems to be within all of us an innate yearning to be lifted momentarily out of our own lives into the realm of charm and make-believe."*

~ Dorothy Draper

67

Deep down I knew Roy could never forgive me, but I chose not to believe it, chose to ignore the fact we never made love anymore, that he could barely look me in the eye unless he had to. For Becky's sake.

When Roy's business was still in its infancy, he would invite colleagues over to the house on the last Friday of the month to brainstorm ideas and have a couple of drinks to unwind. It was a rotating bunch of maybe eight to ten people, men and women, but with a core group of four guys. I don't remember their names.

As the months wore on, the brainstorming sessions became secondary to the drinking and eating. Roy was putting on his vegan spreads, subliminally trying to push the company's future in a greener direction, and for the most part was succeeding. Of course there were a couple of people who were sceptical, who couldn't see big enough markets for meat-free products for what was essentially an omnivorous target group, but there was one guy in particular who was outright against it, and who thought the whole concept of fake food was ridiculous and against the laws of nature. As I said, I don't remember his name, but I took some guilty pleasure in setting down meat-based fare alongside Roy's plant-based, and even more guiltily enjoyed the winks I'd get from this guy as he dangled a cold-cut of salami over his mouth. To this day I'm still not sure if Roy fired him for his anti-vegetarian sentiments, or because he caught me going down on him behind the bushes at the back of the garden. One thing I am sure of though, as I stand here on the bed removing each of the photographs from the wall, is that *that* was the night Roy shifted from merely not loving me anymore, to out and out hating me.

Once I've collected all the photos together, I take them back up into the loft and sit by the rose window. From here I can just about see the art deco house across the road, its cruise-ship façade framed within the gap in the evergreens that forms the entrance to the driveway. It's never looked so far away, and I have never felt so alone.

My hands are rough, but I have no cream. It took me two hours to bury Ben last night, and literally blood, sweat and tears. When Rosie took me back to my room I stayed in the shower until my skin pruned, and cried myself to sleep, which thankfully came quickly and dreamlessly, until Rosie woke me this morning with tea and toast, and news that Darryl had left four messages about my solicitor holding up the sale of the house because I hadn't sent her the materials she'd asked for days ago. I don't know what these "materials" are because I haven't been able to access my email, and at this point, I don't really care.

Movement on the grounds of the art deco house. The captain of the ship, no less. I stupidly raise my hand, as if he could ever see me, as if I wasn't so utterly invisible to the world outside of this death veil of evergreens. I watch as a golden retriever bounds up to the captain, followed by a smiling woman in a wide-brimmed hat and sunglasses. So happy. So elegant. I look down at the clothes I was wearing days ago, because the clothes I had on last night I needed to bury in the hole with a dead man's body, along with Rosie's bloody clothes. I can still picture us, standing naked over Ben's concrete grave, Rosie telling me what a "sweet" job I'd done, before walking me back to my room at knifepoint, our sweaty bodies gleaming under the light of a fattening moon.

I wonder if the captain and his wife would notice if I smashed through the rose window and jumped—

I turn toward the loft hatch, to the sound of Rosie knocking on my bedroom door. It must be lunchtime.

68

D*ay six*. Or is it *seven*? I honestly can't tell anymore. Perhaps I should've notched the bedpost after all. When I come out of the en suite I see that Rosie has left me my tea and toast, but also an empty glass tumbler. I wonder if she wants me to start watering the lilies, which have begun to shed their petals. There has to be a point when it simply isn't worth bothering to keep something alive, and I wonder when Rosie will reach that point with me. Soon I expect, but not quite yet.

Yesterday Rosie mostly left me alone, only disturbing me to deliver my meals, which were more substantial than any I'd had on the previous days. Breakfast was the same, but lunch was a reasonably good-looking cheese omelette, and dinner an impressive Provençal chicken and veg dish, even if it was served straight from its oven-ready roasting tray with some of the cellophane still attached. Roy would have hated it, but that wasn't why I flushed it and the omelette down the toilet. I couldn't get Ben's grisly murder out of my mind, or the sea-sicky feeling I had when I poured the wet concrete over his face. At least Rosie brought me a packet of cigarettes. They helped to take the edge off both my hunger and my nerves.

Unfortunately, my pleas for my phone and access to email were not as well catered for, and I was met with the calm but firm reply of: 'We'll discuss those things tomorrow, Dina. Today is about resting and regaining your strength.' At least Rosie didn't ask me to put the pictures back on the wall.

After I force myself to eat a slice of toast, I shower, and as I'm towelling my hair dry, I hear a light knock.

'Dina?' Rosie calls. 'You ready?'

'I'm dressed if that's what you mean.'

'Great. Did you eat the toast?'

'Yes.'

'Great. Always a good idea to line the stomach.'

'Line my stomach?'

'You see the chest of drawers?'

'The chest of drawers? Umm, yeah.'

'Great. Pull out the bottom drawer, would you?'

I sit on the edge of the bed and reach down to the bottom drawer, tug it open. 'Clean towels, thanks.'

'No,' Rosie says. 'Beneath the towels.'

I lift out the top towel, a second and a third, then recoil and rush to the door and pound my palms against it. 'Rosie, what the hell are you playing at?'

'Been thinking, Dina. It's so silly that I can't let you have access to your phone and laptop, you know, so this whole house thing could be ticking along happily while we work through this process together. I texted Darryl and said I – by which I mean *you* – was having some personal issues and would get back to him asap—'

'You have no right! Let me out of here, Rosie!'

'Listen, asap could literally mean this very afternoon, but what I've come to realise is, when I say you're a liar, Dina, what I really mean is you're a fucking awesome liar, and I could keep asking the same question over and over and you'd just feed me your bullshit lies over and over and I'd be like, whoa, I should just set fire to this fucking house and walk away.'

'Rosie, listen to me—'

'But then I'm like, hmm, Ben was a lost cause, but you, Dina? You I can see on the other side of this. I think that whatever it is you're hiding – from yourself, not just me – I think whatever it is you're hiding you are secretly *desperate*, oh my God, *des-per-rate*, to get it off your chest, and as your sponsor it's my responsibility to facilitate that purge.'

'So you think locking me in a room with a litre of vodka is the answer?'

'It's highly irregular for a sponsor to be forcing someone who's in the programme to drink – Justin would literally shit a sheep, can you imagine? – but in this instance, Dina, I think it's highly appropriate.'

Utter madness...

'So, drink the vodka, Dina, all of it – and I'll know if you haven't, trust me – and when it's all gone, we can have a little chat and then I'll give you your phone and laptop back. How does that sound?'

I wither against the door, slide down it until my head is buried in my knees. It sounds crazy, that's how it sounds, because it is crazy.

'Dina?'

'The only thing I'll purge if I drink that vodka is the contents of my stomach. Burn the house down, I don't care anymore.'

'Nah, I have faith in you, Dina,' Rosie says. 'Call me when you're done.'

69

When I finally uncrumple myself from the floor, my hair is dry and my cheeks are soaked from my tears. I fall onto the bed and bury my face in the pillow, allow myself to be distracted by the kaleidoscope of colours that spring from the darkness behind my eyes. But not for long. I get up and cover the vodka bottle with the towels and close the drawer again. I'd wondered where Rosie had hidden it. Mystery solved. I look at the empty tumbler Rosie brought me this morning along with my tea and toast, and a second mystery is unpicked. I light a cigarette.

How have I come to be in this hideous position, and how far back in time would I have to travel to change it? What if I'd not opened the door to Detective Wallace, and let the news of Chapman's early release pass me by? What if I'd not gone to the AA meeting, or called Rosie from the top of the scaffold tower? What if I'd just slapped Grant Chapman around the face? Would that have been enough?

Of course not. The mark of a slap fades all too soon, and I wanted him to wear my pain every day, to look in the mirror, as I do, and be reminded of the thing he'd done. What he had taken from me. There is no point in time I could go back to. My malice would have brought me to some version of here, with or without Rosie's help. But as much as I know I am the orchestrator of my own demise, and that I deserve to be trapped in this hell, there is still something deep inside me that is fighting to be free, whether it deserves to be or not.

I finish my cigarette at the window, reminding myself that the bottle of vodka in the drawer had been in my freezer for months without me touching it, and that this is no different.

But it is so very different, isn't it? I'm different. Completely in tatters compared to who I was back then, when my only worry was the impending early release of the man who killed my daughter. How trivial an issue that seems now.

My cigarette burns down without me noticing, and I let it fall to the paving below. I'm about to light another when a black four-by-four pulls onto my drive and Mr Delevingne climbs out.

'Dina, who's this just pulled up?' Rosie asks through the door.

I walk over. 'Mr Delevingne. He's buying the house.'

'Well, not today he ain't. Get rid of him.'

'And how am I supposed to do that while I'm locked in here?'

'He's knocking now, Dina. Talk to him from the window, unless you want us to fill the other hole in the basement.'

I grab the damp towel from the bed and wrap my hair up, go to the window. 'Hello?'

Mr Delevingne backs away from my front door and removes his fedora to look up at me. 'Mrs Young.'

'Mr Delevingne,' I reply. 'I'm sorry I've just got out of the shower. Have you been knocking long?'

'Long enough,' he says in his southern lick. 'Now what's all this nonsense I'm getting from your lawyer. I don't think I could've been clearer about the speed with which I wanted this sale to go through – I got contractors lined up and I mean to oversee the breaking of ground, so to speak, before we fly home. Stonewalling me for more money will not work in your favour, Mrs Young. As God is my witness it won't.'

'I promise you, Mr Delevingne, I'm as eager to get this sale done as you are, but I'm having communication issues with my solicitor—'

'Well, let's see if I can't simplify things for you. If you haven't gotten your issues rectified by the end of business hours one week from this day, I'm withdrawing my offer.'

'Please, Mr Del—'

'I'm already offering you grossly over what the house is worth, and for the happiness of Mrs D I am gladly doing so, you understand. But do so understand that there is a point at which my wife's happiness crosses horns with my bullish pride, and that is the point I will not go beyond. Are we clear, Mrs Young?'

'One week from today.' I nod, but it feels more like I'm bowing my head in defeat.

Mr Delevingne straightens his fedora back in place and descends the front steps.

'Wait, Mr Delevingne! What day is today?'

He shakes his head but doesn't stop. 'One week, Mrs Young, and not a minute more.'

I watch from the window until he reverses out of the driveway, then drag the towel from my head and bury my face in it.

'Seems like you really need your laptop and phone,' Rosie says. 'I'll make sure they're both fully charged for when you finish that bottle.'

I scream and throw the towel at the door.

## 70

I've been sitting by the rose window for perhaps two hours or more, partly to get as far away as I can from the bottle of vodka, but also because the loft is the only place in this entire house that doesn't trigger a memory of Becky, and I wanted to conjure her up all on my own. Trapped within this ever-spiralling nightmare, I seem to have forgotten how to remember her without the visual echoes that stalk around every corner and beyond every door, like an acetate overlay, and so I imagined the loft would be the closest to feeling what it might be like living somewhere else, somewhere Becky isn't stitched into the fabric. I don't mean that to sound callous, or that I'm trying to push her to the back of my mind, it's just that I see her everywhere in this house and it's a torment, like the Saab torments me with Roy. I needed to be reassured that the future I'm fighting for is real, and that only my loving memories of Becky travel with me, and her tormenting ghost remains anchored here. But so far the only thing I can recall that isn't a memory attached to this house is the weight of her inside me, and that feeling draws me low.

Sounds truly awful, thinking of her in those terms, but no

more so than the fact I once had a daughter, and now I don't. That thought draws me lower.

And what of it all anyway! Even if I drink the damned vodka, I'm still not going to be able to give Rosie what she wants, whatever that is. But, hey, let's entertain the notion she doesn't burn me alive in my own house and instead gives me my laptop and phone and has done with me. I'll at best buy myself another week with the Delevingnes, and I'll still have a dead body to exhume from the concrete grave in my basement, which I will then have to dispose of somewhere without getting caught and imprisoned for murder! Because what could I say? *You have to believe me, Detective Wallace, I didn't kill him, it was Rosie Rey. I just buried him.*

Dear God, Rosie could just as easily turn this whole thing around on me – say that I'd forced her to give me an alibi for Chapman and his solicitor. After all, she had no motive, and me... I had all the motive in the world, and a dead body buried in my basement.

I scream into my palms, the heat and exhaustion of this hellish loft threatening to render me unconscious. I swoon, and in the brief second I drift back to clarity, the vodka pretends on my moistureless tongue, and at that point I know I've come undone. I'm going to drink the vodka, but not for Rosie or to be free of this house, I'm going to drink it to be free of my head, my thoughts, my pain. I'm going to drink it to be gone from this fucking reality, because my life has been an illusion up until this point, and I've only just come to understand, the way my husband and my daughter came to understand, that I have never really been here at all.

71

I t's dark when I rouse, half-dreaming that the captain's golden retriever is trying to drag me away, only to discover that it's Rosie. She's sitting on the end of the bed, tugging at my leggings.

'Wakey, wakey, Dina,' she says. 'I've brought you another drink.'

I don't speak, but I swallow, can feel the rasp in my throat and a familiar tang in my nostrils. I've vomited somewhere.

'Here you go, Dina. Drink up.'

I twist my legs over the side of the bed so I'm sitting next to her. Take the glass without question. I've not been asleep for so long that the thought of more alcohol is repulsive to me, though when I take the first mouthful my gag reflex spasms. A second mouthful calms the reflex and soothes my throat. The third reignites a welcome buzz and I feel a lazy smile creep onto my face. 'Rosie,' I say.

She stands and holds out her hand, her eyes bright in the moonlight. 'You can bring it with you,' she says.

'Cool.' I take her hand and she pulls me up. 'Where's Roy?'

'He's downstairs. I'll take you to him.'

Halfway down the stairs I stop to take another drink, squint at the monstrosity beside me. 'Whasat?' I ask Rosie, the echo of my voice trapped in the glass.

'That's a scaffold tower, remember?'

'I got one those,' I mumble. 'I tried to...' But the thought dissipates as we move on, through the beautiful moonlit entrance hall, the kitchen, and to the basement door. 'He down there?'

'He sure is,' Rosie says. 'Just stand there while I get the light. Okay, take my hand now, Dina.' I take her hand and she helps me down into the basement. Or is it the loft? So hard to tell, it's like a kiln in here.

'Roy?'

'Let's sit you down,' Rosie says, and walks me over to a tiny little chair, and I laugh when I realise it isn't tiny at all. The chair's in a hole. 'Here, let me take your drink and I'll give it back to you once you've sat down.'

'S'okay, won't drop.' I cup the glass to my chest, and Rosie lowers me down, into the chair. 'See? Didn't drop none.'

'Good girl,' Rosie says.

'Good girl, good girl.' I take another drink. 'Roy?'

'Can we talk about Roy, Dina?'

'Uh-hmm, old mister happy...'

Rosie crouches. 'Is he happy?'

I snort. 'No.'

'Why is that?'

I shrug. 'Dunno.'

'Dina, look at me.'

'I am. Why you got a knife, Rosie?'

'Tell me why Roy's unhappy.'

'I don't wanna talk about Roy anymore.' I go to drink but Rosie slaps the glass from my hand and it smashes across the concrete floor.

'Hey!' I look up and Rosie slaps my face. 'Ow, fuck, Rosie.' I start to cry, to wake.

'Tell me why Roy's unhappy or I swear to God I will stick this knife in your fucking neck, Dina.'

'Okay, okay!' I cry, getting a flashback to something horrific. Something bloody. 'I was unfaithful.'

'How many times?'

'Once.'

'Once?'

I shy my face away from the blade, my head ringing from the slap, the booze. 'Few times, can't remember.'

'Was that because you were a drunk, Dina? Was that why Roy looked so sick of you in those photos, because you were a sleep-around drunk?'

I nod, begin to sob.

'So why didn't he leave you?' Rosie asks, now pacing around me. 'Did you keep promising to get sober? Promise to clean yourself up?'

'Couldn't stop, even if I wanted...'

'So why didn't he leave you? Even my useless dad found the balls to leave my mother.' Rosie passes in front of me, the tip of the knife aimed at my face.

I sob even more. 'He stayed for Becky, not me.'

'See, don't it feel better getting it all off your chest, Dina? This is the process!'

I sniff. 'Are you gonna let me go now?'

'Let's see, shall we! Here's the biggy!' Rosie squats in front of me. 'What made you want to get sober?'

'I... I'd just had enough.'

'Ohh, so close, Dina! I was nearly out the door, but then, you know, you fucking lied again. Want another stab at it?'

'It's true, my doctor said if *I* didn't quit my liver would.'

Rosie nods seriously in my face. 'Yep, uh-huh, the doctor

said you should, yep, the liver thing, better quit, yeah, okay.' She stands and paces, batting her head this way and that, weighing my reasons, the knife swishing back and forth as if doing the same.

'I'm telling the truth, Rosie,' I say, terrified to look behind me to see what she's doing.

'So you're telling me it was for health reasons?'

'Yeah, yes.'

'Hmm, in that case, Dina, I think you deserve another drink.'

My body contracts as the cold liquid pours down me, soaking my hair, my clothes, stinging my eyes shut. Sobering me in an instant. At first I think it's vodka that Rosie has doused me in, but when my eyes spring open at the clattering sound in front of me, and I see the petrol can go tumbling into the stairs, I realise with horror that it isn't.

'Rosie, please, God, no.'

Rosie appears in front of me again, a lighter sparking playfully in her hand. 'So what you're telling me, Dina, is that in the few short days after your daughter is mown down by a drunk driver in the street, and your husband drops dead of a heart attack, you decide to go on a health kick? Yeah, calling BS on that shit.'

'Rosie...'

Rosie comes a step closer. 'Any normal person on the planet – *especially* a world class alcoholic such as yourself – after witnessing their whole family die before their very eyes in the space of days, would, I'd suggest, want to drink themselves into a coffin with immediate effect.'

I cover my ears. 'Stop it.'

Rosie crouches before me, ignites a flame and marvels at it. 'Your whole fucking family, dead, and you wanna get sober...'

'Please, stop it,' I cry.

'Little Becky, crushed against the school railings...'

'Shut up!'

Rosie holds the flame in front of my face. 'Last chance, Dina. If I can't help you, perhaps God can.'

I reap in a breath, the petrol fumes reaching deep into my lungs as I lean forward and scream: 'SHUT UP!'

A cold silence follows, as we both stare at the lighter I have just extinguished with my scream. Rosie looks at me and laughs, but I am filled with fear and rage. I strike out, snatch her hair and drag her with all my strength into the hole, and she plunges, her head thudding against the concrete lip on the other side. I spring from the chair and scramble to the stairs, expecting to hear her young feet slapping after me, but all I hear is her weakened voice call my name.

I crash through the basement door and spill into the kitchen, drag myself up again and make my way into the entrance hall and to the front door. I fumble with the latch for what seems like a decade, a growing wave of frustration building in my throat with every failed attempt to work the lock. I finally remember to check the bolts, but both the top and bottom ones are open, which means the door is locked, and Rosie has the key.

My only other way of escape is through the bifolds in the lounge, and I always leave the key in those. I stagger-run across the entrance hall towards the scaffold tower and start to negotiate the spiderweb of struts that have been blocking the lounge door for so long now, and crack my forehead as I try to duck beneath one. I'm dizzied, enough to buckle me at the knees had I not grabbed onto a vertical section of the tower, and then I will myself on, into the dark and unfamiliar lounge, but only to find the key missing from the lock and the bifolds stubbornly resistant to my attempts to work the handles. I want to cry, as I remember giving the key to Rosie when she moved herself into my home, my life.

I'm about to check the windows when a chilling scream erupts from somewhere in the bowels of the house, and I am frozen to the spot. There's silence for a moment, when all I can hear is the faint drip of petrol falling from me onto the concrete floor, then a second terrible cry rips through the dark – Rosie shrieking my name – followed by her crazed and feral declaration that I was going nowhere.

It's too late now to escape. I have no other option than to hide. I run to the scaffold tower and haul myself up, plant my foot onto the first strut, then the second. Hand over hand I climb, and at some point a drunken flashback sparks in my mind, to the night I'd scaled the tower and had to call Rosie to help me down. Even now, fleeing Rosie as I am, the thought of climbing down again is far more terrifying than the thought of climbing up, and I can't believe I'd even attempted it. But then I remember. The darkness driving me to the top of the tower that night, and why the return journey had held no fear...

I'd had no intention of climbing down again.

72

A breathless minute later and I hear Rosie's footsteps emerge in the kitchen, a chair scrape across the floor.

'Where are you, Dina?' she calls out. 'We were actually getting somewhere, I think.'

I peer over the edge of the scaffold tower platform and see Rosie enter the moonlit entrance hall, see her notice my wet footprints soaked into the concrete floor. See the knife blade glint in her hand. I crane my head back in again, my heartbeat ricocheting around inside my chest.

'We can finish this right now, Dina. Put this nasty business behind us and get on with our lives, how does that sound?'

It sounds like she's directly beneath me, that's how it sounds, and my body clenches at the thought, tighter still when I detect a faint tremor chime through the tower. She's climbing up, dear God, she's climbing up here and she's going to cut my throat open and I'm going to bleed to death next to a puddle of my own congealing vomit, the vomit that had stopped me from—

No, Rosie's not climbing up, she's climbing through, into the lounge, following my footprints. I draw in a shallow breath and fight the urge to scream.

'Come on, Dina, this is silly,' she calls, her voice sounding more distant. 'You can't hide in here forever.'

And she's right. I have nowhere left to go. I hear furniture shifting in the lounge, the sweeping of the curtain rail, and then Rosie's slow footsteps returning.

'How curious,' she says, her words drifting up from beneath me again. 'Your footprints seem to have disappeared, Dina. It's like you've evaporated.'

A tap-tapping rings through my bones. The knife blade chiming against the tower. Of course Rosie knows where I am. She's tormenting me.

'You coming down, or are you going to make me climb up there?'

I glance around at the arch window, to the full moon that's framed within it. I realise now, if I had the ability to travel back in time, that it would be to here, to when I'd climbed the tower last. If only I'd had the courage to finish what I'd set out to do, to throw myself off and end it all, I'd have never called Rosie. Never invited her into my life. Never done all those terrible things... But I'd been too drunk to even get that right, and I'd vomited before I could—

'Okay, Dina,' Rosie says. 'Have it your way.'

The tower begins to tremble as Rosie begins to climb, but I am through with fear. I can't erase the things I've done, but I can escape this nightmare. I sit myself up, onto my knees. All I have to do is lean forwards...

'There you are,' Rosie says from somewhere behind me, but I do not turn to look. I'm swaying now, moving closer and closer to the point I won't be able to stop myself from falling. I hear Rosie clamber onto the platform, and faster and faster I sway, leaning out farther and farther, until I know I'm done with it all.

Done with Rosie, with life, with me. I close my eyes. It's finally over. I let myself fall...

'Dina, no!'

A clatter of feet, followed by a bright stinging in my scalp as Rosie pulls me back from the edge by my hair. I lunge forward with a scream, trying to wrench free of her grip, and a second sting flares as the tip of Rosie's knife sweeps down my brow, my cheek. I clap my hand over the burning cut and fall onto my side and curl myself into a ball, waiting for the frenzied attack I'd seen from Rosie before, but to my disbelief, no attack comes. I stay that way for how long I don't know, panting, eyes clamped shut. Why doesn't she finish me?

And then I realise why, when I see the congealed vomit streaked across the scaffold tower platform.

73

I peer terrified over the edge of the platform, and see Rosie lying on the concrete floor below, her right leg hinged at a sickening angle to the knee, the knife a few inches away from her open hand. From this distance I can't tell if her eyes are open, or if she's alive or dead, until she coughs weakly. I duck back behind the platform, wincing from the pain of the cut that traces my brow and bloody cheek.

'Dina...' Rosie's voice carries to me, a pinched whisper that doesn't sound like her at all. 'Dina... I... I can't feel my hands, Dina...'

I physically shiver, but risk a second look, even though I'm convinced I'm going to see Rosie already climbing the tower again. But no, she's lying in the same position, on her back and unmoving apart from her expression, which is a mixture of disbelief and confusion, like Becky awakening from a deep sleep.

'I can't feel my legs, either,' she says, and coughs a rivulet of blood from the side of her mouth and I can't bear it any longer.

'I'm coming, Rosie. Hold on, I'm coming.'

With my hands slicked with blood, sweat and petrol, I

somehow manage to climb down from the scaffold tower. My mothering instinct resurfacing perhaps, to conquer my fear of falling, or more probably my guilt. I kneel beside Rosie, not caring which.

'Oh, Dina, look at your face,' Rosie says. 'I didn't mean to, I promise. I would never hurt you. Petrol's mostly water... I was just trying to make you...'

I take Rosie's hand and it's lifeless as a mannequin. 'You stopped me from falling. You should have let me go.'

'I only ever wanted to help you—' Rosie coughs and another trickle of blood spills from her mouth. I move closer and raise her head onto my lap, stroke her face.

'You couldn't help me,' I tell her, as a tear – or is it blood? – falls from my cheek into Rosie's hair.

'You're not a lost cause, Dina. My mother was a lost cause, blaming me for Dad leaving us. That's why I killed her – not because I hated her, because I loved her. I couldn't bear to see her tormented for another day, unable to stop drinking, to stop hurting me, even though she knew I didn't deserve it. Torture for both of us. But you... you can still come back from this.'

I push her hair from her forehead. 'Too far gone now, Rosie.'

'No, Dina. Just... just admit the things you've done and forgive yourself, that's it.'

'But I can't do that if the things I've done are unforgivable.'

'I'll forgive you, Dina, I promise.'

A sob racks my body and I have to look away from her, my watery eyes settling on the arch window, on the moon. *It's like God staring down at me...*

'On the day I collected Becky from school, I was late,' I tell Rosie, my hand on her cheek. 'I was late because I'd been drinking all afternoon, and I'd passed out on the sofa, and I might never have turned up at all if the cigarette I'd been smoking hadn't fallen onto my arm and burned me awake.

Anyway, as we were walking home, playing that silly game of not stepping on the cracks, I drunkenly stumbled into Becky, causing her to stumble, and bless her, she tried so hard to get her little legs back underneath her, but she couldn't quite make it, and by the time she actually fell she was in the middle of the road, and when she got to her feet, Grant Chapman's car—'

'Stop, Dina, you don't have to say any more,' Rosie pleads. 'I forgive you, I forgive you, and you have to forgive yourself. You're not that person anymore.'

My tears are still falling in Rosie's hair as I look down at her. 'You don't understand, Rosie. I can't forgive myself, and you can't forgive me either.'

'I can, and you can, Dina.'

'No, Rosie,' I say, 'because after that, I did something much, much worse.'

## 74

It was two days later, and I'd taken a packet of cigarettes and a bottle of vodka into the Saab. I had to get out of the house, you see, because I couldn't bear Roy's eyes on me for a second longer, and I couldn't bear the house itself, which wherever I looked I saw my dead daughter. The daughter I had killed.

I'd spent a couple of hours in the driving seat, drifting in and out of consciousness, my in-between rants and rambles steaming the windows against the bitter December chill. At some point Roy must have come out to check on me, to wake me, because he was suddenly standing in the open door of the Saab and he was shaking me.

'What did you say?' he was shouting. 'Say it again! What did you just say!'

I was disorientated, of course, and didn't know why he was so angry, and so I tried to push him away so I could reach for the vodka, which had fallen into the footwell. But before I could get my fingers around the neck of the bottle, Roy slapped me across the mouth and threw me back against the seat.

'You fucking drunken bitch!' he screamed into my face. 'You

knocked her into the road? You killed our daughter? You killed Becky?'

'What? No...'

'That's what you were crying about just now, in another one of your fucking stupors. You said you knocked her into the road!'

'I didn't—'

'I just fucking heard you, Dina,' he roared at me, 'the actual words coming out of your mouth!'

'I mean, I didn't mean to, it was an accident – or maybe she tripped, I can't remember—'

Another slap around the mouth, and then another. I covered my face, but only so Roy couldn't see me, and I waited for the slaps to become punches, deserved punches, but they never came. When I finally roused the courage to open my eyes, Roy was kneeling on the driveway, clutching his arm and biting his lip in pain, face growing redder and redder.

'My pills,' he said through his gritted teeth, his white breath short and sharp in the freezing air. 'My pills...'

I slipped by him and staggered into the house, swaying from room to room as though on a boat in a storm, in search of his elusive heart pills that seemed to be in a different place every time he needed them, because I was always drunk while I searched. I finally found them in his briefcase, and ran back outside to find him sprawled across the driver's seat of the Saab, clutching his chest. I darted around to the passenger side and lifted his head up onto me, cracked open the pill bottle and spilled a few pills into my palm.

'Quickly,' Roy grunted, his bottom lip protruding, waiting for me to drop the pills onto his lolling tongue. But I didn't.

'Can you ever forgive, Roy?' I asked him. 'Can you?'

He couldn't speak, but he could shake his head, spittle raging from his mouth.

'Please, Roy, you have to. I can't live with myself—'

'Then die,' he managed, his face as red as blood. 'You killed my daughter, should've been you...'

In that moment, I knew I could never bear the shame of anyone knowing what I'd done to our daughter, and so I closed my hand around the pills, and let my husband die in the seat next to me, and that's what got me sober. The shock of how I had failed as a wife and mother, how far I had fallen as a human being. And as the shock dulled over time, the shame kept me sober, but even that I could feel wasn't going to last, and I so wanted to stay dry. To keep the pain bright.

But then when I found out Grant Chapman was going to be released early, I knew I was in trouble. You see, he's the only other person alive that knew what I'd done, seen me knock Becky into the road. Made no difference that he only mounted the pavement in an attempt to miss her. A dozen witnesses agreed with my version of events, and at three times over the legal limit to drive, who was going to believe him, and to what ends? That's why when Chapman got sent down for a miserly two years, he winked at me. Not out of malice, but as a *fuck you*, to acknowledge that I was just as much to blame, and that his sentence was fair, as was mine.

'And that's when I met you, Rosie, my love, my sponsor,' I say, crying so hard now as I look up at the moon, as I struggle to maintain the pressure over her nose and mouth. 'You don't deserve this, after the life you've had, but it has to be this way. Don't hate me.'

When I remove my trembling hands, I lean down to make sure Rosie isn't breathing. I kiss her eyes.

It's a struggle to drag her down to the basement, a different kind of struggle to find her All Stars and put them back on her feet where they belong, but I know what I'm doing now with the cement mixer, and once Rosie is in the other hole, I make quick work of burying her.

Afterwards I shower and bandage my brow and cheek, drink two mugs of coffee at the kitchen table to sober me up sufficiently so I can drive. I then erase all traces of Rosie from the house, stuff every single item she brought with her into her suitcases and load them into her car. I haven't driven for so, so long, but I somehow manage to drive Rosie's Beetle down near the train station and park it in a little side street. I wipe the steering wheel and the door handle clean with the hem of my T-shirt, and lock it and walk away, heading back along the river, where I toss her keys into the moonlit water.

<h1 style="text-align:center">75</h1>

THREE DAYS LATER...

Alcoholism is fine if you're doing it for the right reason, and I'm of the same opinion about sobriety. Eighteen months ago, I finally ran out of any good reason to stay drunk, but today, I think I've run out of any good reason to stay sober.

I reach across the kitchen table for the tall glass of vodka I've poured, which I've been staring at for some time now, but the glass doesn't reach my lips.

Ahh, saved by the bell. The doorbell. I'm not expecting anyone, but I can guess who it will be.

'Detective Wallace,' I say when I open the front door. 'Another hot one.'

'Hello, Mrs Young,' he says, dabbing his forehead with a handkerchief and briefly glancing at my bandaged brow and cheek. 'Do you have a minute?'

'Would that be a doorstep minute, or do you need to come inside?'

His awkward smile says he remembers this exchange, but also that he does need to come inside. I open the door wider and glance towards the kitchen.

'I'd offer you one, but I'm guessing you're on duty,' I say.

He looks at the glass of vodka, the bottle next to it on the table. 'Is there someone you can call?'

'You mean like my sponsor?' I grab a glass from the cupboard and waggle it. 'Water?'

He nods. 'Is she around?'

'Rosie?' I place his glass of water down in front of the chair opposite mine. 'She left a few days ago.' I take my seat, gesture for him to do the same.

'Thank you.' He places the iPad he's carrying on the table, swings off his jacket and hangs it on the back of the chair. Not a flying visit it would seem. 'Did she say where she was going, or who with?'

'What's this about?'

Detective Wallace takes his seat. 'We're looking into a missing persons report, a Benjamin McCauley?'

'Sorry, am I supposed to...'

'He's a regular attendee at the community centre AA meetings.'

'That's probably why I don't recognise the name.'

'Well, that's how you met Ms Rey, so I thought I'd ask.' He sips his water.

I want so badly to drink my vodka, but I have a terrible habit of talking too much when I'm under the influence, and I feel like I'm talking too much as it is.

'And I understand that Ms Rey and Mr McCauley had something of a relationship at one time, and that she was possibly the last person to be seen with him, at the Crown pub, six nights ago. McCauley had left his daughter with a neighbour, and then never returned home.'

'That's awful,' I say. 'I hope he turns up soon, his daughter must be frantic.'

'She's back with her mother now.'

'Sounds like the best place for her.'

'What do you mean?'

'An alcoholic that works in a pub,' I say. 'It's not a recipe for success.'

Detective Wallace shifts in his chair. 'How did you know he worked at the pub?'

'Oh, umm...' Because I bloody met him there once! It's no good, I take a drink of my vodka, heaven and hell in a single sip. 'I just assumed that's what you meant. Is there anything else I can help you with, Detective Wallace?'

He holds me in his gaze for a moment, then tugs down his necktie and opens his shirt collar. 'Actually, Mrs Young, I think there's something I can help you with.'

'For God's sake call me Dina.' I take another sip of my vodka, a larger one this time, and return the glass to the table with a little more force than I'd meant. He stares at the glass and then me.

'Okay, *Dina*. And call me Remy, won't you.' He wipes his forehead again with his handkerchief and folds it back into his pocket.

I pick up my glass. 'Okay, *Remy*, how can you help me?'

'Well, we went to Ms Rey's flat—'

'*Rosie*, for God's sake.'

He lifts a hand to apologise. 'Rosie. We went to Rosie's flat, but she wasn't there. We checked with her neighbour, and they said she hadn't been there for some time.'

'Obviously, she'd been here.'

'Until recently, yes, but her neighbour said she hadn't been home at all, and they were worried about her. So we broke in.'

'And?'

'She wasn't there, and it looked like she'd packed some clothes, some toiletries, and we couldn't find any luggage to speak of, so...'

'So you think she's gone on a little trip with this guy?'

'I hope so, Dina, for his daughter's sake, I hope so.'

'What's that supposed to mean?'

Detective Wallace – *Remy* – looks around, at the kitchen door, the ceiling, then semi-whispers, 'She's definitely not here?'

'I told you, she left days ago. What are you getting at, *Remy*?' I take another sip, staring at the iPad he's brought. *Stay calm, stay calm, Dina.*

'I told you I had concerns about Rosie's mental stability, based on her medical history and the irregularities raised by the prosecution at her trial—'

'And I asked Rosie about that, and she assured me it was self-defence.'

'And you believed her?'

'Yes. Her mother abused her, burned her with cigarettes and blamed Rosie for her husband leaving, and after years of suffering, Rosie finally decided to defend herself.' I lean forward. 'Rosie was a product of her upbringing. It wasn't her fault.'

'And what about Rolland Childress?'

'What about him?'

'Somebody stabbed him in the neck and then burned his house down.'

'So you claim, but I noticed you wouldn't show me a coroner's report to confirm that.'

'What reason could I possibly have had to lie about something so serious?'

'I don't know.' Another drink, a little spills down my chin and I cuff it away. 'It was a bluff. You were trying to trip me up because you didn't believe our stories about a movie night. You thought we were lying, but we weren't.'

'You're right, Dina, I did think you were lying, and I do still think you're covering for Rosie regarding her whereabouts on the night of Rolland Childress's murder.'

I lean back in my chair and scoff. 'Murder...'

'Yes, Dina. Murder.' Detective Wallace – I refuse to even think of him as *Remy* now – opens up the iPad. 'We searched Rosie's flat, to see if we could find a hotel booking or train tickets for somewhere, but instead we found this.' He slides the iPad across the table.

'What is it?' I ask, but don't bother to look.

'It's a legal document that Rosie took from Childress's home before she set fire to it. We found it at Rosie's flat. This is just a photograph, obviously.'

'If you say so.' I unscrew the cap of the vodka bottle and top myself up.

'It contains all the information regarding your daughter's trial, including Childress's handwritten notes that raised concerns about your drinking on the day of your daughter's death, and that—'

'Lies.'

'And that there was a conflicting statement taken on the day that suggested you might have, *accidentally*, Dina – I am not trying to cause you any distress – that you might have *accidentally* knocked your daughter into the road and into the path of Grant Chapman's car.'

'Lies!'

'Now this is incidental. There is no question that Chapman was over the limit to drive, or that he mounted the pavement and caused the death of your daughter, but what I'm saying, Dina, is that Rosie had read all of this, and may have come to the conclusion that you were also responsible for your daughter's death and that alcohol had played a large part in that.'

I stand and throw my glass into the sink, where it smashes royally. 'I want you to leave now.'

Detective Wallace stands with me, but keeps his distance. 'I believe that Rosie, for whatever reason, took an unhealthy interest in you, and got you mixed up in something that was completely out of your control—'

'I don't know how many more times I can say it.' I pick the vodka bottle from the kitchen table, and he raises his hands, thinking I'm going to throw it too, but instead I take a deep drink, then shout, 'We were together having a movie night, for God's sake!'

'Childress's fingerprints are on the file, Dina, as are Rosie's, and we found the file at her flat. There's no other explanation.'

'We. Were. Together.'

He nods. 'Okay, okay, Dina. Can we sit back down for a second, there's something else I want to show you. Please.'

I take a few calming breaths, and fetch another glass from the cupboard, sit back down and pour.

Detective Wallace doesn't retake his seat this time, but instead crouches next to me with the iPad. 'We also found this, on Rosie's laptop. She'd downloaded it from her phone.'

'What is it?'

'Here, a short film, just watch.' He angles the screen towards me and presses play.

At first it's just darkness and I can't see much of anything, but then a pool of light comes into focus. A streetlamp. Then a figure emerges as it approaches the light, a pathway, a park bench, followed by a sickening swell in my throat as I recognise the orange T-shirt Grant Chapman had been wearing on the night I killed him.

I turn away to drink. 'Complete and utter bullshit.'

'Please, Dina, just a few moments longer.'

I do as he asks, and turn back in time to see myself stumble from the bushes, the awkward exchange that follows before Chapman attacks me and I have to squirt the acid in his face to escape, then Detective Wallace pauses the footage, just as I climb to my feet and turn to the camera.

'I believe this is you, Dina.'

'You cannot possibly see that, the face is entirely in shadow.' And it's true. Nobody could tell that was me. I only know because it *is* me, and I was there.

'I believe that this is you squirting acid into Grant Chapman's face—'

I shake my head fiercely. 'No…'

'But I also believe you had no intention of killing him, Dina – please, Dina, just watch.' He hits play again and I watch Grant Chapman writhe on the ground, and soon after, I have disappeared into the shadows. 'Keep watching.' And I do, as the camera comes on and on, and Grant Chapman's writhing body gets bigger and bigger, until the camera is almost in his face, and a girl says, 'Jeez, I just saw what happened, let me see, honey, let me see.' And after some more flailing, and the girl coaxes Chapman's hands away from his blistering face, she says, 'This is what you get for killing an innocent child, you fucktard.' And then the nozzle of a squeezy bottle is plunged into Chapman's moaning mouth like warm milk into a crying baby, and the camera spins wildly, briefly catching the wheels of a silver racer in the blaze of the streetlamp, and then all goes dark.

I stand from my chair again and turn away, hugging the vodka bottle to my chest.

'I don't think for a second you intended for Grant Chapman to die, and nor do I think this was in any way your idea.' Detective Wallace places his hand on my shoulder and I flinch. He removes it. 'Sorry. Was this all Rosie's plan? Did you even know that you hadn't killed him, Dina?'

I swig from the bottle, my head shaking, tears falling.

He tries his hand on my shoulder again. I let him. 'I doubt you'll serve any time for this, Dina. It's clear you've been targeted by a very sick young lady who's been playing out some maternal revenge on your behalf, and she needs to get psychiatric help before she hurts anyone else. We'll get you a good solicitor, take a statement—'

'No,' I say.

'It'll be fine, Dina. If you're worried about Rosie – did she do this to you?' He gestures at my brow and cheek and I pull away from him.

'No,' I repeat.

'She'll be in custody very soon, I can promise you that, and if you just tell the truth, and with the evidence we have here against her, and her medical history, I've no doubt Rosie will corroborate coercion and you'll be—'

'I said no.' I take a couple of deep swallows from the bottle and point to my cheek. 'Rosie didn't do this, I did it to myself, and whoever is in that footage, it isn't me or Rosie. I've told you, we spent both of those evenings together, watching Kate Winslet and Leonardo DiCaprio – who is sex on a hickory stick, by the way – and we have witnesses that corroborate this fact.'

'Dina, we took this footage straight from Rosie's laptop, and we have her fingerprints on Childress's file, which we also found at her flat. This isn't going to wash, I'm afraid.'

'Detective Wallace. *Remy*. If Rosie has carried out some revenge fantasy on my behalf, she's done so without my knowledge. If she paid somebody to carry out that horrific attack on Grant Chapman, then she did so without my knowledge. And if she paid somebody to murder a solicitor and steal a legal file from him to somehow further this obsession she has with me and the death of my daughter, then she did so without my knowledge. All I can verify is our whereabouts on the nights these crimes took place, because we were together, and that's the only thing I can tell you. The truth.'

He shakes his head and smiles, but it's bitter. 'It isn't the truth, though.'

'It's the only truth that *I* know,' I say, taking another

mouthful of vodka. 'When Rosie gets back from her jaunt with the alcoholic – who might be acting as her accomplice in all this, if that has even crossed your mind – you can ask Rosie for her version, but either way, it has nothing more to do with me.'

Detective Wallace stands there staring at me for a moment before his eyes fall away, then collects the iPad from the table and folds his jacket over his arm. 'You're playing a very dangerous game in defending her,' he says. 'I hope it doesn't come back to bite you.'

'I'll show you to the door,' I say.

Detective Wallace steps outside into the sun, squints up into the cloudless sky. 'I suppose there's *some* truth in all of this,' he says.

I should just close the door, but I can't help myself. 'Some?' I ask.

He nods, only half turning to me. 'The contradictory statement Childress had on file, from the person who claimed to have seen you knock your daughter into the road. They were telling the truth.'

'If that were so, he would have called them as a witness.' I go to close the door.

'I think Childress may have felt that you'd been through enough, perhaps instead used the statement to bargain down his client's tariff. But they were telling the truth, Dina.'

'You cannot possibly know that, Detective, you weren't there, so you can take your ludicrous speculations and please leave—'

'You don't remember, do you?' He still doesn't turn to face me, and seems more interested with the entrance to my driveway. 'Me driving you home that day?'

'I do actually. So what?'

'You had a small bottle of vodka in your bag, and you drank most of it on the way home.'

'It's called grief.'

'And while you were drinking, you were doing an awful lot of talking, and saying how it was all your fault, all your fault.'

'What on earth are you implying?'

'And then later that day we took Chapman's statement, and for some reason he kept on insisting that he never mounted the pavement, and I remember thinking at the time what a stupid thing to contest, considering where the car ended up, clearly on the pavement, and then he was convicted and I never gave it another thought, until just now.' Detective Wallace turns to me.

'I'm closing the door,' I say, knowing full well that I won't be able to. 'What happened just now?'

'Reading Childress's file, and that contradictory statement. If I'd known about that person's statement at the time, I would have put it all together back then.'

'And do what exactly?'

He shrugs. 'Absolutely nothing. Chapman was a piece of shit, and you'd just lost your only daughter. Whether or not a jury knew the details of how that tragedy came about, it wouldn't have brought her back.'

I swig from the bottle and a tear spills from my eye.

Detective Wallace slips his jacket on, his attention returned to the entrance of my driveway. 'Besides, I'm sure you've tortured yourself over it, and for some people, that can be a worse sentence than any judge can give.'

'What the fuck would you know about it?' I scream, and throw the bottle at him. He doesn't even flinch it misses so wildly, smashing against the side of the Saab. 'You think losing a wife is anything like being responsible for the death of a daughter!'

He glances towards the Saab, towards the smashed bottle of vodka, adjusts his tie, cinching the knot back tightly to his throat. 'My wife died of cancer, and no, I don't think that's the same as losing a daughter, especially how you lost yours, Dina. But a month before she was diagnosed, I left her for another woman, for a relationship that didn't even last two months, and when I realised what a fucking stupid thing I'd done, when I realised how much I loved her, I tried to go back to her but she wouldn't have me, and I couldn't be with her when she died. So I do know about torturing yourself.' He looks off again. 'Congratulations, by the way.'

I can't speak for fear of sobbing, can barely muster the energy to follow his gaze.

He points. 'Old boy just collected your SOLD sign. You'll be out of here soon.'

I step outside to see the white-haired old man from the other day load the SOLD board into the back of his little van.

'No, I've taken it off the market.'

'Decided to stay?'

I close my eyes and faintly nod.

'I can understand that,' Detective Wallace says. 'Sometimes it's hard to let go of the memories.'

*"I am just a copier, an impostor. I wait, I read magazines. After a while my brain sends me a product."*

~ Philippe Starck

It's fully dark when I wake, and at first I'm disorientated, forgetting that I'd spent the rest of the day smoking and drinking in the Saab, talking to Roy. I don't know how many times I've apologised to him in this car, hoping for some ghoulish message to come through from the other side, a sign that tells me I am forgiven. Of course, there never is one, but I do take some comfort from the act of confession itself.

When Detective Wallace reminded me today about our journey home, on the day Becky died, it all came back to me. Not the words I had used to confess to him what I'd done, but the feeling it gave me. The telling of the truth. The unburdening. The taking of responsibility. It was almost a religious experience that I didn't want to end, and I remembered thinking, as soon as Roy gets home I would tell him everything, tell him the truth about who I really am and unbottle myself of the lies and whether he chose to leave me or not wouldn't matter. I would be emptied of it all, and under the eyes of God, be absolved.

Selfish to the bitter end, of course. There wasn't anything I could confess to Roy that he didn't already know. He knew I was a heavy drinker when we first met, and that we both hoped as we moved on together, Roy's straight-backed approach to life would somehow rub off on me and drag me along my desired career path. I know I certainly hoped so, it's just a shame it didn't turn out that way.

I flunked my Art and Design degree, despite Roy's help, but I still threw myself into the interior design world, subscribed to every magazine and openly dreamed, to anyone who would listen, about my plans to one day run my own business. True creative talent didn't need a certificate, I would tell Roy, who grew tired very quickly of my "all talk, no action" rhetoric.

He first started out with a great deal of enthusiasm and encouragement, trying to nurture within me a pragmatic approach to interior design, something financially tangible to anchor to the creative aspect of the business. But all I gave Roy in return, as I wafted around the house with a vodka and tonic in one hand and a cigarette in the other, were famous quotes from long-dead designers and daydreams of how I saw the house coming together thematically, conceptually, and spiritually. Roy's work gatherings became the arena for my lofty ideas for the place, but where Roy used to engage in these conversations, he then started to avoid them, and by the end was actively saving people from getting trapped in a corner with me.

It was never my idea to open up the ceiling space in the entrance hall, Roy wanted to remove a bedroom for some reason, I forget why. And the basement... Roy was going to turn it into a growing room, to cultivate a crop of organic shiitake mushrooms, if you can believe it.

But the one thing we both knew and never, ever discussed, was that Becky's learning difficulties were due to her underdeveloped brain, which was caused, probably, if not definitely, by my heavy drinking and smoking throughout the pregnancy. I feel sorry for Roy about that. There really was nothing he could do or say to stop me. It was my body, and he was being like he always was, a tiresome overanalyser and a joy-suck to be around. Rosie asked me how Roy didn't leave me, and the answer is, because of the drug charge he had against him, a charge I assured him would factor heavily in any custody battle we had over Becky. He couldn't risk losing his daughter to a mother that needed to sleep with a glass of vodka by the bed, just in case she woke up sober in the middle of the night, and I can't say I blame him.

I reach for the bottle of vodka beside me on the passenger seat, light a cigarette, and as I sit here in the Saab, which I haven't legally been able to drive since the first week Roy bought me it and I reversed it, drunk, into a postbox, I come to a profound understanding of what it is I must do to have any hope of saving my soul in the eyes of God. Tomorrow morning I am going to call Detective Wallace and I will confess to everything I have done and damn the consequences. It's the only way. And I am not doing it to make myself feel better, I'm doing it because if I ever see my daughter again, I need for her to know that I love her and I am sorry, and I can only do that if I'm able to look her in the eyes, and I'll only be able to do that if first I am able to look at myself.

Yes, tomorrow. Tomorrow, tomorrow, tomorrow...

## 77

TWO WEEKS LATER…

It is so wonderful to be painting again, to have the creative juices flowing. I'm positively giddy with joy!

Seafoam, Parakeet, Persian Green – I've mixed them all by eye for the leaves, and used Bumblebee, Flaxen and Tuscan Sun for the flowers. I hope Rosie doesn't mind, but I bought a pair of white dungarees to wear while I'm working, to become something of a canvas, a narrative if you will, of my journey in colour. I also bought myself a pair of All Stars. Flamingo Pink. I wouldn't want her to think I was copying.

The doorbell. I lean out of my bedroom window and see a woman in a wide hat at the front door. 'Hello?'

The woman looks up at me. 'Hello, Mrs Young, it's Mrs Delevingne.'

'Dotty! Come on up, the door's open.'

A few moments later and Mrs Delevingne is standing in my bedroom doorway.

'Dotty, how wonderful to see you.' I kiss her on both cheeks, and she studies mine.

'Dear, whatever happened to your face?'

I touch my scar. It angles down across my brow and onto my cheek, and looks as though it has been knitted together by the scar I have on my eyelid. It's still quite raw, so I can't yet apply concealer. 'Just a scratch,' I say.

'Dear, that is no scratch, and I'm no nurse, but I'd say that needs looking at, lest you want a raggedy scar on your pretty face for the rest of your life?'

'I barely notice it,' I say. 'Can I get you a drink?'

Dotty looks at my glass on the bedside cabinet, the bottle of vodka next to it. 'It's a tad early for me, dear, and besides, we're flying back to the States later this afternoon.'

'Of course. I'm sorry about the sale of the house.' I go back to my work, choose a thicker brush this time.

'I'm sure you have your reasons, Dina, but if you should change your mind at all in the future, I want you to know you can call me, anytime. Our offer will still be there.'

'That's so sweet of you, Dotty, but I doubt I'll ever change my mind. This house holds too much history for me. Too many memories...'

'I understand, dear. It's funny, walking along this landing and not seeing my mother's bedroom anymore, and yet it still feels like it always did.'

'Of course, that was your mother's bedroom we removed, to gain the double height in the entrance hall.' I take a little Tuscan Sun and apply it to the petal I'm working on.

'She died in that room. Peacefully in her sleep, thank the good Lord.'

'It's how we'd all like to go,' I say.

Dotty walks over to the corner of the bedroom, to where I'm working. 'What is that you're doing, dear?'

'Well,' I say, stepping back to stand with her. 'It's a flowering vine.'

'It's a very creative way of disguising the crack.'

'Isn't it?' I smile at her. 'It's the subsidence crack. It runs right the way through the house and down into the basement. I haven't got the money to fix it, so I thought if I'm going to have to live with it, I may as well turn it into something beautiful. Come on, I'll show you.'

'I really should be getting along, dear,' Dotty says, but I take her by the hand, and take my glass of vodka in the other.

As we go through the kitchen, I point above the cabinets. 'You see, I've made the vine look like it's coming through the ceiling, and down there by the skirting, so it looks like it's growing through the floor. I've done the same thing in the snug.'

'I see,' she says.

I open the basement door and flick on the light. 'You'll have to excuse the mess, I'm in the process of converting the basement into an interior design studio.'

Once we're down there I show her over to the corner, where the crack disappears into the concrete floor. 'It's a lot harder to paint on bare brickwork, but I think it gives the flowers a three-dimensional quality, don't you? It's like the crack doesn't even exist anymore.'

Dotty doesn't answer, and I can see her looking at the cement mixer and the leftover bags of sand and cement. I had laid a dust sheet over the two ugly holes the builders had filled back with concrete, and moved everything on top. It looks a lot tidier now, I think, and I can picture how the studio will look when it's finished.

'I should be getting along now, dear,' Dotty says, and so I walk her back upstairs.

I open the front door for her, but before she steps outside she turns to me and says, 'Are you sure you're all right, dear? You don't seem well, and drinking this early in the day. It's not good.'

I knew it. Dotty's old, but she has a keen mind. I may look okay on the outside – a little outré, perhaps, but all creatives have their quirks and eccentricities. No, she has seen deep into the heart of me and can sense, as only a mother can, the darkness of my loss.

'I don't know if I've ever mentioned it,' I say, 'but I've recently lost my daughter, Becky.'

Dotty touches my hand. 'You have, dear.'

'I was collecting her from school one day, when out of nowhere a drunk driver mounted the pavement and tore her from me, crushing her against the school railings.'

Dotty covers her mouth with a trembling hand.

'And then two days later, my husband Roy died of a heart attack – well, they said it was a heart attack, but I'm convinced it was a broken heart that killed him. He just couldn't take the pain of losing her that way, and...'

When Dotty has left, I close the door and sip my vodka. For some reason I always feel a little better for talking about the tragic way I lost my family. It does no good to bottle things up.

Standing here by the front door, the arch window appears cathedral-like, and I'm reminded of a school trip I once took to France. It's where I got the idea to remove the bedroom above to create the ceiling space in the entrance hall. It's strange, Dotty mentioning that her mother died in that room, because it has triggered a false memory, where it wasn't my idea to remove the bedroom at all, it was Roy's, something about not wanting anybody to sleep in a room where another person had died.

The memory obviously can't be true, or why else would I take such comfort in having a completely different opinion on this subject than Roy? A lingering presence is not a ghost, it's an idea of a person, which in itself is merely fiction, fabrication, design, and one day I'll take my place in the tapestry of this house and become part of that design, because one day, like

Dotty's mother, I will die here, and the thought of becoming a ghost is, for some reason, terrifying.

THE END

# ACKNOWLEDGEMENTS

Thanks must go to Dom Wing, Les Robertson and Michelle Tregarthen, for their continued interest in my stories. To James Wills for his early editorial insight. And, as always, to my first reader and wife, Lesley.

# A NOTE FROM THE PUBLISHER

**Thank you for reading this book**. If you enjoyed it please do consider leaving a review on Amazon to help others find it too.

**We hate typos**. All of our books have been rigorously edited and proofread, but sometimes mistakes do slip through. If you have spotted a typo, please do let us know and we can get it amended within hours.

**info@bloodhoundbooks.com**